ACROSS THE DREAMING NIGHT

JUDITH WHITE

ACROSS THE DREAMING NIGHT

V

VINTAGE

The author gratefully acknowledges the assistance of
Creative New Zealand for a grant received in 1998 and
The Sargeson Trust for her fellowship held between 1995 and 1996.
She would also like to thank Gordon McLauchlan for the generous
use of his studio, which enabled her to finish this novel.

The assistance of
Creative New Zealand is gratefully
acknowledged by the publishers.

ARTS COUNCIL OF NEW ZEALAND *TOI AOTEAROA*

A VINTAGE BOOK
published by
Random House New Zealand
18 Poland Road, Glenfield, Auckland, New Zealand

First published 1999
Reprinted 2000

ISBN 1 86941 412 8

Cover design: Dexter Fry
Printed in Malaysia

Your children are not your children.
They are the sons and daughters of Life's longing for itself.
They come through you but not from you,
And though they are with you yet they belong not to you.

The Prophet
Kahlil Gibran

CHARLOTTE'S STORY

He'd been coming into the salon for some time to have his hair cut and tinted, just a semi-permanent rinse, because it's going grey. He usually came on a Friday evening, our late night. So, right from the start, I was running my fingers through his hair, which is thick for a man his age. Not that I really noticed him much at first — I mean, he was so old. Forty-three. Forty-four in June, actually. His name is Quentin, but ever since I saw his name in the appointment book — Q. Stanley — I've thought of him as Q. At the time 'Q' felt mysterious somehow, like questions and quirks and quandaries, and I imagined it standing for something exotic like Quasimodo or Quixote. When I found out it was Quentin, like the uncle in the Famous Five, I just kept calling him Q. I asked him and he said he didn't mind at all.

It all started one night when I was working late. Mum and her boyfriend were supposed to pick me up. I finished about an hour before the salon closed, and waited outside for a while before going back inside to phone them, to see why they weren't there, but there was no reply.

Q was having his hair done, and heard me say to Jeremy that they hadn't turned up. I was just going outside to wait again when Q asked me where I lived and I told him. It wasn't far and I usually walked, but not in the dark. He said he was going in that direction and that he'd give me a lift, if Mum or Steve hadn't turned up before he'd been done.

Anyway, in the short distance from the salon to my place we got talking, just who we were and everything. He told me that he was some sort of manager in a corporate trust place or something, in the city. I knew he'd be something like that because of the way he dressed, like Dad used to, with a suit and tie and always looking fresh and clean and busy. And then I told him a bit about me, and I was still talking when we arrived home, and after ages he turned the motor off and suddenly, even though the motor wasn't loud, it was *so quiet* and I didn't know what to say any more. So I grabbed the door to go and then I went, 'Oh no!' He said, 'What's up?' and I told him I didn't have the key. Because I thought they were going to be coming home after picking me up.

We waited for a bit but we didn't know how long they'd be. Then he asked whether there was a window we might be able to get in. But first of all he had to ring his wife on his cellphone. He told her he was tied up in a meeting. 'You lied,' I said to him. 'Sometimes it's easier,' he said. 'If I told her I was helping a beautiful young hairdresser break into her house when her parents were out, now, what would she think?' I could see him smiling in the light of the street lamp and he reached across and touched my cheek. Just a little flick with his finger on my cheek like scratching a bit of crumb off it.

Well, anyway, we got out of the car and walked down the path through the trees to the house. I tried the door just in case but no, it was locked. The house was dark except for a light Mum leaves on in the hallway, to make it look as though someone is there. But there was a full moon and lights coming through from Mrs Gardiner's next door. It felt like I was a kid again, playing hide and go seek. Around the bushes we kept bumping into each other and saying, 'Oops, sorry.'

All the windows were shut until we got to Mum's, which was open just a fraction. Q said that I could stand on his shoulders to reach the catch. He took off his jacket and bent over with his face in the leaves, and I took my shoes off and climbed onto his back, then he stood up for me to balance on his shoulders. I could feel spider webs in my face so they must have been all over him.

Anyway. I reached my hand in and released the catch, opened the window, and then.

Well.

I suddenly heard all this breathing and stuff, and grunting, and there we were, me standing on the shoulders of this man I hardly knew, both of us looking in through the window at this shadow of a big fat milky white bum captured in full glory from the hall light through the bedroom door. Heaving up and down in the air. And the grunting. And then Mum, saying urgently, 'Oh Steve, Steve, there's a noise, Steve. There's a noise.'

I scrambled down and slithered off Q's back. I knew he must have seen and heard because his chin was more or less on the window sill but I didn't have to say a thing. We just went for it.

The light went on and we dived under this big bushy tree pressed against the wall of the house. Then we heard the squeak of the window opening further, and Steve's voice saying, 'Anybody there?' As if we'd say we were! Then in a more muffled way, saying, 'Nup. God, hon, try *relaxing* and blow the burglars.'

Up until that day I hadn't even realised they were doing it. It might have even been their first time, who knows. But I was so embarrassed. And I didn't know what to do. I knew I couldn't knock on the door because Steve got mad if I forgot the key, even though that time it wasn't my fault, because they were supposed to pick me up. And then I realised I'd left my shoes there, under the window, and Q's jacket, and that I'd have to go back and get them. But we didn't know whether they were going to come out and check around or what. I just started crying and crying.

Q put his arms around me and held me, not tight, but as if he was putting a shell of protection around me, so I could still move within it. A bubble of protection. And I think, probably out of surprise more than anything, I stopped crying; I was so amazed at the magic of his arms around me. But then, in the silence, all the breathing and grunting started up again, really loudly.

Q said, 'Stay here and I'll get our things, they won't hear us now,' and he darted off under the bushes while Steve was going, 'Oh God,' over and over as if he kept remembering something terrible, and then more terrible and even worse than that. And Mum — I could have died — Kiri te Kanawa's grandmother practising her scales. I was so ashamed and by the time Q came back with my shoes I was crying again, with my fingers stuck in my ears. Q said, 'Look, let's go and have a cup of coffee somewhere until they're done, so that everyone can calm down.'

He was so kind. If it had been a friend of mine, or a guy my own age, it could have been worse, like, different somehow. I suppose, I don't know. But Q seemed understanding about it; he didn't say how disgusting or anything, but he was quiet and thoughtful over coffee. It felt as if we'd known each other for longer and that we'd been through something together. I didn't feel like going back to the house ever again. He handed over his cellphone so that I could ring them to say I was on my way home, so they'd know I was coming. I started thinking they might guess that it was me under the window. It was awful. If he'd said, 'Come with me to America right now, the plane goes in five minutes,' I would have gone. I know it. Without any doubts at all. I would have gone, no goodbyes or anything.

But Q said that of course they wouldn't think it was me, and that they probably thought they'd only imagined the noises anyway. I still didn't want to ring them so he said to tell them, when I got home, that I'd gone to have coffee with a friend after waiting for them to pick me up from work. 'And that's true,' said Q, smiling. He took my hand in a friendly way, just briefly, and gave it a big kiss. 'Isn't it?' he said.

The next morning at work he phoned to see if everything was all right. I said that yes, it was. In fact, Steve didn't even yell at me for forgetting the key. They were up and dressed and watching television when I got home, as if nothing had happened.

There were two empty wine bottles on the table and they still hadn't done the dishes, though. It turned out they'd forgotten they'd arranged to collect me. They looked at each other and laughed and said oh no it completely slipped my mind, yes me too. Mum came and gave me a hug and said she was sorry. I told them I'd rung, and Steve looked at Mum and said, 'I didn't hear the phone, did you?' And Mum said, 'No, you must have rung the wrong number.'

'But I tried several times.'

'We didn't hear it once, did we?' and Mum said, 'No, we didn't,' and looked at me as if to say, well there you are then. You couldn't have rung. It was obvious whose side she was on.

Not long after that, Steve started staying overnight at our place, first of all on a Friday, then the whole weekend. Then more and more of his stuff moved in, his shaving stuff in the bathroom, and his stereo in the sitting room. Pot plants. And souvenirs like a kangaroo standing by a thermometer, and some hanging shell things. Mum was even doing his washing. I didn't want my clothes swishing around with his, his undies and everything, so I did mine separately.

He's so horrible. He'd sit there watching television with his legs crossed so you could see the pure white bits on his fat thighs under his shorts with little pointy pink pimples over them. And right from the start, after the first few times, he spoke to me in a horrible way. He's a school teacher, same as Mum, and he's probably used to talking to his students like that all day. I'd hate to be in his class. He did it to impress Mum, to show her that although I didn't have a father, he'd act in the way he thought one should act, not that he'd know.

He's never been married — no one else would have him, probably. He'd go at me, 'Don't speak to your mother like that. Help your mother with the dishes. Pick up your things.' And I hated him sleeping in Dad's bed. I just don't know how she could do that to Dad. I kept thinking of his big fat bum in the light of the hall. Knowing that Q saw it too somehow helped, somehow made me feel less lonely, even though I didn't say, what exactly did you see, or compare notes or anything. Luckily Robin was staying with a friend, but I can see that was probably planned anyway. I can see that now.

Robin is fourteen and I tried to talk to him about Steve, but he didn't know what I was on about. Robin quite likes Steve because he takes him fishing at the wharf in the weekends, and goes to athletics and stuff with him.

Anyway, after that time, I kept waiting for Q to come to the salon, or ring me again, but then when he didn't, I told myself not to be so stupid. I told Brigit about him and she couldn't believe he was so old. It's not that we don't know any other guys. So I'd almost nearly forgotten about him, and if I'd never seen him again, that would have been it. But one day I was looking in the appointment book and boiiing! there was his name — Q. Stanley — same time on a Friday evening, for a semi-permanent rinse and a cut. In two days' time. I started worrying that something terrible might happen to prevent me seeing him. All that waiting.

But suddenly it was 7.30pm on Friday and he was walking in through the salon door. I was holding a towel and just stood there. I wanted to go up and say hello, but there was this whole room of hairdressers and clients between us. Then Mrs King said, 'Is something the matter, dear?' and there she was with the water all trickling down, with her eyes blinking and her soft purple tongue out a bit and catching the drips, and her hands trapped like lumps under the plastic cloak, trying to wipe her face.

That night I was planning to catch a cab, so he offered to take me home again. On the way he asked how things were with Mum and Steve and, well, I just started going on about how I hated Steve so much and when we got home I was still going, so he said without even turning the motor off, 'Come on, let's have a cup of coffee, shall we?' I went, 'Okay.' But instead we had a glass of wine.

Two glasses of wine actually, in the end. Wine really goes to my head, especially since I hadn't eaten since lunchtime and this was half past eight. I told him all sorts of things I never tell anyone, about Dad dying on the camping trip when he went away on that long weekend with his mates. Dad was my best friend. You might think he was boring but he was kind and handsome and always nice to all of us, not like Steve. He'd buy you presents when you were sick, or he'd come home and say, just when you thought you were going to do nothing, Let's go out to dinner or Let's go to the movies, and we'd go out as a family and it would always be fun. And he'd ask about school, and he always understood about fights and that, without actually blaming anyone, you know?

It was really lonely when he died. Mum went all brittle, in a way. And tired all the time. I told Q all that. And I couldn't help it, but I started crying and I hadn't cried over Dad dying for about three years. So that was twice I'd been out with Q and twice he'd looked after me when I was crying. He must have thought I was a real crybaby, but he squeezed my hand and said, 'No, of course you're not. Let's go for a walk along the beach, to freshen you up a bit.' I suppose he felt a bit of a dork, all those people in the bar wondering why I was snivelling away like that. Sniffing into a tissue like that.

The beach was just over the road. The moon was almost full and the sea was so beautiful and sparkling. I couldn't stop thinking about Dad, even though it was about five years since he died. Stupid, I know. You must think I'm obsessed, especially when I'm walking along the beach with someone else really nice, thinking about my dead father. Hopeless.

Q stopped and put his arms around me in that same way, and we just stood there for a bit. I couldn't believe it. He was a magician, making a spell. Safe and protected and loved; for the first time since Dad died, I felt loved. Then we walked a bit more and talked about music and stuff, and he dropped me home and that was that. I felt so happy even though I'd been crying all night. I know, I know! The next day at work he rang to see how I was, and asked me what I thought about going flatting. Then I didn't hear from him for another four weeks, until his next semi-permanent, when it was the same all over again. Asking if I'd like a ride home and then going out for a drink.

I suppose you should know a bit about me. I go to tech once a week and work five days a week: late on Fridays and a half day on Saturdays. Sometimes I stay at Brigit's place on Saturday nights when we go out to a party or something. When I said I was lonely I thought you might think I didn't have any friends but there's a whole group of us, kids from school and other guys we've met. But I was meaning a different sort of loneliness. As if I didn't fit in. A tadpole among goldfish and one day something was going to happen to me so that I knew why I wasn't the same. That's what I meant.

So anyway, the next time I went out with Q, as I was saying. He just about did a double take because I'd bleached my hair — I'm always changing it but before it was a dark red and this time I went berserk and had it bleached just about white. I deliberately wanted to look special for him. He kept saying, 'I don't know why you girls have to play around with your lovely hair like that,' but in the end he admitted he liked it. He said it made me look like Marilyn Monroe. I was wearing this lowcut short top and short skirt and he said I'd be the undoing of him. He said I was all peaches and cream. Not like Steve, who'd usually say what do you think you're doing, going off to work with the public like that. Mum doesn't say anything any more. She used to but she gave up.

This time we didn't even head for my place. He took me straight to have dinner down in the bay — there's lots of restaurants and he took me to this really awesome one. He'd already booked a table by the window upstairs, looking out over the sea. It wasn't expensive — I'd already been there with Mum and Robin and Steve, downstairs — but it was nice and friendly.

He asked me how things were at home, and I started telling him how Steve was doing his school teacher thing at me all the time — always going on about me being untidy and staying too long in the bathroom and all that, and how it wasn't fair. Q put his hand on mine and said, 'Don't worry. I've thought about this and I know just what we're going to do.' He arranged to pick me up the next day, Saturday, at one o'clock, straight after work, with the newspaper, so we could go looking for flats. I just went, 'Okay.' It was like I didn't believe it, but that it would be a neat thing to do, with him, anyway, even if I didn't take a flat. He said he'd look in the *Flatmates Wanted* column and mark the ones he thought I'd be interested in, have the addresses all sorted out and off we'd go.

Well, that's what we did. He parked around the corner a bit, because he said he didn't want people to get the wrong idea, but Jeremy was walking out with me and said, 'Isn't that your friend with the fancy car over there?' and I said, 'Oh yes,' and ran over and climbed in the car and I didn't look but I know he would have just stood there and gawked. It was the first time I'd seen Q without his suit. He had a long-sleeved soft green shirt on, open at the neck and I could just see some hairs on his chest and he smelt clean. That's what I loved about him, always smelling fresh and fragrant. I got in and gave him a kiss on the cheek without thinking and he just smiled and said, 'Off we go then.' Then I realised that that's what I used to do with Dad, when he picked me up from anywhere. Jump in and give him a kiss on the cheek. And I did it with Q without thinking.

We looked at quite a few flats. Some were a bit scummy but there was this really good one — one of those old houses with high ceilings and a wide hallway and a cosy kitchen at the back, all recently painted. The other people there were a bit older than me, but the trouble was that it cost more than the others we'd looked at. They showed me the empty room which had a double bed and looked out into a private garden full of flowers and trees. They sort of interviewed me and then said did I want to ask any questions and I said no. But Q asked a few and after that they all agreed I could move in when I wanted to. So I said I'd think about it, and we went off and Q said why think about it? It was perfect, wasn't it? And I told him about it being too expensive and he said not to worry about that, he would help me out. He put his hands on my shoulders and looked into my face and said it would make him happy to help me. I couldn't believe it. So we went back and I said I'd take it. And Q, then and there, wrote a cheque for the bond and six weeks' rent, even though I only had to pay four in advance. Just like that. It was a bit scary really.

He dropped me off home and I skipped down the path, swinging on the tree branches as I went. I always do that when I'm happy. I felt as if I was in a dream. The front door was open and I went inside. There was no one in the kitchen or sitting room and I called Mum but no one answered. Then Steve came out of their bedroom. He was obviously going out because he had a jacket on and was shaved and his hair, what he had left of it, was slicked back.

'Where's Mum?' I asked.

'She's taking Robin to Tim's for the night,' he said. 'Then we're off.'

'What do you mean, off?' I said.

'Off for the night,' he said, rubbing his hands together, with a wormy grin. His thick tongue didn't quite lick up over his lips but I could see it. 'It's her birthday,' he said, 'and I'm taking her to the Carlton for the night.'

Oh god, I'd forgotten it was her birthday. I couldn't believe it.

'What, all night?' I said.

'Yes,' he said with such a disgusting smirk. 'All fucking night.' He wouldn't dare swear like that if Mum was there.

'What's wrong with here?' I said and wished I hadn't. He was so triumphant and haughty. It was obvious he hated me.

And then Mum turned up in a cloud of perfume, dressed in a new black dress that sliced down between her breasts as if she had none. She'd never have worn anything like that when Dad was alive, not tarty things.

'Oh, Charlotte. You're late home. I'm glad I've caught you,' she said. 'Steve's taking me out for the night. Aren't I spoilt!'

'Happy birthday,' I said in a grumbly way, and I went to kiss her.

She said, 'Thanks love,' and she held her hair so it wouldn't get messed up, craning her neck over to give me her cheek. Then I saw her overnight bag in the hall and realised she was all ready to go right then. The dream was over. I would have to tell her now, with Steve there, all in a rush.

My heart was beating and I nearly didn't say anything. I thought maybe I could just go. But then I took a deep breath and said, 'Um, I'm going flatting.'

Mum just looked at me. Bam. 'Well, we'll talk about it tomorrow night when we're back.'

'I'm moving in tomorrow,' I said. Peoww. It was as if all the little pins holding up the smile and happy mood in Mum's face had been taken out. It just dropped, her whole skin just dropped.

'Come on, honey,' said Steve, taking her by the arm, looking at me with fat snake venom.

'Wait till we talk about it,' said Mum. 'I mean, who are you going with and where? You can't just do this.'

'Well, I am.'

'Well, if you think I'm going to drop everything and help you move in, young lady, you've got another think coming. You're on your own.'

'Okay,' I said.

'Come on, honey, it's all for the best, she's got to go sometime.' Of course he was doing cartwheels, anything to get rid of me.

'How can she do this to me? How can you do this to me?' said Mum. 'Just walk out like this with no warning. After a lifetime. After a lifetime of washing your nappies, cooking your meals, giving you my life, you just . . . you just . . .'

'Madame has always done what she pleases,' said Steve. 'I've told you that. She'll be back when it bloody well pleases her too. So she thinks. Come on, honey. Now look what you've done,' he said to me in a low voice, his teeth stuck together with fury, as if an aside in a play. He picked up her bag and scooped his hand around her bottom, pushing her out the door. Mum was saying, 'We can't go now, we have to sort this out.' But he just kept pushing her on, so she kissed me with toity lips and said in a huffy way, 'Well, I'll see you when I see you then,' but her eyes were swimming in tears, and she suddenly looked tired and quite ugly. All the makeup looked like a mask that you could see through. White and red.

'Thanks for spoiling everything,' said Steve brightly and sarcastically, and they went up the path, Mum's shoes clicky clacking away, clicky clacking away from her life as my mother into a new tarty one with Steve all because of something terrible I'd done wrong. I felt as if someone was pulling roots out of my stomach. Something awful had happened and it was my fault. I was an orphan.

I shut the door and walked around the house. So much of my life had been lived in that house. I went into my bedroom and suddenly noticed the crack in the top corner where Robin had thrown a pill bottle at me and it had missed me and hit the window, when he was about nine. I won't go into all the soppy things, but you know how it is when you start thinking. Suddenly I felt like my blood had turned to mud and it was clogging up in my veins, getting slower and slower and I could hardly move. I threw myself down on the bed with my face buried in the pillow. I put my finger in my pants not doing anything but just letting it slither around in the warm moistness as I was lying there not thinking of anything except how I hated Steve, and then thinking of Q and the new flat and then suddenly the phone rang and it was him.

He asked if everything was all right and I told him, and he said not to worry, to get going and pack up my things, and that he'd be around in the morning to pick me up, and that really things had worked out in the best possible way because

I could pack up without anyone interfering. I felt so much better then. When Brigit rang and asked me to go out and I told her, she went a bit like Mum, all funny. It was so sudden, I suppose. Well it was, really.

I had to get some boxes so I went down to the basement, which is always like entering the pyramids after ten million years. You have to clamber through tunnels of dusty junk before you find anything. I was shifting some stuff when I noticed Dad's old pack crammed into a corner. I thought it would be a good idea to have a sleeping bag in the flat so I undid the straps. It was stuffed with his things, not all neatly as he would have put them away, just stuffed with things all screwed up. Then I realised that he would have had it on the camping trip when he died. It was freaky really and gave me a knotted feeling in my stomach. I sat there on a dusty crumbling concrete wall with the light on and spiders swaying everywhere and I went through the lot. I hauled everything out: crumpled stiff old towels and clothes . . . like his good jersey with the Fair Isle that Mum spent years knitting for him. When I pulled that out it just about fell to pieces. It was full of holes, and little tubular shells where the moths had pupated.

I went upstairs and got a rubbish sack and threw all the clothes out — I knew it would make Mum upset to see them. The last things he was wearing and using. I felt so sad but not in a crying way, just in a deep losing way. You just know that you're not going to see that person you loved ever again, or tell them anything, even. Sometimes I think that if you could just get messages through, it would be much better. Little notes or something. Just to say what you're doing and to ask how they are.

I found his toilet bag with his shaving gear. He always shaved in such a way that his cheeks were pink and smooth. See, even on a camping holiday he took his shaving stuff. Unless Steve's going out he doesn't shave all weekend and he looks like a greasy blowfish by Sunday night. I suppose you think I'm stupid, but I decided to keep the toilet bag, even though the zip was a bit rusty and catchy. But the things in it too, even the toothbrush. Not to use or anything, but just to keep. Even the facecloth, because he would have wiped it over his face probably on the day that he died. I thought that if you had it analysed by scientists, you might be able to find the impression of his face; he might have held it over his face and sighed, filtering his living breath. Like that shroud somewhere.

So I put that aside to be kept, dipped into the bottom of the pack and found a bundle, a shirt wrapped around something heavy.

I opened it up and there was a camera I'd never seen before, in black leather casing held shut with metal domes which I clicked apart. Written inside, in capital letters, was a name: Maatje Steinmetz, and an address in Switzerland. Where did it come from?

Then I realised someone must have gathered up Dad's things in a hurry after he died and picked up the camera thinking it was his. They'd been camping in tents, Dad and two of his friends, in the mountains by a river or something. That's what I'd thought. But maybe they'd stopped in a hut. No, they definitely were camping in tents when he died, because I know he had gone outside to have a pee and someone, Garth I think it was, found him lying on the ground. Dead. They were far away from anywhere, after tramping four hours to get to where they did.

I turned the camera over. There was still a film in it — twenty-one had been taken. I decided not to say anything to Mum about it, I don't know why.

Time was rushing on. It's funny how that happens — you get caught up thinking about things, just sitting and looking at things but you're not really in the present at all but far away, as if you're in a time vacuum and when you get back to earth you realise it's a hundred years later. So I grabbed the boxes

21

and ran upstairs and flew around packing up for real. It was really like packing up to go on a big holiday — I didn't have to take any furniture or anything. I threw my duvet and pillows into my sheets and tied them into a big parcel. I thought that when Q came around I could wait outside with it hanging at the end of a stick and tell him I was running away. Silly.

I didn't even take the things off my wall. By midnight the hall was filled with boxes and suitcases all ready to go. Q was right — thank goodness Mum and Steve weren't home. While that creep was performing his big bum ballet I could get ready in peace.

Q had said that he would be there around nine o'clock but he wasn't. I waited and waited. First of all I just sat on a suitcase, all showered and ready to go. Then I'd go into my room just to see if I'd forgotten anything. Then I had breakfast. After a while I thought something terrible might have happened, like a lethal gas leaking over the city and I was the only person left alive. I looked out the windows but I couldn't see one person anywhere. I switched on the radio and there it was, the usual raving on, no mention of everyone being dead. So I rang Brigit to see how the party went but she wasn't home yet. I couldn't ring Q because he hadn't given me his number. My biggest worry was that Steve and Mum and Robin would all turn up to find me still there and let down and everything. Steve would be so mocking. And because of all the gear I wouldn't be able to pretend that I'd changed my mind or anything. But anyway, thank goodness he turned up.

I was a bit sulky at first but he said he was really sorry. It was unavoidable. He'd forgotten that he'd promised to go shopping with his wife. He would have rung but it'd taken longer than he thought it would.

He took me and my things and we loaded them into my new room, then we had to come back for another load and that was that. The others in the flat were just getting up, and coming out and making toast and coffee in the kitchen. They all just said, 'Hi,' blearily, and make yourself at home, and stuff like that. My room was neat: white walls and clean with a desk and chair, chest of drawers, a walk-in wardrobe and, best of all, a big bay window seat with cushions where you can just sit in the sun, sit and look out into a lovely back yard with hedges and a huge leafy tree and flowers.

'Well, there you are,' said Q. He lay back on the seat with his arms behind his head and gave a big noisy sigh and watched and talked while I put my stuff away and made up the bed, which was a double one. My sheets and duvet only just came over the edges. In a way it was quite weird just talking to Q like that, as if I'd known him for ages, but then I kept remembering that I hadn't and I felt shy.

And then he said, out of the blue, 'Charlotte, you never said whether you had a boyfriend or not. I presume you don't, but you might have one tucked away in the Antarctic or somewhere.' God, it gave me a shock, I don't know why. Because it was unexpected, I suppose. There was a feeling of, uh-oh, here we go.

And then I couldn't believe it. I was lying to him. I never lie normally. He started it by saying about Antarctica. My voice was all shaky. I said, 'Well, there's this guy in Scotland, he's got this scholarship. He's over there for a year. In Edinburgh. He wants me to go over but I have to finish my apprenticeship.'

I was talking about Brigit's older brother, but he wouldn't even speak to me, he thinks I'm such a little twerp. But I just picked the only boy I knew who was overseas. I still don't know why, really. Anyway. It didn't matter. Q just said, 'Good. I'm glad. Do you write to each other?'

'Oh yes,' I said, nodding furiously.

'Good,' he said, smiling. 'That's just how it should be.'

I grabbed Dad's shaving gear from where it was on the bed. 'This is his toilet bag,' I said.

He unzipped it and peered in and went, 'Hmmm,' before handing it back, looking at me with a great big warm smile.

'What?' I said and he said, 'Nothing. You're lovely. Here, pass me that camera — does it have a film in it?'

I turned around. I'd just about finished putting everything away. I gave him the camera and put the empty suitcases under the bed. He made me sit on the bed while he took a photo of me. Then I took a photo of him sitting on the window seat. It was one of those complicated cameras and Q had to show me how to set it. So then of course he asked me how it was that I couldn't use my own camera, so I told him how I found it in Dad's pack.

'Oh, that's a pity,' he said. 'The film's probably too old.' He took another photo of me to finish the film, and took it out. 'It might be okay,' he said. 'As long as your basement is cool and dry. It might have to have special attention; if you like I'll take it to a lab to be developed for you.'

I said okay, as the salon is on a corner by a dairy and no other shops for miles, so it would've meant that I couldn't do it before my next day off. 'But only if you promise you won't look at them first.'

'They might give a clue about the camera. Maybe your father bought it second-hand?'

'Maybe,' I said, but I didn't think so. Dad liked everything new.

After that, Q had to go. I went out to the sitting room and talked to my flatmates. One girl and two guys: Seon, Garry and Todd. Seon was a cook in a fancy expensive restaurant, Garry was a librarian, and Todd was a landscape gardener. They all seemed really cool and friendly.

The next day Mum rang at lunchtime at the salon. She was going berserk, she just spewed at me. I mean, I didn't intend to hide where I was or anything. But when she started on about it . . . I know I should have written down the address before I left but I forgot, and I kept thinking I should ring her when she got back on Sunday night, but with the phone at the flat being in the sitting room, I didn't want to have to talk to her if she was going to spew at me like that in front of people I didn't know. They'd think I was a baby or something. When she gets like that, you can't say anything. It was like that in the salon, and I could see people were beginning to listen to me going but, but, but, and pretending they weren't. So in the end I hung up and I still hadn't told her where I lived. I didn't mean it to be like that but that's how it turned out. I bet she imagined I'd moved in with a bunch of drug addicts and a boyfriend who smashed into chemist shops or something.

Brigit came around after work on Wednesday to see my new place. We sat in my room on the window seat drinking coffee with our chins on our knees, talking and talking. Then Seon came in and said I was wanted on the phone.

'It's your father,' she said. I was freaked because I thought it must be Steve but it was Q, saying that the photos would be ready on Friday and that he'd pick me up that night after work to give them to me, and also so I wouldn't have to take a cab.

When I got back, Brigit said, 'What's all this about your father?'

'Bloody Steve,' I said and she looked at me strangely.

'I thought they didn't know where you were,' she said. She knows me, that's the trouble with friends.

'Joking,' I said. 'It was Q.'

'What? You've told them he's your father? Charlie!'

'I haven't. They just think he is, and I didn't say he wasn't.'

'What? Are you going out with him?'

'No, I'm not. He's getting some photos developed so he's picking me up after work on Friday to give them to me.'

'He's married, right?'

'So what? It's nothing. True.' And it wasn't, but it was weird. Normally we'd be making something out of nothing. Normally we'd be saying, Oh wow, man, he's so cute, he's such a babe, and all that. I started off like that with Q, but now I found myself denying everything I felt about him, and with Brigit, my best friend.

'He's just kind, that's all.' And it was true too, but I couldn't tell her that I thought I might be in love with him. I didn't even want to think about his wife. In a way, she didn't matter. We hardly ever talked about her. I just knew things like her being a nurse, and that one thing they really liked doing together was going out in their boat and sailing around islands and little bays, just relaxing, but that they couldn't do it very often because of her funny hours.

On Friday night after work we went to our little bar in the bay. We ordered the wine and he passed over the photos.

'It's the best they could do,' he said.

'You've looked!' I said. 'I bet you've looked.'

'Honest,' he said shaking his head and crossing his chest with his finger. 'I told you I wouldn't.'

I pulled them out of the packet. My hand was trembling.

The first one was of a girl about my age standing in front of a house with an arm around two people bundled up for the cold: an old man stooped over a stick and a tiny walnutty lady who came up to her shoulder. It seemed as though there was snow all around but it was hard to tell as the colour in the photo was faded with a strange magenta tinge. As it turned out all the photos were faded in the same way, which gave them a ghostly quality.

The next three were of family groups at an airport, definitely overseas because of the signs around the place. Probably parents and little brothers and friends.

The next two were at the same airport. Two girls stood by backpacks — the girl from the first photo with another about the same age. They were both in jeans and both had long hair, the first one blonde and straight and falling down to her shoulders and the other thick and dark and pulled back in a tail.

'I think we'll find these are the stars of the show,' said Q as I passed the photo to him. 'And the camera probably belongs to the blonde one. Don't you think?'

'Maybe,' I said and I shrugged.

There were a whole lot of boring touristy ones. Up around the Bay of Islands, Waitangi and all that, the blonde one sitting on an old bomb of a car with her legs crossed, the Treaty House, beaches from cliff tops, both of them standing laughing absolutely drenched with rain in Queen Street in Auckland, and then the car at the side of a road with tussocky country rolling into the distance, with the dark one standing with her arms folded, watching a man squatting down with his back to the camera changing a tyre. The next was taken at the same spot. This time the man was with two other men standing alongside the girl, and they were all beaming happily, in a jovial way. The man was my father and the other two men were his friends he'd gone camping with, Garth and Simon. In this photo you could just see the back of Dad's car parked in front.

I put the photos down and took a drink. My heart was bursting and I could hardly breathe. I took the last photo from Q again and studied it. Dad looked so healthy and handsome, dressed in his old bush shirt and jeans. He looked young and rugged. Younger than Q. You wouldn't imagine that he was about to die. I gave it back to Q. I didn't say anything about it being my father, but he probably guessed that one of the men was. By this time we were just looking at the photos quietly, but I sensed he was observing me closely.

'You okay?' was all he said, but he reached across the table and put his hand behind my neck for a second.

I picked them up again. In the next photo the three men and the dark girl were sitting at a table in a restaurant. There was a bottle of wine on the table and they were all holding glasses in the air. The girl was sitting closely between Dad and Garth but I could see Dad's fingers curled around the top of her bare arm. It was funny because all the photos had a ghostly air about them, sort of dreamlike and smoky, like at dawn when the colour hasn't quite started coming into the day yet. It was weird with Dad being dead and the photos being like that . . .

This is so hard just talking about it, I mean it was all such a shock . . . you've no idea how I felt when I saw Garth and Dad and the two girls naked in the hotwater springs on the way to the mountain. In the background you could see that they'd had a picnic — there was a cloth on the grass with the end of a french loaf, cheeses, a tomato and beer cans lying all over the place. We'd stopped there a couple of times as a family, Mum and Dad and me and Robin — it's this small river with springs of hotwater boiling into it and it's like sitting in a spa bath. If we were travelling we'd stop there, with our togs. It was a fun way to break the long journey.

In the next one the dark girl was sitting on Dad's knee, still in the water, and he had his nose in her neck. I started thinking that maybe it wasn't Dad because the photos were so ghostly and perhaps I'd forgotten what he looked like. His hands were cupped underneath her big breasts, holding them up to float above the water. He was busy studying her ear but she was laughing into the camera, obviously enjoying herself. Perhaps he didn't even know he was being photographed.

Q put his hand out for the photo. I realised I kept saying 'Oh my God. Oh my God,' like that, so he wanted to see what I was talking about. Finally he reached over and gently pulled the photo from my hand. He went, 'Hmmm . . . I see what you mean.' I almost didn't want to look at any more but I couldn't help myself. She was still on his knee in the water and they were playing. Dad was holding out her hair like a fan, all thick and wavy and you could just see a strip of his face cheekily poking through, with a funny little expression on his face he'd have sometimes, when he was teasing you.

The next photo was a busy scene in a different setting, in a clearing in the bush. One tent was up, and Dad, the darker girl, Garth and Simon were putting up two others. Packs and pegs and everything strewn all around. Dad and the girl were working on one tent, and the two men on the other. No one was looking at the camera. In the following one the three men and the blonde girl were all sitting in a row on a log eating with forks from plates. It looked cold and they all had big jerseys and hats on. The next was of Dad and the dark-haired girl with their heads poking from a small tent, each holding a flap aside, looking quite serious. They both had their clothes on, and they must have crawled out of the tent a bit for the photo. I was trying to see whether in the background they were coming out of two sleeping bags or two opened out, but I couldn't. It was night time, though. The next photo was of me sitting on my bed in the flat, then Q on the window seat, and the last one was of me again.

My mouth so dry. And me thinking, I'm not going to cry, I'm not going to cry. I looked out the window at the sea with no moon and felt as if I'd spent years and years reconstructing a statue from a pile of broken pieces and now someone had deliberately kicked it apart and I had to start looking for the bits that fitted all over again, but to make something else, because all this time I'd been gluing the pieces together inside out. I'd got it wrong.

These were the last images of my father before he died. I wondered how many lies we'd been told. I suppose it was this chick's tent he crawled out of to have a pee and never came back alive. Or perhaps he died in her tent. In the middle of nowhere like that. God, you'd think you could get away with it, wouldn't you, in the middle of nowhere like that. Mum used to say to me, 'Be sure your sin will find you out.' Even if I snuck a biscuit.

I suddenly realised Q was talking to the waitress, ordering something to eat. He didn't even ask me what I wanted.

'I'm not hungry,' I said. 'I don't want to eat, I'm not hungry.' Here I was being angry with him and what had he done wrong?

'The way you were biting that serviette . . .' he said, and again he reached over and gave my arm a huge squeeze. Oh God, I would cry if he did that. I suddenly felt as if I had nowhere to go in the world. Like an animal that had popped its head out of a burrow one day to find there'd been a nuclear holocaust, that all around there was a vast desert of nothing, absolutely nothing everywhere, with the colour all drained like in the photos and needing to drink but not knowing where the water was, or whether it was safe, even, to go out.

Q was talking. I didn't know what he was saying. His words felt far away. I just looked away from him out to sea. Then I realised it was me that had been smashed to pieces, it was me I was having to put back together again quickly, while the glue was still wet.

Q was paying the waitress and he had his hand under my arm, picking me up.

We walked out of the bar and down to the beach, the same old story over again, Q walking along the beach with me all freaked out.

We were just walking along the beach, just walking silently, until he said, 'Charlotte, do you want to talk about it? The photos.'

And I just exploded into sobbing and sobbing and I wrapped my arms around him bellowing and broken and then I kissed him, kissed him properly on the mouth and he sort of pulled away but I grabbed his head and kissed him then and we just ate each other, our tongues hungry and wild and our lips and tears pouring into our mouths drinking and then I undid the buttons of his trousers, my fingers fumbling but undoing the buttons and he put his hand firmly on my hand and whispered Charlotte sweetheart. No. But I did I slipped my hand under his undies through the hairiness and he was all big and burning and hard and he said, Charlotte sweetheart, no, it wouldn't be right, but he was breathing in that way, and I just had to, crying and crying on tiptoes oh please please please trying to pull him down under my skirt and nearly falling over holding me gasping whispering No my little darling my little love, just let me put you near me, against me, just for a second, just to feel you I said and then thump we landed against the sea wall his back jolting up against it and he said in a stronger voice, Charlotte little one, and then it hit me, what I was doing.

I pulled myself away from him, running through the thick sand and into the sea, crashing through until it was past my knees to my waist and my breath sucked out by the cold, and I threw myself into the water and swimming out and out and out until Q caught up and grabbed me around the waist. I kicked and shoved him away and screamed at him to go away, and he slapped me hard on the face.

'Charlotte! Shut up!' He put his hands under my arms, I was choking and half vomiting and he hauled me over and grabbed my head and we were both on our backs with his legs kicking beneath me. We stopped when the water was up to my waist and he put his arms around me and said he loved me but that we had to go back in and talk. There was lots to talk about, he said. He was just in his shirt and undies. I started shivering then, really shivering and I couldn't talk.

When we got back to shore there was a group of people running towards us to see if we were all right. I suppose I'd made quite a bit of noise with all the screaming. And oh God, there was a policeman, too, with a torch. They kept saying to me was I all right and was this gentleman bothering me? They didn't ask whether I was bothering him. I said of course not and Q said that I'd just had some bad news and had become a little hysterical. Oh God — the photos! They were in my bag and where was my bag? The policeman shone his torch around the sand and there was Q's suit coat and a bit further away his trousers where he'd stepped out of them before chasing me and, thank goodness, my bag just lying there. Imagine if someone found them. Someone who'd known my father, or any of us.

We were all walking back along the beach. Someone came from somewhere with two towels and we rubbed the worst of the wet off.

I could see Q felt a bit silly in his shirt and undies and just his socks on. More people were coming and others were settling to sit down on the sea wall, as if they were gathering to watch a show. Then a policewoman turned up and she asked if she could speak to me for a moment, in private. And she said that if Q was pestering me, now was my chance to say, and not to be frightened of him, that they would take me home if I needed them to. And I told her that no, truly, that he had saved my life. That he was rescuing me. And it was true. It had just occurred to me. Q had saved my life. She seemed a bit disappointed in a way, as if she was the one who wanted to save me. We returned to the group where Q was putting his trousers on.

'My shoes . . .' he was saying. The policeman ran his torch over the sand until he spotted the shoes, lying there in the sand as if someone had finally taken the giant leap for mankind but had vaporised in the process. As for my shoes, they were lost, sodden in the sea. I didn't even care, even though they were good ones. Q picked up his coat, put it around my shoulders and said, 'I think we'd better get this little lady home.'

We started walking away, a bit wobbly because of all the shells and things hurting my feet. I could feel everyone gawking and wondering what was going on. It was all a bit embarrassing.

Back at the car neither of us said anything. We were both totally blasted by what had happened. Q just drove off, towards the flat.

I started thinking that he probably wouldn't ever want to see me again after what I'd done. I started thinking it was over, and I was feeling so stink. How could I do such a thing, putting my hand down his pants like that? Then I thought of the photos of Dad and that chick at the hot pools and I was wishing that Q hadn't come out to the water to save me, I was wishing he'd just walked away, and got in the car and driven off never to come back. A jogger or an old man walking a dog would have found my body on the beach the next morning. Then everyone would have had something to gawk at. I started thinking that I'd take some pills or rat poison or something. I looked out the window at everything going past, all the lights and houses blurring past like a life that didn't matter.

At the flat I thought he'd drop me off and go but we both got out and he followed me up the path. Thank goodness everyone was out, with us both so wet and bedraggled. We went to my room and closed the door and he said, 'Whew!' I wouldn't look at him, but he picked up my chin and gave me a big kiss on the lips, not a passionate one but a firm friendly one, and then on my forehead, then on the top of my head.

He said, 'I don't know, Charlie, what are we to do with you?' He kissed me on the head again. 'You get into something

33

dry while I make us a nice hot cup of coffee.' I found a sloppy jersey of mine that fitted him okay. He took off his singlet and shirt and socks to rinse and spin and throw in the dryer while we had the coffee. When he came back I was in my jeans and sitting on the window seat, with my knees up.

'I found some brandy in the cupboard; I thought we deserved some ooomph in our coffee. I'll pay them back tomorrow.' He sat at the other end of the window seat facing me and we both cupped our coffee in our hands and sipped. He'd made it with hot milk and it was sweet and yummy with the brandy.

'Good coffee,' I grumped. It was the first thing I'd actually said since we'd been back.

'A Quentin special,' he said. 'Guaranteed to do the trick.'

'What trick?'

'Anything you want.'

'Oh yeah?' I said. He looked really funny sitting there in my jersey and suit pants and bare feet. His feet were bony and white, with hairy toes, and rounded short toenails. Refined feet. My feet looked like toys, the toenails painted red. My big toe touched against his, and his toe gave a little wiggle against mine. At first I pulled mine away but then I just stroked the tip of mine over the tip of his. His nodded in response, then it wandered right around the edge of mine; they were two bald piglets sniffing each other, checking each other out. Then his big toe tucked itself under mine and came up between, linking together. He gave a tug.

'Aha. Got you!' he said. But I pulled his foot towards mine. 'No . . . I've got you, so!' And then we both said together, 'We've got each other.' It was so silly that we laughed and our feet rubbed and snuggled up together, and for a flash of a microsecond everything was perfect. But then I remembered it was terrible. So did he.

'Charlie,' he said. He'd suddenly started calling me that.

Anyway. I said, 'What.'

He said, 'It's very complicated.'

'What is?'

'People. People and their feelings and . . . and sex . . . It's not just straightforward. You can't just . . .'

'What?'

'Well, on the beach. It wasn't that I was rejecting you.'

I still had half of my coffee left, muddy liquid that I could dive into and disappear, to hide from him. This sounded as though it was going to be a lecture. He was just like Mum and Steve and the rest.

'Charlotte?'

'What?'

He sighed. Good. Let him suffer.

'You were extremely upset. And I don't think that that is what our relationship is all about, is it? And, well. I am married. I know that doesn't mean much these days but it does make a difference to me. It does mean at least you have to try. And anyway, there's your boyfriend in Scotland . . .'

I glanced up. 'Very funny . . . Sounds like excuses to me.'

'Look. Don't think I don't understand. I do. I understand your confusion. What happened tonight in the water took me back to a similar incident in my life, but for a different reason, for a much worse reason, when I wasn't much older than you.'

'Here we go . . .' I sighed loudly and deliberately. 'But anyway, how do you know it was much worse? You don't understand what I'm feeling. How can you compare?'

'I'm sorry,' he said, really patiently. 'But let me tell you anyway. Just so we understand each other. Do you want me to carry on or not?'

'Yessss.' I waggled my head and rolled my eyes at the roof.

'I just want us to understand each other. I want us to know everything about each other. You're not helping.'

'Go on then . . .'

'Well . . . now you're making it sound silly.' He started talking fast. 'I went out in my father's boat, just a little fourteen-footer with an outboard motor and a bit of a cabin, and I sat at the back there and went for it. Past the bluffs of Napier where my parents lived, and out to sea. It was a splendid day with a soft swell and after a while I couldn't see land in any direction. Just the deep dark sparkling blue of the sea. Everywhere. And the endless blue of the sky. But I kept going. Chugging along, further and further out to sea. It was a bit like you tonight, except I'd thought about it a bit longer and also I had a vehicle to take me further. I hadn't thought of what I'd do when I got there, when I got to the point where the petrol ran out, right out in the middle of nowhere. I'd taken sandwiches, I remember that, and a bottle of whiskey. Banana and date sandwiches they were. Whiskey and sandwiches. I'd planned that much, at least.'

'And then you found God? Or did you forget the thermos?' I was being a little shit, I know. It's a wonder he didn't give up then and there. He ignored me and went on.

'Well, I've no idea for how long I'd been going, when I suddenly noticed out on the horizon a black shape, a strange shimmery dislocated blackness. I thought at first it was another boat, a yacht with a black sail. I started imagining it as a symbol of my own death, in a romantic sort of way. A black yacht coming to spirit me away. I made it the focus for my direction until I realised there were three shapes out there. With great fins. I shut off the motor so as not to draw attention to myself and moved to the centreboard, just slopping about in the sea, with the sucking and slurping of the water around the side, watching these three great animals coming towards me.'

'Sharks,' I said.

'No. Not sharks. I knew them then as killer whales. Orcas to you. I'd read about them being the scourge of the seas, responsible for overturning craft, biting men in two with their great teeth. And here I was, in a tiny little boat under the searing sun in the centre of all this blueness . . . with these ferocious things approaching.'

'Ferocious! Come off it.'

'Charlotte, I *thought* they were ferocious, don't you see?'

'So?'

'Well, they came up to the boat, just a few lengths away. A mother and her two calves, all black and glistening. I was bloody terrified, I can tell you. The mother's fin rose higher than the boat's cabin. I just sat there, barely breathing, trying to look as inanimate and unappetising as possible. They circled the boat a couple of times, doing little dips and dives, spluttering and snorting, observing me. I remember the mother's eye and this sharp sense of really being observed. And then to my amazement they swam on their way. It was as if the mother had wanted to show the young ones what a human looked like. But they left me a nervous wreck, I started shaking and shaking as if I were cold although it was stinking hot. I took a swig of my whiskey and looked out after their disappearing forms. It occurred to me then how ironic the situation was. There I was out in the watery wilderness with the express intention of ending it all and I was trembling like a leaf over a passing family of whales . . . Well, you know . . . So I took another swig of whiskey, threw the rest overboard and headed back for shore.'

'What a waste of good whiskey. So how did you know where shore was if you couldn't see the land?'

'I had a compass,' he said. 'But I eventually ran out of petrol and started paddling for a good deal of the way back. I was pretty buggered and wasn't making much progress when, just on sunset, these chaps coming back from a fishing trip spotted me and gave me a tow for the rest of the way.'

'And here endeth the first lesson. The parable of the orcas.'

Q pulled his feet out from under mine and stood up. He put his hand out for my cup.

'I haven't finished,' I said, although I only had a mouthful left. 'Where are you going?' I'd overdone it. His face was pale and tense. He left the room and came back dressed in his shirt. He sat on the bed putting on his socks and shoes.

'Don't go,' I said.

'It's late,' he said. 'Past your bedtime.'

He straightened up but slowly as if in pain. He ran his fingers through his hair all stiff and messed up from the salt water, patting it into place. It was as if he was trying to remould himself back to the memory of how he was, the clothes and the hair and everything, but he couldn't quite remember how to hold himself. The colour too needed touching up and sharp lines cut past his nose and mouth. When older people get tired they look ancient.

'I thought we were going to talk.'

'I was trying to, Charlotte. I was bloody trying to.'

'About whales.'

'Well, sweetheart, if you hadn't been so involved in yourself, you might have realised that I was trying to tell you something else as well. I've been a fool. I guess I don't know how to relate to children.'

'Bastard!' I mumbled. 'You're as bad as Steve.' He took his jacket from the chair and put it on. The finishing touch to a droopy old scarecrow. As he turned to go he bent down and picked up a folded piece of paper with my name on it. Someone must have slipped it under my door before we arrived and we hadn't noticed. He handed it to me.

Charlotte. Your mother rang. Doesn't sound too happy. Call her. Seon.

'Oh God,' I said. 'Mum. How did she get my number?' I'd meant to ring her.

'See you, Charlie,' Q said.

'Please Q, I'm really really sorry,' I said, getting down from the window seat and crossing the room to go to him. 'I know I was being horrible. I couldn't help it. I just felt so mixed up about everything, that's all. About the beach and the photos and everything.'

'I know,' he said.

He lifted a hand as if to touch me but let it drop, as if he'd just discovered how heavy it was. He took a deep never-ending breath inwards and the whole room seemed to diminish, as if he had sucked it into his lungs. The room suddenly seemed too bright and dense, like a pinprick of light and we were two minuscule suspended dots, Q and me, getting smaller and more and more dense. And then he breathed out again, and shook himself and said, 'See you, sweetheart. Look after yourself.' I realised I'd been holding my breath too. It was as if he had taken us to the edge of a black hole and then thought better of it, or didn't know how to pass through. But now he was out the door, and out of the house and I could hear his footsteps striding to the car, then the purring of the motor into the night.

I'd blown it. Well and truly blown it, you could say.

I lay in a huge bath after that, just lying like a blob, turning the hot tap on with my toes to top it up. Thinking and thinking. Finally I went to bed. It was about midnight and still no one else was home. I felt so mixed up. The house was quiet and scary. Little noises outside and scratching leaves against the window. Sudden frightened bird noises. Creakings and scamperings.

I was thinking that a week ago I still lived at home. If I hadn't left, none of this would have happened. I wouldn't have gone down to the basement and I wouldn't have found the photos. I wouldn't have dived into Q's undies and I wouldn't have dived into the sea, and I wouldn't have been so pissed off with Q that I didn't listen to what he had to say. I just made fun of him the whole time and I couldn't believe that I didn't even ask him why he was so down that he wanted to kill himself. I just thought, oh yeah, everyone thinks of suicide at one time or another. Something goes wrong and you think, oh well, better go and jump off something. Better go and dive into something. Better eat something, drink something, blow something apart. But you don't in the end. Well, most people don't. And he didn't. Twenty years or so later and he was still here, wasn't he? So I thought, what's he on about?

I suppose it was a good story about the whales, but I didn't want to be sucked in to a lecture. That's the sort of thing Mum does. An illustration to drive the wise and worldly point home. But I knew it made sense as there I'd been, swimming out to sea, or thinking of taking rat poison and then next thing I was scared of the noises in the house. If you really wanted to kill yourself, you wouldn't be scared of anything because you'd just think, oh all right then I'm going to die, so what? Really, no one wants to die, they just want things to get better. But anyway, I knew he was intending the story to lead to something else, and I spoilt it. By being so selfish.

Perhaps I was scared of what it was he wanted to say.

I suppose what I really wanted was for him to say amazing things about *us*, to start talking really deeply about the two of us.

After midnight, the sounds around become different. You can almost tell, without checking the clock, when midnight passes. As if the language of the night changes. This night I could hear noises, like footsteps in the house, and water. Flowing water.

I lay there watching the leafy starlight on the wall above my bed. Finally I went to sleep but I had these weird dreams. There was one with Q holding me in his arms, and it was as if I was so tiny and light and he was running along this beach but almost flying. I could hear him breathing fast in my ear, sort of like when we were together on the beach that night. But in the dream, he was panting loudly from the running. There were all these people chasing us but a long way away, and then all of a sudden, Mum and Steve were standing in front of us like a brick wall. Q dropped me, and I started falling and falling and falling and then I woke up.

Then there was this other funny one, though I'm not sure whether it was a dream or for real. But what happened was, I was sitting at the bay window in the room and it was either moonlight or just before dawn. A funny sort of light. I could hear water flowing like quite a large river nearby. Suddenly this huge shadow of a great bird went across the window. There was a moment when everything fluttered into darkness, and a whooshing of wings. I got a real fright and jumped off the seat, but then all was quiet again and I looked out the window and there was this hawk swooping at something, a mouse or something on the lawn. It lifted up into the air and swooped away.

Again it seemed that the wings filled the whole window. It must have been a dream because I've never seen a hawk in the city before but it seemed so real. And all the time the river, or broken pipes gushing somewhere. I don't remember going back to bed but the next thing I was waking up to someone piercing a torchlight through my brain. I opened my eyes and it was sunshine bursting through the window. Sparrows were chirping on the sill and someone was making toast and it was Sunday.

PART ONE

A hawk makes small adjustments against the wind, its feathers ruffling, its wings spread above the trees, the ferns, the cabbage trees clattering like blunt teeth. Far below the river roars, almost unseen except for an occasional sparkle through overhanging trees reaching across the gorge. The hawk shifts to soar with the rising heat from the road that cuts a twisting scar around the contours of the hillside. Its radar head twitches this way and that as it scans the roadside for lizards or mice darting through stones among the weeds growing there.

One side of the valley opens into farmland. The road forks onto a gravel byroad that coasts down towards the river over a rickety wooden bridge to the small settlement of farmhouses, church and pub scattered around the plains beyond. A man clutching his hat sits on a tractor ploughing a paddock, and people leaning on cars parked on the cooler side of the pub complain of the wind and the enervating heat. Women hang out washing behind farmhouses, or pull weeds in the shade of their gardens while a child collects empty cicada cases in a jar.

Not far from the bridge, beneath a long stand of macrocarpa, a young woman is bending to pick up a wooden post, her small frame bowing under its weight as she carries it towards a hut. She pulls a towel from her shoulder and wraps it around the part of the post that she is to hold under her arm, before positioning it horizontally, directed at the hut. Then she runs. She is thrown backwards to the ground as the post rams the door. She repeats the performance but with the same result; the door stays intact. She casts a furtive eye about, then dumps the post and runs across the paddock into a nearby house. Returning to the hut with a key, she opens the door and studies the inside lock. She closes and rattles the door, then opens it to examine the lock again. Then she focuses her attention on the windows.

This time she folds the towel in two before placing it over her head. She picks up the post, braces herself, then swings the post upward to smash the window, showering shards of glass. For a moment she stands paralysed, like a nocturnal animal caught in headlights. Then she shakes the towel from her head, throws it down over the glass, and cautiously steps across to pick out and throw aside a few jagged shards from the window frame. Reaching in, she unfastens the catch of the window, leaving it open and hanging loose.

She enters the hut through the doorway, and comes out again, unfolding a double sheet which she spreads over the grass in front of the hut. Several times she scurries to and from the hut, each time returning with a dried marijuana plant almost her own height, which she throws onto the sheet. The last plant she shoves halfway through the window, then shakes it before sliding it on through. Outside again she gives the bush another sharp rustle before tossing it to join the others on the heap.

She goes inside again and sweeps the pathway through the door, then leans on the broom handle, surveying the scene. She gives the towel a wary flick, then flings it upon the pile of plants, which she then bundles up into a giant parcel, finally pulling opposite corners of the sheet to secure a tight knot.

Hurrying now, she returns the broom to the hut and locks the door. The empty window swings in the wind, banging against the frame. Papers inside the hut blow across the room. She squats down and grabs the bundle from behind her, hoisting it onto her back. It's not so heavy but awkward and she staggers over to the trees, leaving it there while she runs back to the house. Not long afterwards she's out again. She locks the house, puts the key under the woodpile around the side and jumps into her little car, driving bumpily over the grass to collect her loot from under the macrocarpas.

✳

The hawk drops to the bridge, curling its talons around the wooden railing, its feathers fluffing in the wind. Its eye catches movement farther up the river, where a woman bustles outside a tent and a man is slumped in a canvas chair reading yesterday's newspaper. His licked-greasy lunch plate sits in the cleavage of a nearby log and two empty beer cans lie in the grass by his feet. His mind, weighted by the beer and the hot annoying wind, struggles to concentrate on the article he is reading.

He neither senses nor notices other eyes peering at him through the foliage behind. His own eyelids lift and drop, and he flicks his head violently, scratching his florid face, sticky with stale perspiration. He repositions himself on the chair, which is cutting uncomfortably into the flesh behind his knees, then spreads leathery arms to open and refold the paper back on itself. He finds an article about the growing opposition to Muldoon and the proposed Springbok tour but before too long his eyelids have fallen again. His hand flops and slithers from the paper, from his bare thigh, to dangle beside the chair.

Released from its anchor, the newspaper slips from the plump thighs to cover one jandled foot which lifts to rub the ankle of the other, shifting the paper further towards the river, where the wind like an anxious finger riffles through the pages,

44

flicking them over and over until the newspaper is spread open like wings, tugging skyward. Finally one page, then another and another rise and tumble clumsily, until the air is full of great wayward butterflies setting out on their first uncertain, drunken flight.

※

Further up the valley a truck rumbles on its way, an old Ford painted white and decorated with large crude yellow daisies with red centres and twirling green vines. Inside the cab, a man with thick hair falling onto his shoulders keeps glancing from the road ahead across to his wife, who is suckling their child. He is noting that the baby's head is no longer smaller than each of her breasts. He is thinking once again of how beautiful they are, his wife tired and pale and tender as she teases the side of the child's lip with her nipple when the drinking subsides and finally stops altogether.

Easing her breast away, the woman nestles the baby down into the crux of her arm but leaves her blouse open, her bare tanned chest adorned with necklaces of tiny colourful beads and her blonde hair loosely hanging in silken plaits, the colour of beer through that last special sunshine before twilight. A beer would hit the spot right now, with the windows of the truck closed in a vain attempt to shut out both the rattling din and the dust of that tiresome parching wind. The mother runs a finger into the corner of the sleeping eye of the little girl where dust has accumulated in the last tardy tear.

'Josie,' the man says, 'We'll stop by the river, have some lunch.' She drops her head back onto the leather seat and lets the endless greenery blur into a mesmerising doze, and her husband leans forward and puts on a tape and thinks that blowing through the jasmine of your mind is one way of putting it, one way of describing this devilish wind, but he could think of others far less poetic. Just up ahead, as the road begins its descent, he spies a hawk with its wings outspread hovering seemingly motionless before them.

'Look Jo, a hawk,' he says, as the remaining page of newspaper, which has missed being swept away by the river, which has avoided being tangled in a tree, which has lifted and rested upon bushes and ferns, lifts and twists and tumbles through the air to the road, swirling in the funnelling wind, and — just before the road curls around a bend — spreads itself splat across the windscreen of the truck, eclipsing the cab into twilight.

The man shouts, 'I can't see, I can't see!' He plants his foot on the brake, hitting deep gravel, clenching the steering wheel to hang in there, hang in there as the woman screams and hurls her legs upwards so that her feet are braced against the dashboard, her thighs and breasts cushioning the baby who is already crying as she is tossed and jolted in her mother's arms, as they go beyond the gravel and the roadside weeds and ferns, and over.

For an instant, the rattling and jittering ceases. There's an eerie silence which hangs there, which fuses them, the three of them, into an eternal bond of knowing that they are one, inseparable. In that moment, while he desperately wrestles to regain control, while he still has hope, they manage to glance at each other, he and she, just a flicker of a terrorised glance, until the first impact: the bursting door, her grunt as her head thunks into the windscreen, then upside down with legs in the face and Jo limply leaving as he tries to grab her and the baby's soft tugging ankle in his hand while the lashing branches and ferns, the slithering crunch, the smashing of teeth into a roaring mouth.

over stones and rocks under fibrous sweeping roots of tendons and tendrils draining from the river of bleeding into the plunging dark through stars of fizzing sea stars floating. Floating past gliding past pointing rocks to sea into a thundering pounding silent thundering pounding silent needle cutting night.

✳

The hawk yaws and rises as the truck wobbles along the side of the road and over the embankment, until it hits that first rocky outcrop and flips onto its back and downwards as the woman's body is thrown from the opened door. The truck batters through ferns and bush, between trees, skewing around and finally rolling onto its side, arriving with a wheel lodged in a gushing sucking pool in the river, like some cumbersome beast intent on having a drink.

'Godallbloodymighty whatevaa's the . . .' says the man with the florid face, jumping out of his chair with dribbling open mouth, his legs apart and arms flexed as he prepares for the Japs who've got him after all. A figure is thrashing through the trees but away, away from him.

Then he says, 'Whaa? Oh . . .' as he sees Lilian in her togs erupting from the tent. 'Crikey, Lil. Whatever the bloody hell was that?'

They stand and examine each other's faces. They register the horror of realisation that even dozing by the river, in the most secluded spot in the bush, one can never be sure that a humdrum existence will not be shattered by the intrusion of the unknown to change everything, whether for always or a day; to force their upheaval from comfortable lethargy.

'I suppose we'd better go and have a look,' says Lilian, flicking her finger into her togs to yank them over her peeping buttocks.

'Aw, it was probably nothing,' he says. 'Earthworks up at the bridge or something.' But at that moment, among the sounds of the wind and the river, they hear the screaming of a baby.

'I'll just get my purse,' says Lilian. 'And get something decent on.'

Across the bridge, the man on the tractor lets go of his hat and turns off the motor to listen. People leaning in the carpark stand upright, and women drop their washing or put a hand on a knee to push themselves up from the weeding. The boy collecting cicada cases puts the lid on the jar, and everybody listens.

Fishers of men, the long liquid thread of his self unravelling and pouring through darkness into darkness.

Dragging.

The flesh of breath gathering. The crunching shoes of the fisherman along the shore. The scraping shuffle around his head. The fisherman hauling in a catch, his own broken mercuric self, the old boot of his self. Fingers skittering over his skin, a burning thumb prising his eye open to light around a transparent face in a child's silken scribble of tangling sunshine and lapis stones for eyes and a mouth saying wind and water this is my blood and crying oh Jesus dragging along the scraping stone. The boiling freezing water.

Curled over, curled over into sleep, head resting on the dog earth's gurgling stomach and all the time the baby . . .

Back at the farm, the young woman packs the bundle of plants into the boot of her car, slams it shut, gets in the car and drives down the long tree-lined driveway. She stops to open the gate, drives through, then swings it closed again. Then she heads towards the bridge, where she crunches into a shingly clearing. She toots the horn three times, then again twice.

By the river, a youth pauses in his dragging of the groaning body from the water's edge, cocking his head towards the bridge. At the second signal, he heaves the injured man onto his side, then hurries around to the flipped underside of the truck. With his foot on the chassis he hoists himself up to the buckled door and, with the running board in his stomach, stretches into the cab to reach the crying baby jammed between the floor and the bulkhead. Clutching the child to his chest, he jumps into tussock and runs. Over stones, over logs dripping with desiccated weed. To the place where he knows he can cross the river, at first balancing from boulder to boulder, then cradling the baby as he wades waist deep. It is there that he notices the blood streaked across his t-shirt. He dips himself under the water and, with one hand, vigorously rubs and tugs at the stain. The baby gasps with the shock of the cold, drawing renewed energy for a cry that uses the last iota of breath and holds there until a miracle provides more air to start again. The young man splashes his face, then takes handfuls of water which he swishes around his mouth then spits out, and another and another which he drinks, then another which he lifts to slap at the baby's face before striding on until the water is frothing around his thighs, his knees, and he is running across the baking stones, his jeans pouring, the baby rigid with screaming under his arm. He pauses to grab his shoes and socks sitting side by side on a log, then scrambles up the slopes, bramble tearing his arm and the baby's leg, his bare feet scrabbling through the crumbling bank to meet the dirt track which leads upwards then across the road to the waiting car.

The girl has already started the motor and reaches over to open the door to let him in.

'Bloody hell, Matt, what the fuck have you got there?' He clambers inside, dripping wet and bleeding from the brambles. She switches off the motor, plunges her fist into her waist and shakes her head. 'Oh no you don't, sonny boy.'

'I saved it,' he announces triumphantly, still puffing.

'What are you on about? I said to be ready, didn't I? I said to be *ready*. Where did you get that thing? We'll have the whole bloody world out looking for us.'

'I told you, I rescued it.'

She gapes at the distorted crimson screaming face. 'I knew you'd be trouble. It might look like a skinned gnome but it's somebody's baby. You know, desperate parents and all that. God, I can't believe this.'

'They're dead.'

'They're *what*?'

'There was an accident. A truck over the side back there. Just now. It just happened.'

She undoes the clip behind her head and holds it in her teeth as she scoops stray strands around her neck, retwirls the long thick black hair into a knot and clips it back into place again.

'So that's what it was. I heard it. Oh fuck. Fuck and fuck.'

'Well, what was I to do, leave it there to die?'

'I don't care, I'm not interested, Matt. Put it somewhere. Put it in the grass there. Someone will find it. Or go. But I'm not going back. I *told* you I'd be in a hurry. Go on. Go. I just can't believe this.'

They are sheltered from the wind in this clearing, this hurricane centre; they are the oven-heat eye of the vortex as the wind tosses the trees and ferns and bushes creaking and hissing and rustling as the hawk swoops higher into the sky, over the ridge into the next valley, and in the distance they hear the rumble of the tractor grinding its way up the metal road towards the bridge, and not too far behind, the cars from the pub.

'Bloody hell,' she mutters, turning the key and revving up, skidding out of the clearing and over the bridge towards the fork onto the main road.

Matt yanks a couple of tissues from a box at his feet, and secures himself with the seat belt. He spits on the tissue and dabs the plump white skin around the bleeding leg of the child, then looks for other signs of injury.

'Just a few scratches,' he says. 'A nasty scrape on its shoulder here . . . and across its neck there. Lucky.' He peers into the sopping nappies, which he holds out with his finger. 'Hey, it's a girl, Fritha. A baby girl!' He jiggles the still crying baby on his knee then puts her over his shoulder, rubbing her back.

'What shall we call her? Miss Moses from the bulrushes. Butterfly! Hey, Butterfly Baby, don't cry.'

'Can you bloody well hear yourself, Matt?' says Fritha. 'This is the last straw. You're dead meat, Matt. We're going to have to leave it somewhere.'

'Her.'

'It.'

'Anyway, don't panic. We can just take her to the police or a hospital somewhere. I can't see why we didn't take her back to the house and call an ambulance in the first place.'

'No, you wouldn't. You bloody well wouldn't see anything.'

'Poor thing. I think she's thirsty.'

'So what are you going to bloody do about that, have you thought of that?' Fritha growls, her knuckles white with anger as she grips the steering wheel.

Matt leans over the back seat, rummaging among the jumble of gear until he finds a warm bottle of Coca-Cola.

'Better than nothing,' he says, lifting the cap off with his teeth, spitting it aside, to the floor. He takes a couple of deep swigs himself then puts the bottle to the little girl's mouth, lifting it carefully to her lips. The crying eases as her lips swivel to drink but she chokes as a great swoosh of fizz flows into her toothless mouth. He snaps another tissue and scoops away the mixture of spilled coke and long strands of saliva from the prolonged crying. Then he realises that his finger dunked in the bottle is just as effective.

'She's sucking the blood out of my finger. You wouldn't think she'd have such a pull, for a little one,' he says.

'We'll leave it in a toilet at the next petrol station,' says Fritha stonily.

'I know!' says Matt.

'What?'

'Dylina. We can call her Dylina. No, Dylana. Or Dylanna . . .'

'What are you on about, Matt? We're not calling it anything. It's not ours, can't you see that?'

'We could keep her just a little while.'

'It's not a kitten. Parents or not, it'll have aunts, uncles, grandparents — people who know it's missing. Look at you. It's soaking wet, bawling its head off and you're feeding it Coca-Cola, of all things. Poison. You have no spare nappies, no bottle, no change of clothes, no bedding. Yes officer, sir, this is my baby, it's just that I'm not sure yet which way up to hold it, or what it eats.'

'What have I done wrong? You dump me by the river, a truck goes over the side, I rescue a baby and you go berserk. As if it's my fault.'

'You mean it's mine? Oh yes, I see, it's all my fault. Let me think now. We have a very pleasant couple of days with my parents. They feed you to the hilt, even though they're about to leave on holiday. We leave when they do and stop to have a nice swim on this hot day. Then I realise I've forgotten something, so I go back. When I return to pick you up, you arrive with a bloody baby, and show it to me like a kid with a tadpole in a jar. Look what I've found by the river, Mum.

God, Matt, there's a part of you got stuck somewhere, on the way up.'

'Okay, okay, we'll just take her to a police station or something.'

'We can't.'

'Why not?'

'Because it's too late. They'll ask questions.'

'So what?'

'Because you don't have any answers, that's what.'

＊

Small waist, belt, flat stomach, crisp uniform. A cool hand holding his wrist, dropping it, flop, onto the sheets.

I'm very sorry to have to tell you this, Quentin, but we have lost Josephine. In the accident. Thrown out of the truck.

His mother and father at his bedside. Did he hear them practising the statement over and over, toying with the words in a variety of constructions, different structures, as if a grammatical exercise? Or was it his own mind anticipating their announcement? In the accident, during the accident, as a result of the accident, Josephine was fatally injured. We are so sorry, dear.

We. We are. So sorry.

Quentin darling, Josie's dead.

The cold hard words like icebergs in a winter's heart.

We regret to inform you that your application to lead some sort of life with your wife and family has been turned down. Do try again.

Have they told him yet? He doesn't know. They are sitting there, a unit, two concrete blocks mortared together by time and habit, their concern a heavy clammy hand held over his face, holding his eyelids closed, his nostrils and mouth struggling to draw in oxygen.

And yet he can visualise them, see his mother in that pretty yellow dress exposing her plump drooping shoulders, see his father in the pale blue open-neck shirt, running his hand over his shiny head, his face with that ashen pallor reserved for situations of immense emotional strain, too large to be diverted or distracted by a flippant remark into some ghoulish arena of humour.

There is only one question now. Where is Georgia?

He observes himself with disinterest, as if he is floating idly beneath the ceiling. He can see the long hump of his body under sheets, the black misshapen face with missing teeth, the tangle of tubes and his wired jaw. He can see his pain, as if a coil of jaggedly serrated metal is being unwound through the top of his head. It is finite, he has faith that it is finite, that the coil will come to an end and the pain will cease and he will be able to ask the question: Who is looking after Georgia?

It wasn't so many months ago that *he* had been the visitor at a hospital bed, with Jo propped among pillows, holding the wizened creature whom they grew to know as Georgia, both blinking at the miracle that had overnight transformed them from couple to family.

Now some smudging finger has interfered with the scheme of things and he has been hurled back into the bosom of another era, thrown into the bewildered arms of his retrieved parents, back into a family where the dynamics and characters have already ossified in the natural progression of life.

But they are standing up, both his mother and father are standing up, responding in that way married people do, to invisible commands and signals. They take turns to clutch and squeeze his hand, and lean over to kiss him on the cheek. His father's breath has a faint sickly aroma of alcohol, and he says, 'Keep your pecker up, old son.' Quentin can hear this perfectly well. His mother says, and he can hear this too, 'We'll be in again tonight,' and her hair scrapes across his face like blunt pins.

But he wants to know about Georgia. Just where she is, who is looking after her.

'Ssssh,' says his mother, coming back to the bed. 'We'll be back tonight.'

He drags his eyes open. 'Look at me,' he says. 'Look at me. All I want to know is where Georgia is. That's all. I know about Jo. I just want to know about Georgia. Please just tell me that. I just want to know. Is she with Jo's mother? Yes or no?'

'Oh dear,' says his mother, pressing and pulling at her forehead. 'Perhaps we should call the nurse. Excuse me, nurse,' she cries into the corridor. 'Oh excuse me, our son, our son seems to be getting terribly upset at our going. Oh it's all unbearable . . . Unbearable.'

The nurse with the small waist and flat stomach bustles in, in a busy detached way, like a firefighter who has the luxury of insulation and an oxygen mask in a fire. 'Now, Quentin, what is the matter?'

He tells her. He tells her that all he wants to know is where his daughter is. She searches his eyes, looking for house keys in a smoke-filled room, and she turns to his parents. 'He's trying to say something. There's something he wants to say, and he's frustrated because he can't make himself understood.' They all stare at him as he settles in affirmation of the nurse's diagnosis.

'Georgia,' he says. 'Where is she?' He reads the fear on their faces. His mother pulls her shoulder to her cheek, and says to his father, 'Oh dear, I can't understand a word he's saying, can you?'

His father looks blankly at her then back at him and says nothing. But they know, he is sure they know. From the murky ocean of sedation he feels a stirring of a thick silhouette of fear. Already Jo inhabits this other territory, drifting like dislodged seaweed. But not Georgia as well. No. No, no, of course not.

He sees the nurse squeeze her eyes at his parents, pucker her lips, give a barely perceptible nod. Don't worry, is the message. I'll handle him. Off you go. They kiss him again and turn, his father's brown arm across the back of his mother's gathered skirt, and his impression is of an old four-by-two board stuck across a curtain to prevent his passage.

PART TWO

They are in a sitting room, Quentin balancing a cup of tea in a saucer on his lap. Lilian pushes the trolley across the teal blue carpet, confronting him with plates of food. Sponge cake with raspberry jam and thick whipped cream spilling from the centre, mashed bacon in chutney on toast, date scones and chocolate fudge squares.

Lilian's husband sits there, puce with embarrassment, his fingers too large for the delicate china cups. 'Look, Lil, maybe it wasn't, we was in shock.'

'No. No no,' she says. 'No no, I *know* it was a baby. What do you think I am, that I don't know a baby when I hear one? We heard the crash, remember? Well, you were fast asleep anyway. We'd just had a bite to eat. It was really hot, but windy, really windy, a hot dry wind. He'd fallen asleep reading the paper and I was getting into my togs to have a swim. Well, not a swim exactly but just to sit in the water to cool off for a bit. And we heard this almighty crash that seemed to go on and on.'

Quentin scoops a spoonful of sugar into his tea but pushes his hand at the food. 'No, thank you,' he says, then, registering her disappointment, forces himself to take a piece of savoury toast.

'Look, son,' says Harry, licking the end of his thumb. He holds his cup like a boxer with a sparrow's egg. 'We was in a state. Here we was sitting there by the river, all peaceful like, not a care in the world, if you know what I mean. I mean, it could have been the end of the world, and we wouldn't have known. When we go on holiday we just like to get away from it all and relax. Let the old hair down and not have to think about anything. Don't we, Lil?'

'Yes,' says Lil, nodding, as if betraying a secret. 'We do.'.

Quentin looks about the room, at the parade of small fussy ornaments along the mantelpiece, the pelmets, the shelves above the bar. He sees the stern look as Harry slurps too loudly at his tea. Harry, ruddy-faced and fat, sits awkwardly among it all, a sculpture roughly chiselled out of pumice amid cheap English china.

'And we hears this crash, as Lil says. And well, I think at first it's earthmoving at the bridge, like, and then we think, well, Lil thinks, we heard this baby crying.'

'No, you heard it too,' interrupts Lil. 'You heard it too.'

'Well, like, as we say, we was in shock. But anyway, Lil gets dressed, puts a skirt on, and we head off through the bush and there you was. We got there pretty quick, like, before the folks from the town. And there was just you, no baby, lying in the water, your head on a smooth rounded rock like it was put there, like you'd chosen it to have a wee snooze like, but your face was in a hell of a mess. Like the river was your blankets, and you was having a bit of a kip there.'

'And then we saw your wife,' says Lilian in a whisper, her spaniel eyes searching his face.

'Ah yes,' says Harry. 'Yes, I'm sorry lad. Yes.'

Quentin is learning to become accustomed to this. The strained moments loaded with pity and sentimentality, and trite words from strangers trudging across the marshlands of his pain.

He says quickly, 'Was there anything else? You say you heard a baby crying . . . did you look for one?'

58

'We was too busy looking after you, lad, and shocked over the young woman and all that. And then the people from the town came.'

'I looked,' says Lilian. '*I* looked. I looked in the truck. And around about. A woman, you see, a mother's instinct, to protect a child. But like he says, there was nothing, no one else. And then there was all the to-do, to get you out, and the helicopter coming, and in the end I thought I might have been mistaken but I wasn't. You didn't look too good. I told somebody, I think, that I heard a baby, but it seemed a bit silly, and they must have thought I'd imagined it but I didn't.' She looks earnestly into his eyes. 'I didn't. Well, I didn't, did I? Because when I heard the baby crying I didn't even know there was one. So that proves it, doesn't it?'

'Well, whether we heard it or not, it . . . she . . . must have been swept away, lad, in the river. Well, it's obvious, ain't it?'

'Did you hear or see anything else . . . anyone else . . . around that morning? Were there other campers, other picnickers?'

'You see, lad, no, we specially chose a quiet spot, away from it all. It's not the normal picnic spot, it's off the beaten track, like. Away from people. No toilets or taps. Like we said to the police.'

Quentin gulps his tea, his strong sweet tea, clunks the cup in the saucer. He is feeling drained, utterly exhausted again, a sharp ache running up his face. 'I think I'd better go.'

'Just a minute, lad,' says Harry. 'Just a minute now. It just suddenly came to me just then, just then when we was talking. But it's probably nothing. But I was thinking, lad, and it just suddenly come to me. I was sleeping and we'd just had lunch. And there was the crash.'

'Yes . . . yes . . . ?' says Quentin, not at all hopefully.

'And I remember thinking it was the Japs coming to get me . . . like, after the war . . .'

'Harry,' says Lilian. 'Not *that* again.' She looks at Quentin, pursing her lips, frowning conspiratorially.

'He had troubles, see, after the war. He was in Singapore, and it touches them, the war. They're never quite the same. Shocking really. There's more victims than they make out.'

'Crikey, Lil, let me think a moment.' He rubs his round chin. 'There was someone running, crashing through the bush. There was. Well . . . I think there was . . .'

'Harry.' Lil covers his rounded mottled hand with hers. 'Ssh,' she says. 'Don't get the boy's hopes up.'

'No, of course. It was a thought,' he says. 'I suddenly remembered. But maybe not . . .'

'No,' says Lil, shaking her head at Quentin. 'Maybe not.'

Dizzy. He wasn't feeling well, he shouldn't have come. The false hopes.

'Sorry lad,' says Harry. 'It was just a thought, but . . .'

✳

He is perched on a large stone, a lichen-covered mossy boulder, bulging from the grass at the side of the river. Green grass. The vibrant succulent grass that lovers choose for picnics.

This is where it happened. He has finally located the gouging tracks of the truck as it swerved from the road down the bank, crashing through bush to the river. He has spent some time searching for clues. He has found a brown rubber monkey that whistles when it is squeezed. This had been on the dashboard of the truck, ready to entertain Georgia. He has also found a soggy book by Carlos Castenada, its pages almost fused together. Jo had been reading this. She'd picked it up at a second-hand bookshop. It is so saturated that there's probably not a trace of her within it, no molecules remaining from her fingers as they turned the pages. He tosses it into the water, a sodden brick sinking, rising, bumping rocks, rolling over, bobbing and sinking, disappearing . . .

There are few signs of the drama of a family destroyed. Somebody could walk by and notice nothing. The more astute might wonder at the gouge down the hillside but already that is softening, already there are seedlings appearing in the mud.

He has little memory of the tragedy.

He remembers the truck being plunged into twilight, his vision of the road cancelled in a single thwack.

He remembers rushing water. As he sits here today, the gurgling of the water touches him with a sense of horror, as if it were responsible somehow.

He reconstructs the truck's path through the trees . . . if only it had been directed a little to the right or to the left, it may have been halted before the river, and Georgia may have been saved, and possibly Jo.

He runs his fingers through the moss, which, as he looks more closely, becomes a forest within its own terrain, its own rugged geography, its own impenetrable density.

The river rushing, babbling, boiling with bubbles like spit.

Like spit, like fury on a man's lips.

The bark of a tree with its elephant eye, ogling him.

If only these trees could speak, could somehow communicate with him. And that shrieking bird overhead . . . did it cock its head nearby as he lay in the pouring water, as it watches him now? He was the intruder here, that day and this.

Sandflies scramble around his ankles, above his socks. Blood smears under the hair of his legs. He finds it strange that these small pinpricks of irritation should even be noticed above his other, deeper pain.

He slides from the rock and trudges a little further, the long grass wet around his jeans. A willow has fallen across the river, clad in moss as if in an attempt to clothe itself, its trunk shooting myriad young stems with leaves, some green, some sad soft yellow.

The smell of dank kitchen cupboards.

His feet stumbling and tripping over vines and wet rotting branches.

He is unable to take the narrow path any further because of the bank; the water falling into fizzing rapids over sharp and jagged rocks. He flinches at the thought of Georgia's delicate skin scraping across these boulders. Like a pear in a blender.

Had they searched properly? *If* she had tumbled down this river — she must still be somewhere. Her body . . .

The sky now grey, now blue. An autumn day. The river clear, then plunging into black green. The boulders like secrets, holding shadows, dark places.

Tattered things wave from branches, streaks of mud-strewn debris hanging like hair. A willow shivers in a breeze, clinging to the last of its leaves. It seems the tree is a living animate thing, filled with fear, endeavouring to remain still in his presence. The trembling leaves give it away, escaping one by one, jumping reluctantly, like frightened parachutists.

Quentin finds himself leaning, exhausted, against a giant log, a tree up-ended from the side of the hill, its bark scored by insects. He stands there, idly fiddling, thinking and not thinking, scuffing away at the bark with his fingers. He lifts a lump from the tree. A green hunk of the soft fleshy cortex is wrenched away, revealing damp highways of holes and tunnels. He is drawn into a disinterested observation of the chaos he has created. Worms lift uncertain heads from a mush of chewings; shiny-plated brown larvae recoil from the light. Minuscule white mites and yellow millipedes speed on a flurry of legs.

Quentin picks up a stick and pokes at a network of dew-drops dangling on a lacy spread, prods into a white fur of mould. He watches ants acting out their civil defence strategies, carrying transparent eggs and young to safety. Black pearly eggs and tiny yellow ones. He becomes a monster. It gives him satisfaction to wreak havoc upon these helpless beings. He starts tearing into the rotting tree. He, too, has the power to destroy a delicately balanced system of life, a complex structure of organisms existing in harmony.

The truck heading across the bank and down the hillside was no more or less significant than these panicking bugs.

This rotting tree is a fertile compost heap feeding a humming society of living creatures . . .

. . . and an icy vice grips his stomach as he suddenly visualises Georgia lying tucked under a log or in a small hole, caught between rocks. Georgia dead and rotting like this log. A microcosm of life feeding upon her. Until now he has imagined that, should he find her body, she would be lying peacefully, eyes possibly open or closed, somewhat scratched and battered by the crash and the journey in the water down the rocky river. He has imagined her in her pink dress, her chubby limbs splayed in floppy abandonment like a doll dropped from a pram.

For some reason, until now, he hasn't taken account of the process of decomposition. Once again since the accident, he is assaulted by another indignity, another horrendous affront to his sensibilities. He grabs a large branch and repeatedly pounds the log and its tiny villages. With his fists he pummels at the tree, an animal noise rising from the pit of his stomach. Why hadn't he died too? If only he knew for sure that Georgia were dead, he would jump, he would slip into the deep river and let himself be taken.

Then he is still. His face rests across the pulverised log.

As he lies there, he has a vision of an angel, a figure of glass, transparent — gossamer hair, ice-blue eyes, pink lips —

pulling him from the water, drawing him as if he were a raw egg, from the water. As he is being pulled now from his body. He becomes so incapable of the will to move that he suspects he is the observer of his own welcome death. Georgia, he whispers, as a toddler crawls towards him, a fat baby in blue overalls, her cheeks wine red and a string of dribble hanging from her lips. She is like a cherub swimming underwater, her limbs pumping, and he can see crumbs and a smear of Marmite around her mouth, her eyes large and smiling and he can smell her as she nears him, as she is about to bury her face into his, as her face merges with his, passes through him and is gone. He does not lift his face; he knows she is gone. A spider scurries across the bridge of his nose, and ants already crawl on his skin; one tests with its feelers a dribble of saliva oozing from the corner of his mouth, as an animal might drink at a pond.

How much later is it when he hears the crunching twigs, feels the thump of footsteps walking down through the bush towards him? He has prepared himself for oblivion, and it surprises him that he even registers the intruders, let alone is stirred into any degree of action. His body is flung like a coat across the log. His face, his cheeks, his skin embedded in it. But he opens his eyes, peels his face away. Despite himself, the animal instinct is to check the invasion by an unknown into his territory.

Two people.

A man and a younger woman. Both in heavy boots, the man lumbering along in an olive green swannie, the hood lying on the back of his neck, a gun resting on his shoulder. The woman with her hair pulled back in a swinging ponytail, a red checked shirt tucked into jeans. And a dog running ahead to Quentin, sniffing at his feet, his jeans, his groin.

'Com'ere, Jack,' calls the man, his words gargling in his throat.

Quentin starts to feel foolish now, and confused, as if waking to find himself wandering in a city street in pyjamas.

Rubbing his numb cheek, finding bits of stick and fibre. Ants flee through the hairs in his arm. He sees the mess of tree littered around him, the demolished log in clumps of bark and yellow pulpy flesh. Under his nails, his red, raw nails. He busies himself, hoping they are passing by. He runs his fingers through his hair, shakes his shirt out, rubs down his trousers as they approach.

He catches the man's eye, gives him a dejected nod.

'G'day,' says the man warily.

'Hi,' says Quentin, and nods at the woman too.

'Everything all right here?' says the man.

'Sure.' He is standing upright now, steadying himself with a hand on the tree.

'We were up on the road there and heard a bit of a commotion. Just thought we'd come and check up.' The man casts his eye over the debris. 'Sure you're all right?'

Quentin can feel their eyes upon him. 'I was just . . . just . . . having a walk, by the river. Having a rest.'

'That your car up there? Parked up on the road there?'

'Yes . . . yes, I . . . I'm going now.'

The man puts out a big weathered hand, tanned and sinewy, worn scabs from scratches up his arm.

'No problem, mate. But you understand that we have to make sure that everything's all right, you know? We had a helluva nasty accident here a few months ago and I suppose we're a bit jumpy. We don't mind if city folk come and enjoy the river here, the peace and quiet. But we like to keep an eye on things as well. You know?'

'Sure,' says Quentin, extending his hand to have it flicked like a whip.

'Arthur,' says the man. 'And my daughter, Prue. So what's the story . . . just having a look around?' He looks pointedly once again at the log. 'Looks like there's been a bit of a dog fight here.'

'Yes, I was . . . er . . .'

'We don't stand for any of these magic mushroom eaters around here you know, son. We've had one or two of them, and we don't stand for them around here.'

'No. I'm sure. I was looking for . . . looking for insects.'

'Oh yeah? Endi . . . endimolygist, are you?'

'Yes, something like that.'

The man and his daughter are blocking his way. He would like to turn, wish them goodbye and set off with a wave, but a steep bank obstructs his path. He's unable to move around it because the river there is swirling in a deep green pool. Beyond that, rapids and rocks.

And then he realises that this is opportunity presenting itself: he is being offered answers here in an unassuming way. A helluva nasty accident, the man had said.

He braces himself.

'Any particular insect? Something rare, is it?' The man is clearly uncertain as to whether he believes him; there is an edge of sarcasm in his voice.

The girl is gazing at Quentin intently, with concern. He is unable to cope with concern. It destabilises him, just when he is in the process of hardening, to deal with world about him.

He mutters, 'Well, as matter of a fact I was looking for my daughter.'

'In the log there, is she?'

Quentin looks up as the farmer exchanges glances with the young woman, looking sheepish when he sees they have been caught.

'Any way we can be of help?'

'I don't know,' mumbles Quentin. He must keep calm. His heart is racing as he feels a hot blush spread up his cheeks.

The girl steps forward, touches his elbow. 'Were you in that accident?' she asks. Her honey voice.

He nods, biting his lip, working at his nails, torn and clogged with wood mash.

'The baby. The little girl. Georgia, wasn't it?'

She knows her name. He looks at her.

'Yes, yes. Georgia.'

'They were searching the river, the bush, all around here. Police everywhere.'

'Yes,' is all he can say.

'They did everything they could.'

'But they didn't find her. They didn't *find* her.'

'No, I know.'

'You . . . you were around at the time?'

'Yes, we live across the bridge. Everyone around here knows about it. Most of us were involved in the search. And being questioned and all that.'

The dog has been darting around as they chat, sniffing at the clumps of rotten wood, sniffing at Quentin's ankles, licking at the man's fingers.

'Sit,' snaps the man. The dog perches by his side, nuzzling into his hand. He grasps its nose fondly, like a furtive fumble for security, for something solid and known.

'I'm sorry, mate. It was terrible, what happened. Your little girl. And . . . your young wife.'

'We were down at the scene, helping,' says the girl.

'So you were down here in the beginning. Before the helicopter?'

'Yes. Everyone came as soon as they could. We heard the crash. I got here shortly after. It was terrible, as Dad says. At first we thought you were dead too, and then we thought you might die.'

'You didn't by any chance hear a baby, or see any strangers around, did you? Anyone at all?'

'No . . . hmmm . . . except for the old couple camping by the river. They were here when we got here.'

'Lilian and Harry. I've spoken to them.'

'So what are you doing here now?' the man asks.

'It's stupid, I know, but I was just looking around. Looking to see if there was something I could find, something that everyone else might have missed. You know. Clutching at straws, you might say. I can't believe she could have disappeared so completely. What do you think? You must know the river.'

The man hoists his gun, dips his fingers into the fur on the dog's neck. 'There're some deep patches . . . it's a pretty solid stretch of water. Could have been swept out to sea . . . or caught under something . . . but they searched pretty thoroughly.'

'So you think it's unlikely, then. That she could have been lost in the river without trace?'

'I didn't say that, son.'

'But do you?'

The man shrugs. 'Who knows. Look, what are you up to now? We were just talking about heading back for a cuppa. Been out looking for rabbits. Come back to the house and have a cuppa with us. Can't be too easy on you, all this.'

The dog barks, a single harsh clatter, as they turn back along the path. When they pass the scene of the accident the farmer starts whistling a nondescript tune. His daughter calls needlessly to the dog, slapping her hand against her thigh. It's a relief when they have to clamber up the grassy slope, through the bush, the dog skidding and tearing around an alternative route . . . waiting for them, panting, on a higher ledge, almost smiling as they scramble to catch up.

Quentin pulls out from the weedy verge to follow the ute, the back wheel skidding in the long wet grass. He notices the length of new fencing, fresh as matchsticks.

The road drops into the valley and across the bridge to the township below.

They pull up outside a house surrounded by a fence like a play pen, a low cage of framed wire-wove. The farmer — what was his name? Arthur — and Sue — no, Prue — climb from their ute. The dog jumps from the tray and bounces alongside Prue. Quentin moves stiffly from his father's borrowed Holden and follows them to a picket gate. Arthur clicks open the metal latch and says, 'In you come, son.'

Quentin doesn't notice that Prue is beautiful as her hair swings in a ponytail but he has a stab in the heart for Jo as he walks behind her, up the cobbled path that runs to the house between one patch of neatly mown grass and another, with clumps of early jonquils nodding in the cool autumn air. They scrape their boots on a spade-head embedded in concrete, then take them off anyway. Arthur and Prue sit on the red steps, loosening laces.

Arthur says, 'It looks like the rain's going to hold off.' He clutches a verandah post as he hauls himself up, a hand on his rump. Quentin removes his sneakers, which he leaves neatly in the porch. They all file into the laundry and wash their hands with a worn block of Sunlight soap, passing it one to another like comrades sharing a ritual. Arthur picks up a soggy towel and sniffs it.

'She'll do,' he says as he passes it to Quentin. 'Mum's probably got a dry pink one inside, but what she doesn't know . . .' He winks as Quentin dries his hands and passes the towel to Prue.

The dog whines outside but doesn't pass the barrier from the doorstep to the wooden floorboards of the hallway, the kitchen large and cosy with a fat black kettle simmering already on the coal range. A woman is bending at the open oven, prodding meat. She turns around and stands up, her face red and shiny from the heat.

Arthur saying, 'Mum, we've got a visitor.'

She clangs the fork against the roasting dish and props it dripping against a saucer on the bench, then wipes her hands on her apron. She peers at them, looking with surprise at Quentin.

'Mum, this is Quentin. Quentin — my wife, Elsie.' She smiles at him warmly, shyly.

There are three cups and saucers on the table and a square tin displaying a picture of Milford Sound. Prue is reaching into a cupboard for an extra cup, saucer and plate. She takes plump queen cakes from the tin and puts them on another plate. Pours water from the kettle into an enamel green teapot with a graceful swan's neck and a chip in the spout, and slips over a woolly striped tea cosy.

Quentin feels as though he is part of a scene in a wax museum, set into motion with a key. The kettle is still simmering on the stove, and the steam drifts rather than shoots from the spout. The man, Arthur, has grappled his way out of his swannie and thrown it over the back of a chair. Elsie unties the back of her apron and lays it over the swannie. Arthur pulls out a chair for Quentin, then himself, and they all sit at the table. Elsie pulls a handkerchief from her pocket and dabs her face. Prue, in the red shirt, passes the cups around. Her ponytail long. Auburn, copper. And Quentin. The stranger.

Quentin looks at his hands. Once again he is sipping cups of hot tea. But at least this time the cup is solid. Their sympathy has not extended to the special china, though if Elsie had known he was coming, it probably would have.

Arthur is talking about the price of wool. Whether it is rising or tumbling, Quentin doesn't care. He has just bitten into a soft and fluffy queen cake, still as warm as blood.

Elsie is watching him. He assumes she is trying to place him. Finally she says, 'Are you a stock and station agent, are you?' This is a community where everyone knows everyone. And their business. Quentin sees Arthur once more using his eyes to transmit messages, shaping an exaggerated frown at Elsie. Quentin has become adept at catching eye language. People flicking eggs at each other through the air.

He explains that he'd been wandering around the river.

'Arthur and Prue ran into me and asked me in for a cup of tea. Very kindly.'

'Oh yes?' This is clearly not enough for Elsie. Her curiosity defies Arthur's bushy grey eyebrows, his forehead, his speaking frown.

Prue intervenes. 'Mum. Quentin was in that accident. The one by the river.'

'Oh. Oh yes, I see, I see.' The flush from the oven heat, which was starting to subside, fills her plump cheeks once more. 'And they never found the baby.'

'No.'

He is improving. He is learning to pull away and back, like a prompt crouching in the wings, watching the performance. Soon he will be able to direct a play that is quite different from this one. One that might be flippant, jovial even. Making light of it. He is still learning. To be the director.

'I had been hoping,' he says, 'to find something.'

'That was a peculiar day, that one,' says Elsie quietly.

She puts her cup down in the saucer, fastidiously, as if its placement is significant, like a potter making a considered decision. She aligns the handle with the edge of the table, a little shift this way and that. They are all looking at her and she blinks rapidly before lifting her eyes from this project.

'What day?' asks Prue.

'The day of that accident.'

'What do you mean?' says Quentin.

'Everyone on edge, like before an earthquake. Very hot and windy, if you remember. Started off with Soots going missing. Our cat. A lovely cat, black and shiny as a Moor. I used to get up in the morning to make the tea and she'd be there, at the door, waiting to come in. Rattling the fly door to be let in. And that day she wasn't there.'

'Come on, Mum . . . She was nearly sixteen,' Arthur explains to Quentin. 'She walked as if she was on jelly; her poor old pegs could hardly hold her up. She would've crawled off under a log somewhere and gone to sleep. As they do. If Elsie'd let me I would have put a gun to her head in her sleep months before.' He vigorously rubs the back of his head, the prickly stubble of a new haircut. His steely wirebrush hair, though clipped, still manages to give him the tousled look of a man surprised from sleep.

Elsie tightens her lips and lifts a shoulder sulkily.

'Well, anyway, that day she disappeared. That day. And so then there was your accident, and then while everyone was down at the river helping and doing what they could, someone broke into the labourer's hut on Tizards' farm and stole drugs.' She starts to toy with the cup again, pointing the handle towards Quentin.

'Some people are real opportunists. Milking other people's bad fortune. So. Yes, hmm. It was a funny day all right.'

Quentin is disconcerted by the idea that his accident should have created an opportunity for someone to break into a cottage for drugs.

'The young chap working there had been taking the Tizards to the airport, in Napier. It's amazing to think that someone could have been so cunning to even think of it.'

'What sort of drugs?' says Quentin disinterestedly.

'Heroin,' says Elsie. 'Or opium. Something like that. *Drugs.*'

'No, Mum,' says Prue. She shrugs at Quentin. 'Grass. Pot. Home grown. There's a difference.'

'Not quite heroin.'

'No, well. Drugs are drugs as far as Mum's concerned. The farm hand had been growing marijuana in some secluded spot on the farm, and had some plants stashed under his bed where he was staying. The day of the accident, he'd taken the Tizards to the airport in Napier and stayed there overnight himself. When he returned, someone had smashed into the place and taken them. Of course the place was swarming with police

72

looking for the baby. With the Tizards' farm the closest to the bridge, someone'd called in there, not realising they'd left already. They discovered the break-in and the police were on hand. So Bruce, the guy, arrived home the next day to find a welcoming committee and no dope. But there was evidence of it everywhere. They even thought he might have gotten rid of it himself. But the Tizards swear everything was intact when they left, and that their suitcases were in the back of the vehicle and nothing else.'

'So instead of looking for Georgia, they were busy looking for drugs.'

Arthur clunks his cup down and sucks his front teeth. 'Come on now, Prue, there's no point in going over these things. This isn't helping anybody.'

A surge of light fills the room, the weak autumn sun finally finding its way through cloud and between the curtains above the kitchen sink. It brushes lightly across Arthur's face, giving him a warm hue, the hairs in his ear sprouting like the grey feelers of a sea creature in a rock.

'Have another queen cake, son, and don't listen to these women.'

Quentin pushes his hand in the air. 'No, not at all. This is very interesting,' he says. 'Maybe there's some connection.'

'I don't get it, son.'

'Well, what if they took Georgia as a hostage?'

'Who?'

'Whoever stole the grass. And maybe they . . . when they finished with her . . . Maybe . . .' He is silent now but the leap of his heart signals his terror at the thought. His hands are in his hair, digging into his still tender scalp. He is suddenly aware of Prue's hand on his arm, and he lifts his head.

'No,' she says gently. 'No. Impossible. They wouldn't have had a chance. We were all down there as soon as we heard the crash. We got there as soon as we could. I'm sure no one could have taken the baby, whatever Mum thinks. So don't think like that.'

'No, of course. It's just . . . I have to consider every possibility. It's the not knowing, you see . . .'

The sun fades again just as abruptly and the room, which had seemed quite cosy when they entered, is thrown into gloom. Quentin looks up and sees their faces upon his, the two women solicitous and Arthur ill at ease.

'Well, anyway, I must be going,' he says, the chair scraping the wooden floor as he stands up. 'It's been really pleasant meeting you. Thanks for the afternoon tea.'

He is on his way. He'll probably stay at the lake. In a cabin, or a motel. On his way to Auckland. Like he was. A couple of months ago. But the day is suddenly dark. The shadows. Not too long before nightfall. But then he thinks . . .

'The Tizards. Do they live far from here?'

Again the eye language between Arthur and Elsie. But Prue leads him to the window. Outside, the scene is bleak, unwelcoming, unstirring. Sheep nibbling at grass. One lifts its head, holds its chewing, as if it can feel his attention. Prue points towards a stand of macrocarpa some distance away. Through the trees is a snatch of grey, the wall of a structure. She explains that this is the labourer's hut.

'You can't see their house from here, but it's just across a paddock from the cottage. Not far.'

Quentin peers over the line of African violets sitting in wet saucers on the sill.

'So . . . their property is the closest to the river . . . ? Their farm is the closest in the settlement to the bridge, you were saying?'

'Yes, why?'

'So it would be easy for them to get to the bridge and down to the river without having to pass anyone else in the township.'

'I suppose so, yes. But . . .'

'I'm sure there's no connection, but it just seems strange. As your Mum said. Both on the same day.'

'Come on, son.' Arthur digs into his pocket for a large handkerchief which he flicks into the air and they wait as he trumpets into it. 'Look. The cat went missing. You had an accident. There was a burglary. The Tizards went on holiday. I broke a tooth on a meat sandwich. Somebody's grandmother died. A cow jumped a fence.' He folds the handkerchief and puts it back into his pocket. Elsie is tying her apron behind her waist. They all watch as she picks up the spoon and opens the oven, scooping sizzling fat to dribble over the meat.

'That's life, son. Things happen. Some days nothing happens, some days it pours. For no reason except that's life.'

Elsie bangs the spoon against the roasting dish, and exchanges it for the fork on the saucer, to prod the potatoes, kumara, parsnips.

Quentin shrugs. He feels vulnerable alongside the farmer's pragmatism. He feels his eyes soften. Whether of use or not, he'd like to know everything there is to know about that day. Not only the accident but the ripples it has caused in the community. Maybe this way he can solve the mystery.

He is relieved when Prue touches his arm again.

'I was going to go across and look for mushrooms anyway. You can either drive by yourself or come with me, across the paddock.' She clicks open a cupboard under the sink and drags out a couple of enamel bowls. 'You can help me.'

Arthur scrambles back into his swannie, like a man wrestling with a nightmare.

'Oh well,' he says somewhat huffily. 'A man's gotta work. Doesn't get done by itself.'

＊

The grass is dewy around their feet. The focus is the grass, in this afternoon fast approaching evening, the smells and sounds of an evening filling the air. The thick emerald clumps of grass fed by either cow manure or urine, he is never sure. Looking for the beige-grey discs among it. Quentin plucks out a mushroom with his forefingers. Like looking for money in a dream, he thinks. The pink flesh underneath resembling the gills of a fish. Like looking for breath in a dream. Looking for life.

Prue is wandering ahead, her bowl, although larger than his, already nearly full. She waits for him to catch up, pulling blades of grass from among the mushrooms.

'A good crop. We haven't been for a couple of days. Amazing how they come from nowhere. They're yummy with bacon. Do you like them?'

'Yes, I do,' he says. Thinking of Jo. Sitting at the table with her fork poking idly at a heap of black oozy mass. 'This is *evil* stuff,' she had muttered, as he laughed and encouraged her to eat. 'I've *always* thought they were evil. How can you eat anything *black*? They smell like the insides of caves.'

He'd persuaded her to try them, then coaxed her along until she had finished. 'You see!' he'd crowed. 'It's all conditioning.'

She'd been pregnant with Georgia at the time. He wonders now whether she might have sensed something; whether he had encouraged her to go against an intuitive sense that eating the mushrooms would channel some negative force.

He can hear the melancholy bellowing of cattle, a plaintive collective cry. He stands and listens.

'What is it?' asks Prue. 'Is there something wrong?'

'That mooing. It sounds . . . like a sort of contained mass panic. Desperate.'

He feels he could raise his head and join in; there is a quality in the timbre that resonates with a hollow aching in his chest.

She listens too.

'Oh, that. They're rounded up in their pens for the saleyards.

Weaners. Separated from their mothers. It's a bit of a racket, isn't it? You get used to it. I don't even notice it, though when I was little it frightened me. How are your mushrooms? Here look, there's a cluster over here.'

They squat down together, her parka touching his knee as they pick the mushrooms.

'So where are you heading?' she asks him, dropping a handful of mushrooms into his bowl. Her fingers are stained brown. And his are too, he realises. His nails torn and frayed from the episode earlier.

'Well . . . I'll stop somewhere tonight. Possibly at the lake. On the way to Auckland. I've got a job up there.' At least he doesn't have to explain about the accident. 'I'd just finished my degree at Vic. Everything was going so well. We'd been having a holiday before tackling work. This new job . . . reasonable money . . . we were feeling so settled. Amazingly, they've held on to it for me. I start in a couple of weeks. Just part time to start with, as I get tired. Everyone has been . . . kind. Accommodating. But to tell you the truth I couldn't care less about the job. Nothing matters any more. Apart from finding Georgia.'

He picks a mushroom which he absent-mindedly tries to spin in the palm of his hand as he holds the bowl against his jersey.

'What will you be doing?'

'Helping to set up a computing system for a firm of accountants.'

'Aha! I knew you weren't an entomologist.'

He looks at her shyly. 'Of course not. Anyway. I've got to find a new place to stay. A flat or something. It's a bit of a move. My mother wanted to come with me. Would you believe it! Twenty-four!' He gives a dry laugh. 'I've been living at home for the past six weeks. Since I came out of hospital. It's time I moved on. Started life again ...' He is beginning to mumble, his voice caught in his chest. 'It's weird living with your parents after you've been away from them. You almost go back to the old roles. Parents and children.'

'I know,' she says.

'You seem to be okay here. Do you help on the farm or what?'

'Yes I do. But I was away at training college for three years. It's complicated, really. Mum was having a few problems . . . depression, sort of. So I'm home for the year to help them out. Give them both a bit of support.'

The evening haze creeps across the paddock, shepherding the twittering of sparrows into the trees ahead of them. He should have left before dark. They startle a sheep which lumbers away from them as they walk, its movement made awkward by fat and wool. It continues to run as they carry on their way, convinced that they are in pursuit, until it finally veers off their course and stands bemused as they pass it by, its jaw stirring from side to side, like an English peer, pausing for thought.

'Stupid things,' says Quentin. 'They must be the most stupid animals in the whole world.'

'I don't know,' says Prue. 'People take some beating.'

They come to the fence under the macrocarpas, and leave their mushrooms at the base of a post. Quentin strips a leaf away as he waits for Prue to climb over. He crushes it under his nose, inhaling the piney fragrance. There's a reptilian quality about the leaf, which resembles a thin green claw. He remembers a huge macrocarpa hedge, thick, clipped and contained, outside his music teacher's house. He'd leave with the pockets of his school shorts bulging with the little round cones, and his fingers would smell like soap. Now he is thinking that the fence is like a musical stave. Prue's boot a crotchet on B, on F, a loop over to the D on the other side, down to G. She stands by, her hand out ready to help as his sneaker wobbles on the wire, but he clutches the post, swinging his leg to the other side and dropping to the damp ground littered with branches and cones like small splitting basketballs. These sprawling trees, with branches exploring the air, are so unlike the neat cultivated trees of his childhood memory.

Not far from the trees is the cottage they could see from the farmhouse window.

'There we are,' says Prue, quickening her pace, dipping her head to avoid a branch. Her hair swinging loosely as she looks back at him. Her face is losing its edge in the twilight, as if she is dissolving. Quentin realises that in the half light she could be mistaken for Jo. He could imagine she was Jo. He stops, lifts his hands above his head to hold a branch, dropping to feel the weight of his body. As if testing his own substance. As if testing for, or ascertaining, reality. She continues to move purposefully through the trees, a silhouette among the shadows now, while the numbed lump of pain stirs once more in his belly. Then dissipates into an all-encompassing fatigue. He crumples to the ground. He feels incapable of taking another step.

But Prue is alongside him, her boots against his sneakers, her jeans up against his shoulder as he sits hunched over his knees.

'Hey, are you okay?'

He scrambles lethargically to his feet. 'Yep, yep. Sorry. My legs suddenly went from under me.'

'You sure?'

'Yes . . . It's just, you know, since the accident. Sometimes I just give out. Without warning.'

He brushes at his jeans, attempts a reassuring smile. 'I'm absolutely okay.'

'Well, anyway, you can have a rest at the hut. We'll try there first if you like.'

The hut is unadorned with garden or trimmings. It is like a child's drawing of a house. Simple. A red corrugated iron roof.

A door with windows either side, an overhang jutting out over muddy concrete steps, and a pair of large gumboots propped upside down against the wall. A trailer is parked alongside, its tow-bar pointing upwards.

Prue knocks on the door.

'Nobody home,' she says. She seems disappointed. 'Oh well, we'll head over to the Tizards'.'

Across a lavish swoop of driveway there is a large old homestead with a wide verandah, surrounded by carefully landscaped garden, old trees and full shrubs. Already there is a light in the front room and a steady rise of smoke merging into the grey sky.

'Come on, then,' she says, but at that moment they hear the drone of a trailbike. It appears through the trees, its wheels crunching in the gravel of the driveway as it approaches, skidding to a halt in a flurry of little stones and dust, too close to their feet for comfort.

The rider is a guy with a mop of black frizzy hair, and a scruffy beard. His jeans and red and black bush shirt are sprayed with mud.

'Hey, Prude!' he calls cheekily. 'To what do we owe the pleasure?' He throws a leg over the bike and pushes the machine towards the hut.

'This is Quentin,' says Prue. 'Quentin, this is Bruce.'

'G'day.' The man gives them a cocky grin as he parks the bike by the trailer, kicking the bike stand into place. He brushes past them, the smell of cigarettes and animal in his clothes. Then he sits on the steps and tugs at his laces. 'So, what brings you? Are you coming in?'

Quentin follows them into a dark room smelling of fresh wood and smoke. The man directs them to a plump and tattered sofa, split in several places as if it were growing too fat for its skin. He goes to a kitchen bench and Quentin hears the distinctive fizz of bottles opening and the next thing a beer bottle is thrust into his hand. Prue is drinking alongside him.

'Cheers, boys,' she says. Bruce takes a swig and crouches in front of a brick fireplace, alongside a pile of folded newspapers and a mess of wood scraps and small logs stacked against the wall. He smashes several sheets of paper into balls and stuffs them into the grate, chatting easily to Prue as he snaps twigs to arrange a teepee around the paper. It lights easily with the first match and they all watch it flare. Bruce is balanced with his elbows on his haunches, his sooty hands clasped together loosely.

Quentin juggles his bottle from hand to hand. No alcohol for a while, the doctor had said. Bruce is talking to Prue about duck hunting with his mates. How many they'd bagged the previous weekend. There was one plucked and gutted waiting for them up in the Tizards' fridge . . . he was planning to bring it over.

Their faces are lit only by the last of the gloom and the flickering red of the fire. Bruce stands up and busies himself at the kitchen bench again, first lighting a kerosene lamp then pumping at a paraffin lamp, which he hangs glowing from a hook dangling from the ceiling. Then he goes over to the sink and runs the tap, washing his hands in a rich lather then splashing handfuls of water at his face, his beard dripping with diamonds as he reaches for a towel.

Quentin is waiting for Prue to bring up their reason for being there . . . he has become an unwilling observer of this man's preparation for evening and meanwhile it is getting late. He has a good hour-and-a-half drive in the dark. He is tired, uncertain as to whether to drink. He lifts the bottle to his lips. The beer is barely cool but pleasant. Perhaps he could sleep in the car, by the river . . .

By the river . . .

81

He takes another gulp, careful not to press the glass rim against his new plate and his still tender gums.

Bruce sits down on an easy chair in the corner. Slaps his hands together, then digs into his pocket for a packet of Port Royal.

'Well, what brings you over to this neck of the woods, mate?' he says to Quentin, rolling a thin cigarette, picking out the stray strands of tobacco, like hairs from a nostril. 'Cigarette?'

Quentin presses his hand in the air, drinks again from the bottle.

'Quentin was in the accident by the river,' Prue explains before he can answer. 'He was wanting to talk to you. He was interested in your break-in. On the same day.'

Bruce looks at Quentin sharply, his eyes narrowing.

'Bastards. Low life. If I could get my hands on their bloody necks, whoever they were. But anyway, what's it to you then?'

Once again Prue speaks for him. He senses she is acting from kindness, feels her move closer towards him on the sofa.

'The thing is, Quentin thought it was unusual that it happened on the same day. And he wondered if there might be a connection. You know.'

'I don't know. I don't get your drift, sorry.'

'Well, they didn't find the baby.'

'So?'

'Well, he was just wondering if the two things were linked.'

Bruce jerks his neck forward, blinking, his mouth hanging open. 'You're saying that I had something to do with the baby?'

Prue shakes her head vigorously. 'Don't be stupid. He was just wondering whether the person who took your dope might also know the whereabouts of the baby.'

He lights the cigarette and draws in the smoke, holding it as he thinks.

'Nah,' he says finally, picking at his tongue. 'Nah. There was no one here, anyway, when we left. I drove the Tizards to the airport.

And Frith and that kid. They left before us. So I dunno. What can I say, mate? I wasn't here. I just know some bastards stole my harvest. It was probably planned, waiting for me to go, eh.'

'Who's Frith?' asks Quentin.

'Fritha. Tizard. Daughter. And her boyfriend or boyfriend's brother or something. The ghost that walks. They'd stayed a couple of nights here — I mean with her Mum and Dad — on their way up to Auckland.' He jerks his head in the direction of the homestead. 'They'd left before us. Nah, mate. Barking up the wrong tree. You'd have to be a magician, and anyway, whatever for? Sorry. Nah, someone knew about the dope, knew I was leaving with the Tizards and jumped in. All they'd want to do would be to get out of here. They wouldn't be worried about babies as well. I mean, it's not that they *knew* you were going to have an accident, now did they, mate? Pardon me, but get real. But I'll tell you what, it'll set them up for a while, that's for sure. Bastards. It was great stuff, too. Bumper crop. The heads! Sticky, man.'

He shifts to the edge of his seat and picks up a couple of logs. Tosses them angrily into the fire.

'Did anyone else know about it?' asks Quentin.

'Yeah, mate. Everyone. I guess I was getting a bit excited about it. Everyone hoping for a free stash. You know. Well, when I say everyone, I mean quite a few of my mates around here. And probably their mates. Prue knew.' He nods towards her and winks.

'When does your court case come up?' she asks.

'A couple of months. A pity whoever it was didn't sweep up after them. Take their evidence with them. Thank goodness they didn't leave me half of it, gotta be thankful for that! We're gonna try and get away with saying someone planted it on me. Sorry, your honour! Don't know a thing. What is that stuff, anyway? Lawn clippings or what? Mixed herbs? Chinese tea?'

They laugh.

'I had it under my bed in the room back there. Five whopping bushes of it!'

'What? Still on the plants?' says Quentin.

The man looks at him sharply, his eyes glinting in the firelight. 'Hey . . . you're not undercover?' he says suddenly to Quentin. 'Checking up on me? Ha ha, just joking, mate. You can tell the good from the bad and the ugly. Ha ha, well, I *think* you can. Boy, I'll tell you what though, mate, any telltales from you and you won't know what hit you.'

Quentin drains the beer and places the bottle by his foot. If Bruce is threatening him, he doesn't care much. If it's a joke, he can't see the funny side.

'Well, thanks anyway. I've got to be going.'

'No, I mean it, man. If this gets out, I'll know it'll be from you, man.' He stabs at the air with his forefinger. 'You won't know what hit you.' He slips his finger under his throat. 'You get what I mean?'

'Sure, sure. I'm not even interested.' He stands up.

'So what's your hurry all of a sudden? You've got your info, mate, have you? Got the evidence you want?'

'Quit it, Bruce.' Prue leans over and pats him gently on the knee.

'Do you know this guy or what? I've got friends, you know. You'll be sorry.'

'*Quit it.*'

'Well, answer me, then. Where's he from? Have you ever seen him before?'

'Yes I have. He's okay. So just shut up and hold your horses.' She glares at him. 'Anyway, we've got to be going. Mum'll have dinner ready.'

Quentin is backing steadily towards the door. The paraffin lamp, until then breathing steadily, suddenly spits and sputters, as if affected by the sudden surge of energy in the room.

'Thanks for the beer.'

'Anyway, mate. None of that was true. I was mouthing off. Course I didn't have any dope. The pigs planted it.'

'Sure. Sure. I didn't believe you anyway.' Quentin is holding the little brass door handle now, round and cold in his hand, turning it behind his back, opening the door. Bruce sits there still, hunched over his knees. He flicks another couple of logs into the fire.

'Ponce,' he says.

'Okay, Bruce, we'll be seeing you then.' Prue jumps up and puts her bottle on the bench. 'I'll tell Dad about the duck.'

Quentin feels a nudge in his back and they slip out into the treacle black night, closing the door firmly behind. Prue pulls a small torch from her parka pocket, and plays a yellow stick of light over their path. Her other hand slips through his arm, and he is aware of his body tensing.

'I'm really sorry about all that with Bruce. I almost saw it coming, as he started blabbering on. That's his trouble, he can't keep his mouth shut and then he gets paranoid. He's a bit of a loose cannon.'

'I thought he might have a go at me.'

'He could have. He's not a bad guy. Just a bit nervy. Smokes too much. Do you still want to see the Tizards'?'

'I couldn't stand it. There seems no point, somehow.'

'Thought so. Come on, then.'

They are having to tread carefully over branches, through the macrocarpa debris which reels before them like a black and white film, shadows slithering over a desolate landscape in a movie. She pulls his arm close to her body with her elbow. Quentin is relieved when they come to the fence, so that he can release himself naturally from her comforting hold. They scramble over the fence and she jumps with a thud into the grass, while he wobbles on the wire and lets himself down warily.

He is suddenly left in darkness as she takes the torch to find the mushrooms. The air is cold, and the sky a lively dance of sparkle; the night, now that his eyes are accustomed, filled with pulsating shapes. He lifts his hand from the post he was holding and starts to walk through the grass across the paddock, like a swimmer kicking off from the edge of a pool. On the other side is a small floating parcel of light — the farmhouse — and his car. The beer has left him drowsy but he is not looking forward to sleeping in the car.

Prue catches up and thrusts the edge of a bowl into his side. 'One each,' she says.

He holds his hand over the soft lumpy cargo to prevent it spilling. Deliberately keeping his distance as he walks now. But she is alongside him, her arm gently bumping his.

Their silence reaches into the dark, joined by the occasional cry of a morepork, like a cuckoo from a faceless midnight clock.

She says suddenly, 'You'll stay the night with us of course. Mum'll have dinner ready for us.'

'Oh no, I can't,' he says quickly. 'I've got to get on.'

'Don't be silly. We've got a spare bedroom. Mum always has it made up with clean sheets in case we have visitors. They'll be expecting you.'

'But you don't even know me.'

He hears a long steady intake of breath.

'More than you might think. I stayed with you until the helicopter came.'

He tenses. 'I see . . . I see, I'm sorry . . . it's . . .'

'I told you quite a bit about myself actually. Just to keep you with us. I chatted to you and held your hand. I wiped the blood from your face with a cloth dipped in the river. You look very different now of course, all cleaned up and alert. And your new beard and your hair short. And thinner, I think. But it's hard to tell. But there's something about you that's the same, even though you were hardly conscious. Every now and then this afternoon I caught something about you that I feel I know very deeply.'

Her voice is soft, tender. He tries to recall its tones, some memory of her soothing reassurances. Some echo of familiarity. He is grateful for the dark as he wipes his eyes with the back of his hand.

'I'm sorry. I don't remember anything. But thank you . . .'

'Everyone did what they could.'

'Did . . . did anyone look after Jo?'

'Well . . . well . . . everyone helped as much as possible. But there wasn't much we could do. She was . . . she was caught in a tree.'

Yes. He knows that. They told him at the hospital when he begged for a reconstruction of the scene.

Perhaps it was Prue he had imagined as the blonde almost transparent angel who had appeared to him as a vision, as the river rushed through him, a creature of light rescuing him from the water.

A dog starts barking as they near the farmhouse and Prue yells at it, her gentle voice suddenly a gravelly roar, as if releasing a wild animal that has been jumping at the gates of her throat to be free.

'Geddin there, Jack!'

Miraculously, the dog stops. 'So, that's settled,' she says lightly, as if her show of strength has settled the matter. 'Have some dinner and stay the night and you can set off early in the morning. Come on . . . Mum'll be wondering where we are.'

As he lifts his pace, his mushrooms dance like little bald men in the light from the porch.

✳

Sleep. Sleep edging away like a bus he has missed, pulling away from the kerb of his consciousness, while he runs floatingly after it, his arm reaching for the rail with which to yank himself up and into the aisle, to be transported as a passenger into his own dreams. But he has missed the bus . . . he is running after the bus, a slow-motion striding . . .

He turns over. The overcooked vegetables and fatty meat lie like mud in his stomach. The beer Arthur forced upon him gurgles uncomfortably. Although he is unable to sleep, he is leaden with fatigue. Once again he pulls at the bead hanging from a string above his bed, dangling like a spider that has died waiting for wind. The light clicks on. 2am. As he lifts his arm, the chilly air finds its way beneath the sheets under the pile of heavy woollen blankets and stirs the warm fug he had brewing there. On the bedside table there is a glass of water and a bottle of sleeping pills. If he doesn't sleep he will be tired for the journey tomorrow; if he leaves it any longer he'll still feel drugged by the medication.

He sits up shivering in the bed, and takes a tablet, washing it down with water. Then another, to make sure, before tugging the light off again. He slips under the blankets, packing them around his neck. He looks into darkness, the blue hue of starlight offering the room amorphous shapes and shadows. Thinking of the dinner and how Elsie had announced quite authoritatively that she did not feel that Georgia was dead, that she was alive somewhere.

'Why do you think that?' Quentin had said politely.

'I just do,' she'd said, pushing her fingers into her breast, into the area he supposed she meant to be her heart. He'd nodded at her without further comment, as he chewed a mouthful of soft lamb. But now as he lies in the bed he feels a delayed irritation as he remembers her earnestness, her audacity even, in offering well-meaning but unfounded hope.

He has already been approached by soothsayers and clairvoyants. He has been told that Georgia survived the journey out to sea, ensnared by the buoyant branch of a tree

88

that had crooked itself beneath her little arms. She was picked up by a passing Japanese squid boat and was safe and sound with her new family in Kyoto.

Another said she had been pulled beneath the water into a tunnel of an underground stream and was lying alive on a ledge in a huge black subterranean cave, crying pitifully as she lost strength. Yet another told him that the little girl had been taken away by a wild dog, and that she was being nurtured along with the rest of the litter in a pit in a woody bank in dense bush.

Rational or not, he had believed each explanation at one stage or another, until one long-haired strikingly beautiful woman sat with him in her lounge, her knees touching his as she gazed into his eyes, one hand lightly caressing his fingers. She had hugged him warmly as he arrived, to put him at his ease. Incense burned in a corner and the music of waterfalls and forest birds trickled and chimed in the background. She solemnly informed him that Georgia had never existed. She was a figment of his longing for life to procreate itself, a projection of the desire for his profound love for Jo to be manifested in human form. Never mind, she told him as he sobbed in his hands, this was quite normal. This was why the accident had to happen, why Jo had to die, because the fantasy could no longer be feasibly sustained. In fact, she said, there really was no such thing in the whole universe as an *accident*.

He had shoved past the curtain of little brass bells, his fingers tearing at the loop of chain across the closed door. He lifted a giant pot plant from the top of her steps and smashed it onto the concrete below. The pot lay like a huge broken eggshell. From it hatched a shattered explosion of black earth, the plant upended with its roots a tangle of evil tentacles that seemed to claw at his heart. He kicked at it as he passed, shooting a missile of clumped soil still further up the path.

He kicked again, violently, as he caught up with it before he reached the car.

As he drove away he saw her standing on the porch, looking bewildered and forlorn. For the duration of the journey home he found himself wondering whether she was right. His life *had* become like a dream. He pulled the car over under a tree, his forehead pillowed by his arms on the steering wheel, as he burrowed his nose into the memory of Jo's skin, nestled his head between her breasts, and breathed and breathed the fragrance which rose like air from water from her skin. The smell of her hair spilling around them as they awoke in the mornings. The piquancy of the breath in her early morning kisses as she first woke, the slightly stale earthy smell of breath that had lain too deeply within her overnight. And the musky smell of her sex, the twisting of his fingers through the coarse curls above that moist territory which offered him anchorage. And through this, through this passage, Georgia had arrived. He'd been present. Yes, he was there. He had seen the bloodied ball of head appearing between Jo's legs, witnessed that first mangled cry, her shivering defiant little fists. It had seemed impossible; she seemed incapable of returning with the burden of the next inward breath. Later at home, they would lie in bed at night listening for her muffled snorts and sucking, at times feeling compelled to get up and check that she was still alive. He thinks of his face in her stomach, blowing raspberries into her fat warm flesh, her giggling kicking vital little body. He wants to check her breathing now — he would do anything, *anything* to be able to check that she's breathing now. He would die to be able to know that.

The house creaks as old floorboards release the day's burden to the night, like a man twitching before sleep, like furtive footsteps in the hall.

90

He turns to the wall, to another layer of darkness, diving through thumping thickets of darkness, to fly over tree tops, over a meandering river to a place where he knows he will find Jo, the place where she left him, where they parted. She is waiting for him, her cool body slipping in beside him, her cool satin skin absorbing his pain. They flow freely like smoke through the deep dark smooth river, like ether in a tormented mind, like blood through a heart. He holds her buttocks in his hands as she slides over him, pressing him through the bed, and down through an explosion of light, plunging tumbling through rushing water, her breath roaring in his ear until he hears their fused cry, a puzzled scream of startled gulls, and then his own voice above hers as he calls into the night for her. Jo Jo Jo. His heart thundering and his whole body sobbing as he clutches her, feeding his aching heart.

Sinking into the abyss.

Dawn is just beginning to filter through the curtains when he is nudged into a soggy consciousness by a small noise. He opens his eyes to see a figure slipping through the bedroom door. A figure leaving the room. A shimmery outline of a woman slipping away. He is capable only of observing this. He thinks for a moment he is back in hospital but he makes no further attempt at interpretation or analysis before he falls back into murky sleep.

✻

Driving. The heater whirring in the car. Around him the earth is white as if overnight the land has sprouted a hide of fur. Polar bear fur. White sharp glass fur. The land has turned to glass. His feet and fingertips hum with the cold and he blows on them, each hand one by one as the other holds the steering wheel. The sky is blue. Sheep huddle together and cows stand in mists of breath. A farmer bundled up in jerseys, coat and woolly hat etches messy footsteps into the frost.

He looks out across the land to see whether there is any sign of Prue or her father. He would have liked to say goodbye to her. By the time he'd dragged himself from sleep this morning she was out of the house. Elsie had insisted on cooking him a breakfast of bacon, eggs and mushrooms but after the hospitality of the night before, her manner with him was strangely haughty — angry even. She slammed cupboard doors, clattered dishes, flicked and lifted the sizzling bacon unnecessarily around the pan, as if determined to find an elusive word, ready to pounce on a trick question. She peered into the food to pick out pieces of shell after smashing the egg too viciously against the rim.

He'd sat obediently at the table while she cooked, her back hunched against him under a long drooping cardigan. When his breakfast was ready she had skidded the plate across the table towards him, then, suddenly embarrassed, fussed with the serviette, placed the salt and pepper too cautiously in front of him.

He would rather not have eaten at all but didn't dare leave a scrap. He wondered whether he had slept in for too long, or whether he had said something out of place. When he asked where Prue was, she had told him brusquely that she was out helping her father, repeating Arthur's mumble of the afternoon before, that work didn't get done sitting around all day.

Later, when he'd gone out to the car to leave, he'd discovered some of his clothes lying crisp and starched by the frost, strewn about in the grass. He opened the unlocked boot to find his suitcase there ransacked. He could not see that anything had been taken, but his once carefully packed case resembled the chaos of a washing basket. He looked back at the house, but Elsie, who'd said a curt goodbye on the doorstep with her arms firmly folded, had disappeared.

He threw in his overnight bag and went around to the front of the car. It was then he saw the word, scraped into the frost on the windscreen. COP. In case he hadn't received the message, there was a grubby page torn from a notebook folded under the windscreen wiper. GET LOST COP. He stuffed it in his pocket. Bruce. It was almost amusing.

He'd prayed that the car would start. As he'd driven away, he'd looked back again for any sign of Prue. Elsie had returned to her post at the doorway, but when Quentin waved she spun around and retreated inside. It was almost as though she wanted to be sure he was aware that he had affronted her. Bewildering though it was, he couldn't bring himself to care.

He blows into his hands again.

Up ahead he sees two hitchhikers, a young woman and a man, heading in the opposite direction. The man has his back to the road, urinating against a steaming fence post. The girl is sitting on a pack, a sleeping bag wrapped around her neck. She stands as he approaches, her eye catching his. He acknowledges her with a small wave as he passes.

He thinks back to Jo — was it only nineteen months ago? — presenting herself to him for the first time through the slow sweep of the truck's windscreen wipers, then melting into a deluge of colour as the rain pelted the glass. She'd stood with her thumb out, rain cascading over her face, her long Indian cotton dress clinging to her body. It was only when she was inside, bleeding great puddles of water, with the truck door slammed shut, that he'd realised she had no luggage.

She had explained how she had been picked up by a grey-haired man with tired eyes and a thin mouth, who'd stopped

93

the car in an isolated rest area. He'd produced a thermos and they drank coffee. He had spread open a greaseproof paper parcel and shared small triangular Marmite sandwiches with her. He packed up the picnic and then without warning, reached over and ran his fingers over her thigh through her skirt. She'd told Quentin that she was impressed most of all in that brief moment by his trembling hand, his fingers shaking uncontrollably, to the point where she felt pity for him.

She picked up his hand firmly and said NO, as if to a child. He broke down and apologised, inconsolable in his shame, so that she eventually assured him that it was all right, a small misunderstanding, and patiently listened while he justified his action with a story of problems with his wife.

Before they'd set off she had left the car to have a pee in a bushy area behind a bank, going further than need be, to be sure of her privacy. The man had driven away, leaving her in that deserted place. She could recall no details about the car apart from its being white. Fortunately she had her passport and money in a belt around her waist but everything else was gone.

She'd told Quentin this as they drove along, rubbing her long hair with a towel he'd pulled from the back of the truck. She was an Australian, and had been travelling for two years, through Asia, mainly India. When they'd arrived at a town he had to stop for petrol, and he gave her a shirt and a pair of loose cotton trousers to put on while her clothes dried. She'd used a piece of rope for a belt to keep the trousers up, and rolled the bottoms up her strong tanned calves.

By the side of the road a hawk lifts from its feasting on the entrails of a possum, tugging at a red string of viscera, like an old woman sewing a stuffed toy.

'Look Jo, a hawk.'

Look Jo a hawk.

The words echo at him from across the valley between then and now. The hawk lifts into the air and slides over a paddock as the car passes by.

As she said later, it had seemed significant that she entered his life with no baggage, cleansed by the rain and soon travelling along the road with him with nothing from her former life except the clothes she was wearing and then, within half an hour, wearing his. It had seemed quite natural that he take her back to his flat where there was a spare room, only to find that in the week he'd been away someone else had moved in. Jo had slept on the couch for the first week and then shifted into his bed. There had been no question from the start that the process had been set in motion by destiny.

Those first few days they had talked, filling in for each other their lives between then and now, with an eager hunger to know everything, as if they were old lovers who'd been on holiday apart. They had covered childhood, parents, religion, schooling and adventures along the way. It was as if they had a checklist of significant attitudes and events. Exchanging information like electrons between them, interweaving memories, ideas, dreams. Meanwhile their bodies waited, fizzing with desire. He had to leave her to go to university lectures, and would find himself sitting at the desk thinking of things she had said, or things he planned to tell her. Their intensity grew. They wandered through the city, looking in shop windows and finding everything hilarious, strangely anachronistic or without reference to their own lives. They walked through suburban streets, arm in arm, at times going for miles and seeing nothing, at other times befriending dogs, enticing cats from under hedges, down from letterboxes.

Towards the end of the day they would start to head towards the beach where they strolled, picking up shells which they would give to each other and receive in a kind of wonder, as if carefully selected jewels. Clambering over jagged black rocks, they'd balance precariously as the sea crashed at their feet, sucking and surging beneath them. More and more they touched each other. More and more the space between them became shared territory. Even after they kissed, they had continued to talk, holding back from the succulent but unexpressed certainty, knowing that everything would change in the metamorphosis from ancient friends to new lovers. They held this time like a firm peach, which sweetened and ripened with each minute passing. Eventually the shared space between them became their own intermingled breath, their own selves lost in reconstruction.

When they finally made love it was as if not for the first time together, but after an age apart.

PART THREE

Fritha swerves off the driveway, parks the car on the rock-hard lawn, opens the door and scrambles out. She flaps her arms, breathing deeply and exaggeratedly, holding her face to the late afternoon sun. Matt is still anchored in the car as she darts around the back of the fibrolite bach, scrabbling under leaves until she finds the round damp wooden lid over the slug strewn drain and pulls out the tobacco tin from its place on the grating.

Yes, it is still there: the key.

Up the rickety old steps to the back porch where she opens the fuse box and clunks on the power switch, then with the long black key unbolts the door, which still sticks on the lino floor as she shoves it open, and the place still holds the musty smell of holidays and stale sunshine. She leaps up onto the divan, reaching upwards to the rusty coiled wire to drag the curtains aside, moving first to one end of the divan, then the other. The windows stick too, screeching as she opens them. She calls out to Matt to get off his chuff, is he going to sit there all night or what?

'Shush,' whispers Matt, but of course she doesn't hear him as he painstakingly manoeuvres himself from the car with his precious cargo, asleep at last.

'I can't believe this,' she says as he creeps inside. 'Going all that way to Wanaka when they could have come here. It's so neat. I'd forgotten just how neat. We used to come here every summer. I bet they've bloody well tossed out the comics.' She bounds to the window and, with her fingers securing the mattress, lifts the lid of the divan, diving into it and hauling blankets and pillows to the floor.

'What d'you know, they haven't.' She stands up, clutching a large pile of well-handled Walt Disney comics. 'There're Phantoms, too. When we got sick of tearing around we'd sprawl around the place on our stomachs with a pile of these and just lose ourselves. And look at the view. You take views and things for granted when you're kids, but look at it. Unreal.'

'Is there a bedroom?' whispers Matt.

'Is there a bedroom? Of course there's a bloody bedroom! Three of them. God, Matt, look at you. Matty Madonna. Virgin Father.'

'You'll wake her.'

'I can't believe this. Puppy envy. Get yourself a puppy, Matt.'

She leads him through the kitchen, through a narrow hallway with great sepia water stains on the walls, like maps. She shows him three bedrooms, two with bunks, one with a double bed. He chooses a bunkroom and gingerly places the baby, who hardly stirs, on the lower bed. He tiptoes out and closes the door.

'Whew,' he says.

He goes out to the car and collects the parcels they'd bought that afternoon, after Fritha's aborted attempt to leave the baby in a toilet block at roadside tearooms and a petrol station. She was determined to be cool about it all. They'd discussed whether they should have a cup of tea, quite naturally, before Fritha took the baby with her to the washrooms, leaving her there as Matt walked out to the car. But Fritha was concerned that there might be a chance of being recognised afterwards, so she decided they should stop the car, go to the toilets, leave the baby and take off. She assured Matt that the baby would come to no harm and that the crying would soon draw attention.

As it turned out, the toilet was occupied by a sharp-eyed old woman who just had to have a peep as she came out and, oh, how old was it, he or she? Oh, they are so unsettled at that age, aren't they? She remembered so well. So exhausting. But why was she *so* unsettled? And oh, what a nasty scratch on her poor wee leg. Was Fritha still feeding her, dear? 'Just Coca-Cola,' said Fritha. The woman gawked as Fritha passed quite brusquely to enter the bathroom. She'd told Matt how she'd closed the door and stood against the wall thinking why the bloody hell did she say that, now that's stuffed it. That's really stuffed it. Walk out without the baby and that old woman with the eagle eye would be waiting to point her out to whoever she's with.

Fritha placed the distressed child in the handbasin. She opened the door a crack and peeped out to see a bus pulling up outside the tearooms. A hoard of people spilled out, heading towards the toilets. Fritha grabbed the baby and tore over to the car where Matt waited, and said, 'Let's get outta here. We'll try the next one.' But the toilets in the next petrol station were locked and to use them they would have had to ask for a key.

'People will have seen us with the baby now,' said Fritha. 'That old soandso, she'd dob me in, I know. What a witch. God, Matt. What have you done?'

It was then that she decided to go to the bach, some distance from the main road by the lake. They stopped in the town and Fritha — it was decided she would attract less attention — Fritha went shopping. She came back to the car several times, loading it up with food for them, as well as disposable nappies, milk formula, bottles and teats, rusks, juice, a couple of tiny t-shirts and two stretch-and-grows. Plus a dummy.

And now the wind has sucked itself back into its genie bottle, leaving the sky blown chalk-dust white and the lake the colour of sad eyes, and Fritha says, 'I'm going for a swim. Coming?'

'We can't leave the baby,' says Matt, 'and anyway, I want to sort this lot out.'

'Suit yourself,' she says. She grabs a towel and is gone. He watches her run across the lawn, through the gate, down the dirt road and the long grassy hillside, to disappear over the bank that drops down to the lake edge. Shortly afterwards he sees her cutting through the water, a distant glistening figure who stops and turns and waves to him, before presenting him with a demonstration of porpoise dives: her round bum then her scissoring legs and did he imagine the dark tuft between them.

He turns to the table and dips into the collection of parcels. So much food. Bolt-hole food. Tins of baked beans and raisins, nuts and cheese. A huge bag of apples. Bread, butter, honey. He pulls out the tin of milk formula. For all her denial of any involvement with the baby, Fritha had insisted that they buy this. 'They can't cope with cow's milk,' she'd told him in the car. 'They get sick. That would be the last straw. Manslaughter. Baby slaughter. Great.' She'd read the instructions on the tin before tossing it back in the bag. 'Over to you, boyo.'

Now he does the same. To sterilise the bottles, he chooses a large enamel pot in the cupboard under the sink and simmers the bottles on the stove. Boils water and takes dollops of the powder and stirs the milk mixture in a plastic bowl. He tastes a spoonful. Hot and sweetish. Pours it into the sterilised bottles. Squeezes over the teats. Two bottles ready. He tips one upside down over his wrist, a ritual he has observed of someone — who, he can't remember — sometime in the past. The milk is still too hot and the droplet leaves a tiny red patch on his white skin. But never mind, two bottles ready.

He opens the door to her bedroom. She is still. He goes in and stands by the bed. So still. Too still. He drops to his knees and stares into her face. The dummy has slipped out onto the crocheted bedspread, and he sees with relief her cherry-pink mouth making a play of sucking. Suddenly her whole body jerks, her arms outspread as if falling. She awakens, crying again, and he is pleased to pick her up and hold her close, soothing her with cooing.

'Okay, Dylina, my little stinker, you are well in need of a bath,' he says, placing her back, screaming and red, on the bed. Her nappy has not been changed since he found her.

The bath stands elegantly on ornate paws but a dry stream of dusty flakes and mouse droppings has collected in its bowl. Matt finds cleaning powder in the cupboard and gets down on his knees to give it a scrub, running the water until the gush of rusty brown becomes clean and clear, swishing around the sides of the bath until it is gleaming. Then he prepares to run the bath but the water is still cold, so he reboils the hot water he used to sterilise the bottles, and adds that.

He goes to the window and finally spots the small figure of Fritha, now dressed, walking briskly around a curve of the lake shore, and he is relieved to see that she's walking away from the house. He doesn't want her scathing insults as he baths Dylina for the first time. Dylina. He is almost sure it is to be Dylina. Dylina or Dylana. Probably Dylina. She is still crying and he wishes she weren't. He picks her up and takes her to the divan, where he won't knock his head on the bunk above, and regards her critically. It was no wonder the woman in the petrol station was suspicious: her pretty pink dress with the gathered smocking is grubby from being tossed around the floor of the truck, from getting wet and then dusty.

He undoes the button behind her soft fat neck and wrestles first one chubby arm then the other from the sleeves. She has a tiny air-cell singlet on as well, and he lifts both that and her dress together over her head, catching them on her nose on the way. He puts them aside then pulls off the fluffy pink pants over her nappy, before unclasping the safety pins and spreading the nappy apart. He is greeted with a pungent smell of ammonia and faeces and is mortified to see an angry red mottled rash between her legs from the prolonged steeping in her own urine. He is learning; there is so much to learn. He leaves her there as he rushes to the toilet and comes back with toilet paper to wipe the yellow mess from her bottom, holding his breath and screwing up his face as he does so. The marble white skin of her legs dives into creases of fat. He hadn't realised babies were so fat.

He puts the nappy aside then swoops her up, holding her out from his body as he takes her to the bath. He holds his arm behind her, but when he eases it away experimentally he is surprised to see that she is able to sit up by herself, like a little slouching Buddha. She looks as if she has been carved from something spherical, fashioned from a boiled egg or a lychee.

She likes the bath. She immediately calms down and regards the water intently, splashing her hands on its surface, trying to grab the soap, which he shoots from his hands in a game for her. She giggles, her first giggle with him. He is so happy. We're going to be happy, he thinks. I'll look after her for ever. He thrusts back the image of the bloodied contorted woman caught in branches of a tree in the bush above the truck, her skirt flapping like a flag, a blonde plait hanging down like rope, like a severed lifeline, too far from him to reach readily or to ascertain whether she was alive or dead. And the man he pulled from the water. Was that only today? It is as if he has erupted from dreaming of his previous life; it is as if fate has presented him with this baby to cherish and nurture for ever. He is the new father. Look at her so happily playing in the water. Fritha will grow to like her too. It will be good for them all.

He lathers the soap and lets his hands slip and slither all over her fat slippery little body, her poor scraped and bruised shoulder and neck, her scratched leg, squelching her arms through his hands, and her feet, and the tiny toes, all the tiny little toes — miniatures — and the fingers too, strange probing miniature doll fingers. He lets her lie back on his arm as he washes her red monkey bottom, and the primitive hairless mound of her sex, splashing her so that she gasps. The water is milky and frothy with soap. He takes her back further and washes the few strands of her fine blonde hair, so fine that it clings like a transparent cap over her head.

'Dad dad dad dad,' he coos at her as he fills the washbasin with cool water to rinse off the soap, then wraps Dylina-Dylana up in a towel, a whole parcel of baby with her ruddy purple fat face poking over the top, a pupating grub, bewildered and upset again as everything, everything in her world is unfamiliar and unknown. She senses the awkwardness of Matt's handling of her, and she senses the frayed umbilical cord, the disappearance of her parents. He pokes into the parcels and pulls out a t-shirt and the stretch-and-grow and a disposable nappy and by the time Fritha returns he is sitting on the divan in the fading light with the clean baby in his arms, gulping the warm milk.

Fritha says, as she walks in, 'Hello, everybody, I'm home. I've had a hell of a day at the office. When's dinner ready? Uh-oh . . . baby still up? Oh my, pretty as a picture . . .'

She plomps herself down in a forlorn old easy chair, among the faded pink flowers and the teal green leaves and the jaded peacock blue background. It swallows her, the tiny Fritha; she seems to be consumed by it. She reaches behind and grabs a book from the bookcase. 'Oh, *this* one,' she says idly. 'I've read this one about eight times. Heap of rubbish . . .' She tosses it aside, then rummages around in her bag until she finds her brush and starts to tussle with her long wet hair.

'Good swim?' asks Matt, taking the teat from the baby's mouth to let her catch her breath.

'Where did you learn to do all that, Matt? I mean, it's not natural, a kid your age, with a baby like that . . .'

He didn't know whether it was a real question or another jibe, so he let it go.

'How would you like some fish n chips? There's a couple of shops on the corner, a dairy and fish n chips. I checked them out to see whether they still existed. It's quite a walk but if we hurry we'll catch the fish n chip shop. They used to be the best I'd tasted — not too greasy and fresh fish. I'd've bought some then but I didn't have my purse.'

'Sure,' says Matt.

'So . . . coming?'

'What . . . in the car?'

'For Christ's sake, it's a pleasant walk. Do you good. Anyway . . . it was always a rule. If we wanted fish n chips, we'd have to walk. We'd tear a hole in the newspaper and eat them on the way home. That's the best way. Though it was also good to eat them by the lake.'

'It's just . . . Dylina. Ah, um, can you get mine?'

'Nope, sorry mate. You comes or you don't gets.' She drops her brush and stands up, then suddenly slaps her thigh. 'Hey . . . just a minute.' She leaves the room and he can hear her footsteps crashing down the steps of the back porch, then shortly afterwards back up again, into the lounge.

'Curse it,' she says. 'It's locked.'

'What is?'

'The shed,' she tells him as if it could be nothing else. 'There's a padlock . . . now wait a minute . . . the cutlery drawer . . .' She pulls the drawer open, shifting a jangle of knives and forks. 'If I remember rightly . . . hey . . . fantastic!' She waves a key with a label dangling from a loop of string as she disappears again. When she returns she is jubilant, lumbering in with a dilapidated old pram which she plonks on the lounge floor. A gaggle of daddylonglegs staggers across the lino, followed by

104

woodlice, like tiny dark toys on wheels, heading for the corners. Fritha places her bare foot on the framework and concertinas the pram upward. She pulls out the mattress and leans from the window, whacking a cloud of dust into the air.

Matt moves from the divan and sits on the arm of the chair, rubbing the child's back. He watches as, several times, Fritha goes across to the sink and rinses out a dishcloth, then comes back to wipe the dust and grimy spiders' webs from the navy vinyl casing. She starts to replace the mattress, then throws that aside and pulls a fresh pillowcase over a pillow from the pile out of the divan, and pats that into the pram instead.

'There you are,' she says proudly. 'Perfect. Get her in there, sonny boy.' She looks at her watch. 'If you hurry, you might get your fish n chips after all. Quick. I'm counting. I'm gone at 100.' She starts counting, loudly and tauntingly.

※

'Well, blow me down, if it's not . . . or is it?' The chap in the fish n chip shop bangs the strainer against the tub of boiling fat and props it up to drain. 'It is, isn't it? Fritha? Little Fritha. You were knee high to a grasshopper last time I saw you. Well I never. Mind you, you're not much bigger now. How many years is it? Eight? Nine?'

Fritha's first impulse is to deny who she is. She hadn't thought for a second that she'd be recognised. The self of her childhood seems shadowy and remote; a character to recall as if from a movie, or from the pages of a favourite book.

'Yeah, probably about eight or nine. Haven't been here for ages.'

'And your Mum and Dad, haven't seen them for a year or two either. They okay, are they? Still in the land of the living?'

'Yeah, they're fine.'

'They still have that bach up the way there?'

'Yeah, but Mum's mother's been sick so she's been spending time with her in Wellington. And they've been busy on the farm. And my brother's got a place with a couple of kids down at Wanaka so they go down there. They're on their way there now, as a matter of fact. We stayed with them last night, and they left this morning the same time as we did.'

'And talking of kids . . . What about you? What are you up to?' He nods through the window towards Matt, pacing along the footpath with the pram. 'Your only one?'

'Um . . .'

She doesn't know, she doesn't know whether to say yes or no. She stares wildly out the window at Matt, who's leaning into the pram, fiddling with the baby, as if the answer might present itself.

The man turns from her and pulls a dripping strainer from the fat, four fish golden brown and crispy. He wipes purple swollen hands down the two vertical skids of yellow grease on his apron, and flicks the cloying strands of hair from his eyes.

'Boy or girl?'

'Whaa . . . ? Oh, um, oh, a girl.'

'Your only one?' he repeats.

'Oh no.' She laughs, awkwardly. 'Oh no. That's not mine. No . . . he's my boyfriend's brother. We're on the way up to Auckland to see him — my boyfriend, I mean.'

'From?'

'Oh, from Wellington.'

The chap folds his immense arms, like thick slugs, and examines her.

'Often wondered where you'd end up. So what are you doing there?'

'Where?'

'Wellington.'

'Oh, this and that. Finished my degree and I've been more or less bumming around since then, being a postie, mainly.'

She glances outside to see Matt standing there, pulsing the pram like a practised grandmother, peering anxiously through the lettering on the shop window.

The chap lifts the strainer of chips, pouring with frothing fat. He arranges the newsprint, places a blank sheet on top and whops down the battered fish. Then the drained chips. Then a cascade of salt.

'Now, let me think,' he says. 'No vinegar, right?'

'Right,' she tells him.

He grins with pride. 'There you are, you see,' he says, his sausage fingers surprisingly deft as he folds over the newsprint into a neat parcel, adorned with ancient news and scantily dressed pin-ups. 'I know my customers.'

'Fifty-fifty,' she says, paying. 'The odds aren't fantastic.'

'Say hello to your Mum and Dad.'

'Sure,' she says, tucking the fish and chips under her arm and diving through the restless fly curtain of coloured plastic strips at the entrance. She gives the chap a wave, and nudges at Matt to get going. 'Let's have them down on the beach,' she says. 'We'll just catch the sunset.'

'She's asleep,' he says. 'Look at her. She's sleeping.'

∗

Crying. Crying and crying. She won't stop crying. Scrambling through the dense forest of night, the two of them, Matt and Dylina-Dylana, pacing and pacing, through the voices and the moving visions from the day before, and Matt is wondering now how long the terror will last. He keeps his panic cornered, clenching his teeth against the inclination to hurl her away and make her stop crying; holding it at bay as something dangerous for them both. He is wondering whether the little girl's mind is bombarded with the same images, whether she will forever smell the rusting metal floor of the truck, hear the roaring of the river, the ghastly cry of her father choking on teeth as he lay at the water's edge?

Hush, little baby, don't you cry . . . Mama's gonna sing you a lullaby . . .
 The words and the tune rise like small birds released from a window of a deserted house.

My baby, the father had been muttering. My baby is crying. And still the baby is crying. Matt paces in his jeans, holding the child against his bare chest, against the tiny useless nipple of his flat chest. The night hangs fat and dense around them and the future coils long and twisting beyond it. Interminably. The bach presses upon them like sand. They are buried under sand, struggling to emerge. Is it possible for this primitive nymph to feel such fury? She is a hard little morsel, hating him. She is refusing him. Scrunched up against him, calling across the night across the night transporting her will across the night to her parents . . . primitive drumbeats into the night, across the clear starless night across the clear throbbing night and he screams to her, bawls at her: Georgia Georgia. He is fighting to sit up, to tear at the visceral tangle of tubes invading his body, his mouth tasting of old tin and drooling with it. Running footsteps and a woman's voice, Come on now, Quentin. Shhhhh. Georgia, he cries, his pain unbearable, a fist turning in his heart. There is the crackle of uniform and other footsteps. A woman's voice saying, Help me with this one can you, and he says, Jo? as he is gripped by fingers and restrained with the sharp penetrating needle and Matt opens the door and goes down the steps to the damp grass on his feet and the cool dark air breathing upon their faces. The squall within Dylina-Dylana subsides, and somewhere nearby a bird rattles in the sudden silence.

'I'll look after you, Dylina, my little Dylana,' he murmurs into her ear, kissing her head. 'After a while, it will be all right.' She smells of flower. That utterly delicate smell of flower, any flower. Her skin is petal soft under his nose. He slides about the lawn in some kind of cruisy dance for two, for which the steps, although unlearned, come easily and naturally, and for which the symphony swells from his head into the amphitheatre of night. Soon he feels a soft yawny shudder, a limpening of her body, a succumbing to sleep. He feels an immense sense of triumph. They have won this demon battle. This time at least.

Reluctant to disturb her, to return inside the bach where she might wake up again, he wanders towards the gate, his hand crooked under her thick wad of nappy. She's a compact package of person. And he feels that she is complementing something within him; he feels more complete as a person than he ever has before. She's a gift to him from God; he'll never abandon her. Never.

Across the lawn to the tree shapes, to the tree by the fence, he slithers down to the leafy dampness and kneels. He gazes out towards the darkening within the darkness of the lake, and he speaks aloud as he holds the baby to his bare heart, her small potato fist rubbing her nose in her sleep as she tussles her head from one side to the other.

'God. Dear God. Thank you, dear God, for handing me this child of yours to cherish and care for. Thank you, God. Thank you. God, I am so grateful that you have chosen me.'

He stops and thinks that yes, he *was* chosen. When you look at it, the unusual circumstances. Fritha announcing as they set out that they were going to stop for a swim, and parking the car so carefully back from the road. Then, down at the river, sitting on the stones and chewing her nails for a while, then suddenly remembering that she'd left something behind, or so she said. She'd suggested that he wait there while she went back. In fact, when he protested, *insisted* on it. And so he did.

He didn't feel like swimming alone, on that hot wind-sucking morning, but he waited for her, for such a long time. He was starting to think that she might be seeing someone — someone she didn't want him to know about, because of Scott. Having sex or something. How long did *that* take? And who with? There was Bruce, the farm hand. He'd seen them sitting on the wood pile under the trees, smoking and laughing like idiots together. But Bruce was driving Mr and Mrs Tizard to the airport; they'd spotted them driving over the bridge when they were down by the water, so it couldn't be him. You never knew with Fritha, who she knew or what she was going to get up to. But anyway, wandering around the river, he'd come across that weird old couple having lunch. Pretending he was spying on them. Hoping to see something . . . interesting. Just to pass the time, while he was waiting. That had turned out to be unfruitful until at the end, after lunch, he could just see strips of her getting dressed in the tent. Her broad dimply bottom as she stood up from sitting on the edge of the camp stretcher, tottering a couple of paces with her togs around her knees as she struggled to pull them up. But no, that's besides the point. The fact is that he was *there* — really for no reason and in the middle of nowhere — when the crash occurred. It was meant to be, that he be there.

He is thinking about it, he is probing into his soul, for there is a nagging doubt that he might not have done the right thing.

Were they dead, the parents? The father didn't look or sound healthy and if Matt hadn't arrived at the scene so quickly he would have drowned. When he'd first come belting through the bushes, a wheel was still spinning and rocks were shifting from the weight of the truck. Matt had dragged the man, choking, from the river, held death at bay by hauling him from the river. Should he be alive now, it is due to Matt. He could say, a swap. His life for the baby. How long would it have been before his discovery? Matt remembers the sound of an approaching vehicle as he and Fritha argued in the car about the baby. He sniffs at Dylina's skull. He rearranges himself to sit against the trunk of the tree, burying his face into the sleeping child's shoulder, inhaling deeply.

For a moment he has the impression of huddling on the bed of an ocean, the surface of which spreads like a dark plate above him. He feels the pressure of the depth, and peers to identify shapeless forms in the suffocating gloom. Someone is drifting by, a tumbling figure from a shipwreck with limbs wavering like seaweed. He recoils as an accusing finger swipes his face. He grabs at the finger to find that he is twisting a leafy twig from a branch above his shoulder. He holds the child tightly, shielding her head with his hand as if from predators, letting her essence waft into his nostrils, until he too is enveloped by sleep.

He awakens with a jolt. Birds are beginning to twitter and light has already started to seep into the day. The tree is grinding at his spine and the soil feels like concrete. Dylana's cheek is moist against his chest. He stares at her. A new day. His predicament grips him first of all with awe, then alarm.

And then he sees what has awakened him. Just a small noise but Fritha, Fritha creeping around the side of the house, with her bag, and now at the car over to the side of him with her hand opening the door so stealthily. She shoves her bag over to the passenger seat, kneeling so he can see her leathery sole poking from the car, and he thinks he can hear the sound of keys sliding into the ignition. If he didn't have the baby, if he could move his body from its frozen lock, he'd spring forward and surprise her by tugging at a toe.

She pulls herself out and walks towards him to the back of the car, digging into a back pocket of her jeans for a key, which she uses to open the boot. She's not removing anything or putting anything in, but poking among a bulging heap there.

'Fritha.'

She gasps and spins around, her hand spread across her throat, her eyes scanning the dawn shadows for the source of the voice.

'Good morning,' he says, waving, as if to clear a misted window pane.

'God, Matt, you fucking little creep, what the fuck are you doing there? You just about killed me, you little creep. You fucking little creep.' She slams the boot down and locks it as Matt scrambles to his feet, clutching a branch of the tree for leverage. The baby in his arms is waking up and greeting the world with a wail. Frith says, 'Here we bloody well go again.'

'Where are you going?' he says.

'Where do you think?'

'What? Without me?'

'Matt. When I agreed to give you a lift up to Auckland as a favour to your brother, there was nothing in the deal about picking a baby up along the way. You're lucky I didn't dob you in. It kept me awake half the night with its non-stop screaming . . . I've been lying there thinking about you, Matt, and you're just such a weirdo.'

'Thanks,' he says. 'Good morning. Welcome to the new day.'

'This is kidnapping, you know that? There's no other word for it. Imagine if you were caught, have you thought about that?'

'I'm taking care of her.'

'She doesn't belong to you. It's not like catching tadpoles in jars, or hedgehogs in a cardboard box, you know. You can't just pick up a baby and go.'

'It's not like that.'

'Yes it is.'

'No it's not. You don't understand.'

'I don't have to. You're nicely set up here. Plenty of food. I've left you money. I'll tell Scott where you are and if he wants to, he can pick you up. Keep it in the family. It's nothing to do with me. I'm just the taxi driver.'

'No. Don't tell Scott, Frith.'

'Huh! I see. It's a secret. You're going to look after this little animal but nobody is to know. Very interesting. Or is it just for a couple of days, is it, Matt, then you'll put it back? Once everyone's had their nervous breakdowns and the lot, and you've had your play, you'll let it go. Set it free. You just want to hold it for a bit, to see what it's like, is that what it's all about?'

The child is giving raucous voice to the conversation as if she has her own version of how things are to be. Matt jiggles her as he talks.

'Don't go just yet. Stay another day.'

'And where will that get us? Sorry, Matt.'

As she paces across the grass to the open gate, Matt reaches into the car and yanks the keys from the ignition, stuffing them into his pocket.

Fritha whirls around. 'Fuck you, Matt, give me those keys.' She strides towards him, her hand outstretched, her monkey eyes blazing, the wild lady from Borneo.

'Fritha, listen, don't go just yet. What if someone comes? Finds me here?'

'You should have thought of that before, sonny boy.'

'Just give me a day to think.'

'About what?'

'About what I'm going to do. Me and Dylana. Just a day to get used to each other.'

'You don't need me around to do that.'

'Just a day.'

'And then what?'

'I don't know. It's all new. And scary.'

'I'll say it is, sonny boy. I'm not sure what it's like in cloud cuckoo land, but from where I'm standing, it's all new and scary to me too. I mean . . . God . . .' She threads fingers through her hair, long strands wisping around her face. She thumps her forehead with the heel of her hand, then sighs.

'Look, you've never even had a proper girlfriend from what I can gather, and now you've got a *baby*. Look, Matt, sweetie pie, you're a lovely guy and all that, but you don't quite see how it is. How things are, how they really are. What normal people do. But you know enough to realise that Scott is going to go off his nut. Of course you don't want Scott to know.'

'He looks after Jason okay.'

'Oh ho. So *that's* what it is. Want to be like big brother. Aha. Look, Scott, I'm grown up, just like you. I'm in the same mess without all the mucky preliminaries. No money and a kid.'

'It's not like that. This baby was given to me. It's not a mess. I just have to sort a few things out.' He drops his lips onto her head. 'I love her.'

'*Shit*, Matt. It's so obvious. What you *really* want is a woman. Most people get a pet. You've kidnapped a baby. And anyway. Anyway. What about the grand plans for you to work in the music shop? Scott didn't organise the job for you for nothing, you know. Just because he's the manager and you're his brother, it doesn't mean to say you can let him down when you feel like it. A job is a job and he's doing you a favour.'

'He'll find someone else. Anyone can do it.'

'That's not the point.' She shrugs. 'But it's your business. I just thought I'd remind you, that's all.'

She's walking towards him, her hand outstretched again, looking him in the eye.

'So, Matt. The keys. Give me the keys.'

He backs away from her. Around the car. He dumps the crying baby on the driver's seat, then retreats into the garden as Fritha holds his eye, a sharp stick of gaze fusing his eye to hers, a shimmering shaft of gaze as he staggers through a shrub and lands against the wall of the house. She mouths as if to a deaf mute: 'Give me the keys, Matt.' She comes close. 'Your baby,' she says impudently, 'is very upset.' He feels her fingers worming their way into his key pocket, delving past the bones of his pelvis into the taut flesh of his underbelly. He swivels against the wall and grabs her wrist with a jelly hand.

'Don't,' he says.

'Now, what have we here? Eh? Eh, Matt? What have we here?' She is like a bush surgeon who has at last located the suspected pulsating tumour. 'Hmmmm,' she says, as if considering a prognosis while her fingers dig and probe, drawing his blood and his breath. Her knee presses into the inside of his leg.

'Stop it,' he says weakly.

She hauls the car keys from his side pocket, singing, 'There you are!' and abandons him, to wave the car keys in front of his eyes, tauntingly.

'That wasn't too bad, Matty baby, was it, now? That was a nice game.'

His lips are as dry as summer leaves, his heart is whamming at the earth, the molten centre of the earth, his eyes are thickening with tears, but it is all right, it is all right, he tells himself, it is all right. Fritha picks up a wad of his cheek and pulls his head down to hers. He feels her tongue slipping into his mouth with a slick flick, as if sampling the inside of a jam jar. She says, 'Yum,' and lets him go, discards him again, turning away towards the car, jauntily tossing the handful of keys from one palm to the other. He takes a breath and it catches at the top of the throat, spasming through his shoulders. Fritha gathers the screaming baby from the car, cradling it as she waits for Matt to come. He doesn't look at Fritha as she hands the child over. He bounces Dylana on his arm and stands there as Fritha speaks, her hand resting on the open door.

'As I said, there's money on the table. I tried to think of anything you might need.'

She climbs into the car and starts the motor. He is thinking that he will probably be okay, he and Dylina-Dylana. They don't really need her. It was just the thought of being alone but then again, he will never be alone again. Now that he has Dylana.

Fritha is cocky, fashions a wave, kisses at the air.

'You'll be fine,' she says. 'Better for both of us. All of us. For the whole theatre company actually — if you count Scott.'

She drives in a slow arc to face the gate. 'Be a sweetie and open the gate for me, Matt?'

He trudges over to the gate, unclipping the loop of number eight wire that straddles the posts, then drags the old gate over the uneven grass. As Fritha drives the little car through, he notices the boot key is still in place.

She waits, hanging her head from the window as he closes the gate again.

'Listen, when you go — well, yes, you know, *if* you go — leave the back door key in the tin under the wooden lid of the drain thing at the back, by the shed. Please.'

He bends over, pulls out the boot key, and slips it in his pocket. 'Sure,' he calls.

And then she is gone, a cloud of rising hanging dust. Matt feels as though a cyclone he has become accustomed to has suddenly abated, and it is only now, when he can stop running for shelter, stop cringing from the battering, that he is able to observe the devastation.

But there is only silence of a sort, a distraught whining from Dylana, and loneliness. The imprint of Fritha's fleeting tongue lingers in his mouth, as if he has been branded by a farmer's iron. He secures the wire over the gate-posts and heads towards the bach, burying his nose into Dylana's wet cheek. Time for a bottle and another bath.

Inside, he pulls the boot key from his pocket, turning it over in his palm. Why would she keep this one apart from the others? Or is he being suspicious about nothing at all? It is of no use to him but he is satisfied that at the very least, Fritha will know that he's had the last laugh. At best, she might return.

'But no more pocket games,' he says to Dylana. 'They make me nervous.' He wants to add, *the bitch*, but can't. He takes the lid from the tin of milk formula and buries the key in the powder. 'Less personal,' he explains to Dylana. 'Now let's change your nappy while your bottle is warming up.'

Some time later he hears the clatter of the gate, then the car pull up outside the bach, the car door slamming. Dylana is bathed and changed and he is sitting on the divan giving her the bottle. He looks up innocently as Fritha barges in with that wild monkey look, her blue eyes darting and furious.

'Hi,' says Matt, as nonchalantly as he can.

'God almighty, I can't bear to look at you. I mean, look at you, Matt.'

'What, you came back to tell me that? I think you mentioned that yesterday.'

She flaps a newspaper at him, then skids it across the divan. 'Have a look at that, smartie pants. You been telling me lies, or what? Just read that and tell me what you think about that, then.'

A blunt knife pierces Matt's diaphragm as he looks at the photo on the front page — the truck, a gathering of people, a man carried on a stretcher with a bottle held high in the air:

ONE DEAD ONE MISSING IN TRUCK PLUNGE.

'You told me both parents were dead.'

'I thought they were.'

Oh crikey and it says one missing.

One dead, one missing, in truck plunge.

He is aware, without looking up, that Fritha's fists are embedded in her waist, her arms like the frills of a lizard ready to strike. Waiting. For a response from him. He scans the article and oh crikey and he picks up the newspaper from the divan to read it more closely and it says one missing.

A woman is dead . . . and a baby is missing . . . a woman is dead . . . Nothing about the woman captured by the branches of a tree like debris after a flood, her blouse open and fluttering like angel wings in a last desperate attempt to fly, her moon-white breasts in raw exposure to the searing heat of the sun, nothing about the peculiar angle of her neck. The man's condition is listed as serious but stable. Listed. The man's condition is listed. His condition is one of many conditions that make up a list. A list of conditions. It sounds like an ultimatum. Police divers are searching the river for a six-month-old-baby girl who is reported as missing. Fears are held for her safety.

Dylana splutters and he takes the teat from her mouth, puts the bottle down on the floor, lifts her to feel her fumbly round feet on his knees as she tests the strength of her wobble-rubber legs. Fritha's feet clamped on the lino, tough dusty feet in roman sandals, the strength of her legs known.

'So?'

'What?' There's a tapeworm writhing around his gut but he kisses Dylana under the chin, the silken junket under her skin and goes pop popopop pop my little poppety poppety pop.

'MATT!'

'God, Frith, you gave me a fright. Look, you've frightened Dylana.'

'No, Matt. Not Dylana.' She snatches the paper. 'Georgia. Georgia Jane, actually.' Waggling the paper under his nose. 'Don't you understand? Georgia Jane Stanley, aged six months. There are people out there now pulling the river apart because of you. With every rock or log those people haul aside they hold in their minds' eyes a private vision of horror. A tiny swollen doll, tongue like a sea slug, eyes like . . . eyes like I don't know what. As they swim beneath the weedy banks probing water holes, they're going to think, is it this time? Every squirming eel is going to be a child's arm, or leg . . . God, Matt. Imagine! And there's a man lying in a hospital bed who not only has to deal with serious injuries, whatever they are, and the death of his wife, but he thinks his little girl is dead as well.'

'Missing, it says.'

'You can't get away with it. I don't know what's in your head, Matt, and it's none of my business but I just thought you'd like to know what was going on.'

'But anyway. It was your fault. I would have taken her to the police or hospital or whatever. It was you. You wanted to go on, leave her in a petrol station.'

'Well, all I can say is that your timing was fantastic.'

'What do you mean?'

'Just that, boyo.'

At last she turns away, and he hears the slamming of the door, hears the thump of her footsteps down the steps. Hears an urgent rustling outside. He swivels around to kneel on the divan, leaning forward to peer from the window, to the garden beneath. Her shoulder blades poking through the muslin shirt as she crawls in the dirt, scrabbling around in the already crumpled shrubs, scuffling through leaves. She backs out, like a cat from a paper bag, sits on her haunches and he dips his head in an attempt to avoid her glare, but there is a brushing of glances like whiskers in the night as she pauses to think, to calculate, where she remembers having the key last.

A sharp smell alerts him to a spill of clotted milk dribbling down Dylana's chin to her chest, and he rises to pull out a number of tissues to wipe it away. He talks soothingly to her, rocking from foot to foot, rearranging her t-shirt, tucking a strand of silk behind her ear. Then he goes back to the window and watches Fritha walking around the lawn, head down, scraping the grass with her feet. Once again she lifts her head towards him and once again he wonders whether he has escaped her gaze. He knows confrontation is inevitable. That porcupine mind of hers, those poisonous sharp antennae.

'Never mind, Dylina-Dylana,' he says. 'We'll be all right. I'll look after you while your daddy is sick. It's all right, my darling. She's a wild one, but she's okay really. Perhaps you need to go to sleep for a while, my littlest.'

He hurries to the double bedroom and dumps Dylana on her back in the bed, tucking the sheet and blanket around her. She immediately starts to cry but he sidles out of the room, rabbiting at her with a babble of pacifying nonsense as he closes the door.

Thumping up the steps. The twisty rattle of the old door handle. Fritha sauntering into the lounge, holding the stance of a miniature cowboy about to shoot. Matt has a panicking urge to run away. To cower in a cave, eating berries and shoots, catching fish and sleeping by damp fires and observing through slits in foliage the fuzzy world tramp by. It is a vision he has entertained before but until now it has always seemed frighteningly lonely. Until now. There is a certain shift about the feeling, he notices, just before Fritha spikes the image with her pitchfork tongue.

'Okay, sweetie pie.'

'What?' he says.

'Gissit.' She steps towards him, holding her hand out like an earnest preacher.

'What, Fritha? No, not again. Piss off. Leave me alone.' He grabs a cushion and leaps onto the easy chair, a foot on each broad arm.

'Give it to me,' she says.

'What are you talking about?'

'The key, Matt. Give me the key, please. You like our little game, don't you?'

'What are you talking about? I gave you the keys this morning.' He springs from the chair as she attempts to wrap an arm around his leg, onto the floor, over to the table where he picks up a kitchen chair.

'Get lost.'

He's crashing around the room holding the chair over his stomach and she says, 'Okay Okay,' slicing her hands through the performance. 'Cut. Cut. Pax. Let's just calm down a bit.'

'I'll go along with that,' he says, warily. She flops onto the divan, folds her wiry arms and chews the inside of her lip.

He drops the chair but stands behind it all the same, like a nervous waiter in a restaurant.

'Right. Let's be serious. Matt, I've lost the key to the boot. Do you know where it is?'

'Yes.'

'Oh, so you do, do you! You do bloody well know where it is! You sneaky little gherkin. So where is it? You're holding me up.'

'Fritha. Stay with me. Please stay with me. Let's stay here together. Just for a while.'

'I'm sorry, Matt.'

'Please.'

'This is weird. *Why* would I want to stay with you, for a start? To play mothers and fathers with the baby you found in the bulrushes? Imagine what Scott would say if he heard you?'

'Yep. You're right. That's okay. I just thought I'd ask, that's all. Stupid.'

'It is, really, sweetie. But it was kind of you to ask.' She added the last like a commentary after the event, an epitaph, even. *It was kind of him to ask.*

'But why don't you stay just one night more?'

'God, Matt! Matt. Come on. Let's not be silly about this. Please give me the key. I want to go now.'

'What about a cup of tea? Have you had breakfast?'

'Okay, I'll have tea and toast with you. All right? Just to please you.'

Fritha lies on the divan with her arms clasped behind her head, a foot resting on her folded knee, staring at the ceiling as if it were a summer sky. Matt makes the tea and toast and brings it over to the table. Two plates, two knives, two cups. Honey and Marmite and butter. The baby in the bedroom, suddenly quiet. There is a desperation within him for this scenario; there is a deep longing that is more than just a hope, but a foreknowledge, a sense of the inevitability of it, as if he were a caterpillar crawling to the steady branch, anticipating the splitting skin, the sleeping growth of wings, the first ungainly flight. He has no doubt that what he has here is the certain outcome of his life.

So much so that he is unable to question it any more.

He has had a feeling about this journey since that Sunday. It'll be good for him, he overheard his father say to his mother, as she shelled peas and he sat with a beer in the kitchen, in from the garden and waiting for dinner. They didn't know he was sitting in the shade of the porch eating plums, the juice like watery blood landing on the white soft skin of his inner thighs, his back thin and stooped like a crescent moon. I was thinking we could sell up here and buy a little unit for the two of us and take a trip somewhere. Club Med or something.

You're talking as if he's not coming back, she'd said. Of course he won't come back. Well, I hope not, for his sake. Did you want to go back home to live after you left? Nah, once he's had a taste of Life, he'll be away laughing. Just needs a push, that's all. Scott'll show him a thing or two.

That's what I'm worried about. I'm not sure that Scott is the best influence, she said. I can't help but worry about him.

He doesn't seem to be going anywhere. He just seems to be marking time.

We all are, said his father, there's no two ways about that, my love. There was a muffling in the sound of his father's voice that told Matt his father would be kissing his mother's neck, a neck he knew was soft like his inner thighs, the juice dribbling there under her full and wavy hair to the wet patch on the porch.

He sat on the doorstep, unbeknown to them, as his mother laughed sadly, and said, Oh Pete, how am I supposed to prepare dinner, you old ram you, and Matt knew that his father standing from behind would have his arms around his mother, his bottle on the bench now, and his hands clasped together under the mound of her stomach, squeezed against the kitchen cupboards . . . nibbling at her ear as she attempted to continue with the peas. Matt could monitor by the nature of the murmuring, his father's snuffling, where they were at in the process.

He wiped his mouth with his shirt sleeve and, taking the last plum stone between his finger and thumb, torpedoed it into the lawn. He stood up and stepped into the hallway. Through the crack of the open kitchen door, he could see his father's bulk cloaked around his mother's back, while she swivelled her head and pushed an elbow back into his paunch and sang, Pe-ete, and said, Dinner will spoil. It's nearly ready. Are you wanting peas or not?

You're the only one that can give me any peace, he said, his words muzzled by desire. When Matt walked in, his father's hand slipped from the dress with such ease and made as if to lean forward to take a pea from the pot in the sink.

Oh, Matt, said his mother. Just in time for dinner. I was just going to call you. By the time you wash your hands, and set the table . . . Just the peas to be done.

In the bathroom he had stared into the mirror. His white curls, his white skin, his lips shapeless with plum stain, his

123

straw-tuft lashes around ice-moist eyes spinning like tops as he clutched the side of the basin, his head dropping from the mirror to the hard ceramic edge. He turned on the taps and let the effervescing torrent swill the dust of his tears away, as he dropped his hands into the water, holding the razor blade against his wrist, against his wrist, against the salamander skin of his wrist, under the water like river surf. The blade biting into the skin, denting then piercing, a smoke thread of red as the blade cut into flesh, a little slit but deep and holding it there under the water, holding it there and unable to slice FUCK IT unable, FUCK AND FUCK to slice the blade across his thin wrist, across the blue pumping byways of his life.

He wrapped his bleeding wrist in a facecloth while he scrabbled in the cupboard for a plaster. Only now did it hurt. He placed a cotton pad over the wound, secured it with a large plaster and pulled down his sleeve, buttoning it at the cuff, just as his father knocked on the bathroom door. When Matt didn't answer, he thrummed the door in the jamb and said, Hey hey Matt. Whatcha doing in there? *I* know what you're up to! Come on, now, you're holding us up . . . dinner's ready.

Matt unlocked the door and his father stood by to let him out. What's eating you? he said, as Matt barged past. Come on, can't you take a joke?

'Fritha. Breakfast.' Pieces of toast lean like cards against one another, on the table. The teapot in its rainbow-coloured knitted cosy. Thick sunflower yellow cups and matching saucers.

He pours a little milk into each cup.

'Dylana's asleep,' he says, as Fritha yawns and stretches. 'She looks so beautiful. So peaceful.'

124

'I must have slipped off. That bloody baby all night. I didn't sleep a wink.' She drags herself to the table, propping her head on an elbow. 'Oh dear. I've suddenly crashed. I can hardly move. All this is too much for me.'

Outside, the lake sits like an oven tray under a crushed tin sky.

'The weather's building up,' he says.

'I know, I know, that's why I wanted to get going.'

He pours the tea and pushes a cup towards her. She takes a sip. 'Eurgh. No sugar.'

Matt jumps up and sidles around the table to poke into the parcels, returning with a packet of raw sugar and a spoon.

'Sorry,' he says. 'I forgot. Have some toast.' It's only when she's mushing up her Vogel's with melting butter, and then peaks of honey, that he takes a piece for himself.

'Is it all right?' he asks. 'Hot enough? I'll do you another if you like.'

'Relax, Matt.' Her teeth clamping into the toast. 'This is great, thanks. Spot on. So. The key? Please?'

'No,' he replies. 'I don't really feel like giving you the key, Fritha, I'm sorry.'

'Suit yourself,' she says, 'You're not going to blackmail me to do anything. I was hoping that I wouldn't have to use a crowbar on the boot, but if I have to, I have to, that's all. But it's a pity. That we have to leave like this. We're never ever going to like each other if I leave on this note.'

'I still can't see what it is to you if I come with you.'

'Because kidnapping a baby is illegal, Matt. I'm not out looking for trouble just for the sake of it.'

'So what, it'd be my trouble not yours. And we wouldn't be caught anyway. The cops don't go around checking on everyone just because they've got a baby.'

Fritha sighs and pushes an eyelid open with her index finger to demonstrate her difficulty in staying awake.

'God, Matt, I'm sick of this. I'm totally and utterly stuffed. Did you put something in the tea? You probably did, to make me stay.'

'Yeah, sure,' says Matt, amused by the thought. He had the Valium his mother had given him before he left, in case he felt unable to cope with the periods of anxiety he suffered sometimes. Just to take you through it, she'd told him. He'd tried one out of curiosity and didn't like the stodgy lethargy it induced.

'I mean, that's the sort of thing you'd do, isn't it?'

'I don't know what you think I am,' he mumbles.

'Well, you tell me,' she says. 'I'd really like to know. *What* are you, Matt? I mean, besides baby snatcher extraordinaire . . . what's in your head? Really?'

'Forget it.'

'No, no, really. Seeing you're so keen on my staying with you, tell me a bit about yourself. I'd like to know. All this is a bit of a surprise, this twist of character. When I've visited your place you've always seemed to be inarticulate and withdrawn, invisible but always present, lurking in shadows, shuffling behind curtains. Your mother pampering you as if you were made of cobwebs. You'd hardly speak to me. You were like a sort of elfin figure, a creature straddling this world and another, a subterranean creature struggling to understand how to perform among humans. It was as if you came up out of a drain or a rabbit hole after a storm or a flood, and lay injured and gasping on the lawn until Scott went out and found you lying there and said, Mum, Mum, look what I've found.' She mimics the high squeaky voice of a child. 'Can I keep it Mum, please. Everyone else has got brothers and sisters except me.'

'Very funny,' says Matt grumpily.

She continues. 'But Mum, I'll look after it, I promise.' Then she adopts a deeper authoritative tone. 'No . . . you don't know what they eat, and it might be nocturnal.

That doesn't matter. Anyway, I can play with it after dinner. Mum, please, please can I keep it. I love it. I love it already.'

Fritha shakes her head. 'Come to think of it, sounds familiar, don't you think?'

'Thanks very much,' he says. 'For being so horrible. You're just trying to make me hate you. But I don't.'

He's been bathing in sulphuric acid all his life, has cultivated his inner core within it, like the tadpole of that frog that has its cycle within the shell of its egg because of the harsh, arid conditions of its environment. And he is disconnected from the process of weeping. The pump doesn't work any more, although a diviner might be able to feel the tug pulling from a deep well of tears.

Fritha can say what she likes.

'You feel threatened by me,' he adds. 'Because you don't understand me. Because I'm different.' This he has learned to say. When he was little, at the end of a day in his mother's arms.

'Of course I bloody well feel threatened by you, and not for the wishy-washy reasons you're thinking of, either. I don't give a fig whether you're different or what. What do you mean "different" anyway? We're all different. *Everyone*'s different. You're not as special as you think. It's just that you've been encouraged to *feel* that you're different. By a mother who couldn't let you grow up.' She sighs. 'I'm really sorry. I shouldn't have said that. And I know I was being horrible before. But it's how *you're* acting with me, Matt. You're holding me to ransom, that's why. You're mucking everything up. You're ruining everything in my life.'

'How?'

'Well, I'm totally confused. I don't know how much responsibility I'm supposed to take for you. You're an adult. If you really have to steal a baby, that's your kinky karma. You can sort it out. I don't want to have to even *think* about it but you're *making* me think about it. You're drawing me in. I mean, the guy in the fish n chip shop: he just freaked me out, recognising me, asking me questions. So rather than our staying here anonymously, already he knows I was here with you and a *baby*.'

'That wasn't my fault. You *made* me go, remember.'

'I had plans, you know, for me and Scott. Something special. I just want to get on with my own life. I wondered whether it was wise for you to come up and have a go at living with us for a while, especially as we've got some sorting out to do ourselves. But I agreed. And it made sense to put our gear on the train and give you a ride. But now you're hassling me to stay here with you. Happily ever after.' She sighs again. 'Whoever would have thought, this time yesterday, that we'd be in this situation today? I dunno. And if I arrive in Auckland without you, what's Scott going to say? I just don't know. It's just a mess. Fuck you, Matt. Of course I'm threatened by you. You're a liability, that's why.'

'I'm sorry,' he says. He'd taken another piece of toast and was smearing it with honey but now he drops the knife and folds the toast over, pressing it flat with his fist as if closing a file.

'Oh well,' he says. He sighs. 'Okay then. Fine.' Then he adds, 'Yes, well, right then.'

'I'm not telling you to do anything. All I'm saying is that I'm off. Up and away. Not because of you. Because of the baby.'

'I have to look after her.'

'Okay. That's fine. That's up to you. What's done is done. It's too late now anyway. Boy, life is crazy.'

'Yeah.'

'So, what do we talk about now, or can I go?'

'Have you finished your toast?'

'Yeah. I've had enough, thanks, Mummy.'

'Look at that weather.'

'I know.'

'Fritha.'

'What?'

'What's in the boot?'

'What do you mean, what's in the boot?'

'What I mean is, what is in the boot?'

'Nothing, why?'

'I've been thinking. When we left the farm yesterday morning our bags and gear were in the boot. After you picked me up, they were on the back seat. You didn't even put all that shopping in the boot. All thrown onto the back seat and around my feet.'

'I can't believe this. Interrogation. I don't have to tell you anything, Matt.'

'I know. I was just curious.'

'Well, if you really want to know, it's a dead sheep. I've stolen a sheep from my parents' farm. Okay? That's another reason I want to get back in a hurry. In this heat, you know.'

'What? You killed a sheep?'

'Yes, but I don't want to talk about it.'

'And gutted it too? What about the hide? When did you kill it?'

'Look, I don't want to talk about it, Matt. I don't feel that great about it. Okay?'

'How did you do it?'

'Matt. Shut up about it or I'll wish I'd never told you. Can you see now why I wasn't that pleased about the baby? Now listen, I'm going to get some sleep. Give me the key and, bugger it, I'll take you up to Auckland. Give me the boot key and we're quits. You've got your own way, as usual. We'll leave tonight just on dark, so we don't attract any attention. Okay?'

'Thanks, Frith,' he says. 'Thanks very much.' The relief settles on him like folding wings.

'I don't know what Scott's going to say. He can handle it when we get there. But it's none of my business, is that clear? And don't mention the sheep again. All right?'

'Do you love him?'

'Who?'

'Scott.'

'Don't be nosy. So where's the key?'

He stands up, goes to the bench and picks up the tin of milk formula. Places it on the table in front of her.

'Oh no I don't, Matt. You're not going to get me to start doing things for your bloody baby. That's where I draw the line, matey. You make up your own bottles, boyo. Now give me the key before I change my mind.'

'I'll get you a spoon,' he says.

He scrabbles around in the cutlery drawer until he finds a long-handled spoon.

'The key to the solution is in the formula,' he says mischievously, handing her the spoon just as Dylana starts crying again.

∗

The night rumbling by. Packets and points and streaks of light. Rain. Spraying fizz of headlights. The slap slap of the windscreen wipers like an uncertain heart. Dozing in and out of sleep. The car a capsule of cosiness. Dylana finally sleeping in the collapsed pram on the back seat, cushioned by their bags and pillows from the bach.

Matt. Wanting to reach out. Touch Fritha's neck, hold his hand behind her neck, to reassure her in the dark, as she drives through the night. The outline of her chin pushed forward, her beaky nose, her forehead thunderous with concentration and thinking, like a myna. Her hands clenched on the top of the shuddering steering wheel.

Matt. Wanting to say, *My darling one.*

My darling one. It would have been perfect if they'd stayed in the bach, though he knows already that life doesn't give you things so easily. But little clues are presented, signs and signals along the way, like a book lying in the grass of a shady glade, its pages riffled by a breeze, giving glimpses of the story to come.

He likes the idea of the anonymity of the city. Where people live in tunnels, in parks, under motorways. In the basements of derelict buildings. Shadow people. Huddling in little holes and burrows. Pulling into the earth. Into the moist friendly earth. The night. The rain whamming at the windows. Passing through the night. Vacated towns. Lights. Distant glimmerings.

Somebody in the car. Somebody else. Matt drifting in and out of sleep. It is past midnight now so they have given up fiddling with the knob on the old valve radio, delving into the buzz and static for a bit of music. Only the uneven slapping of the wipers, the thrumming of the rain, the long snoring breathing of the motor. But there's somebody struggling in the car, like a frenzied cat thrashing from window to ceiling, flailing through the air, and Fritha pulls to the side of the road, bumping along the verge to stop in the carbonthick darkness.

She grasps Matt's arm, holds it tight.

'Matt,' she says, and her voice, matching her grip, clamps onto his delirium, like a vet with a frightened animal. 'Cut it out.'

He's cupped in the bucket seat, cowering under his arms with his knees pressed into his cheek, and the echo of his wailing still wobbling in his ears. He sits up and shakes his head, drops his legs to the floor. Fritha turns on the light, a whiskey-weak glow from the ceiling. 'Matty boy,' she says again, her hand on his shoulder now, beginning to hurt. 'What's up?'

He looks at her, her tough little face in a mess of hair, looks around the car, to the sleeping lump of Dylana, to the chaos of their bags and shopping. One hand clutches the cold metal dashboard, the other the cold chrome door handle that he clicks open, to leave Fritha's fingers flopping loose as he bursts from the car to stand in the tall wet weeds, to be instantly drenched by the rain. The soothing solid rain. The pouring river of rain in his eyes and in his mouth.

'Doctor, we would like to know exactly how our son is doing.'

'Well, he's shocked of course. But, hmmm, yes . . . under the circumstances he's coming along nicely. The jaw . . . and work will need to be done on the teeth. Concussion. The EEG seems to be satisfactory. But, ah, it's not just the physical trauma, of course. He's going to need a lot of . . . tender nurturing. It's not going to be easy for anybody.'

'No.'

'No word on the baby . . . er . . . Georgia?'

'No, doctor.'

'He is currently heavily sedated.'

Tapping the pen on the desk.

'Yes, he . . . he seems so far away. Is he going to be . . . all right?'

'As far as we can tell at this stage, there's no earthly reason for him not to be. But it's early days.'

Twiddling the pen between his index finger and the pointer. Dark hairs on his fine pearskin hands.

PART FOUR

Grubby pink. A wall of mushroom pink, like skin. *His* skin.

Matt slides his fingers from the warmth of the covers to feel the embossed roses and faded green twining leaves, letting the sounds of his new environment sift through his mind. Sparrows, and the occasional whisper of a car, and the groan of a bus. He can smell cigarette smoke and an exotic hint of incense.

He's tired, so tired after the events of the past couple of nights and days. The journey through the night. They arrived in the small deserted hours of the morning, walking up the path under the trees, the yellow street light glistening on every leaf. A cat slipping away from them as they walked up the steps. Matt trudged up the steps with the collapsed pram under his arm, Dylana still asleep. Waking up and now asleep again in the pram. They shuffled onto the big wooden verandah with the spilling creeper and Fritha gave Matt a look that said, Well, boyo, here we go. You've asked for it, Sonny Jim.

She tapped on the dappled glass panelling, then finally rattled the street awake with the lion head brass knocker. A dog a few houses away erupting into barking. The creeper dripping like icicles from the verandah roof. The street empty with long gloomy shadows. The pram cutting into his hip. Then the clatter of chains and the door snuck ajar. Then Scott in jeans and a chest of hair, swinging the door open wide. All bleary and grins as he saw them standing there in the eerie orange lamplight.

Hey, you made it, where've you guys been? Picking up Fritha in his arms and twirling her around and kissing her long on the lips and pulling back and looking at her. Grabbing her hand as he turned to Matt, throwing an arm around his back and squeezing his shoulder.

G'day, Matt, me old mate. Good to see you, mate. His voice rough and fat with cigarettes and sleep. What've you got in your box? Shepherding them into the house with the high ceiling and the long wide hallway into the light. It's so good to see you guys. What held you up? Did you stay longer on the farm? You should have rung. I was starting to get worried. Hey, what have you got there? He let go of Fritha's hand and pulled down the blanket as Matt's fish heart flapped in the bucket of his breast.

The light in the hallway suddenly too bright, too intense and shattering like crystal in a fire. Scott said, *What*? Hey, man, what's going on here? Shards in his voice as he looked at Fritha, accusing Fritha.

Fritha shrugging her shoulders and saying, Nothing to do with me, boyo. I'm just the driver.

Matt's chemistry redistributing itself around his body.

The pink wall.

Like flesh. A hard wall of flesh. Like a big back.

Lying there, remembering last night.

Cleaning teeth while they argued in the kitchen. Already arguing. I am not your brother's keeper, he'd heard Fritha saying. Washing his face, burying his face in the warm wet cloth. Back in the bedroom, about to undress and longing for sleep when Dylana awoke in the pram on the floor by the bed. Screaming. Please don't cry now, he pleaded with her. Not now. Please, God, don't let her cry now.

He lifted her from the pram and sat on the bed. Stood up. Paced. Sat down. Not now. Please, Dylana, not now. He pulled the covers back and shoved her beneath the blankets, because he didn't want to have to go out there with Scott in that mood, so disappointed and angry with him.

He stood up again and opened his door a little, listening down the hall. Fritha and Scott still talking. The muffled screaming rose in volume through the squirming blankets, a little bee trapped in a padded cell. He picked up a pillow. Please be quiet. To cover the wriggling bump. He wanted her to be quiet. That's all. Just to be quiet until Scott got to know her better.

Oh God. Help me, God.

What could he be thinking of doing?

He dropped the pillow, hauled Dylana from the blankets and jiggled her in his arms as she howled with rage, cursing him with dragon-red eyes. Kissing her crimson head. Everybody hated him. Fritha and Scott and Dylana. Please help me, he said out loud. Please, God, don't let me freak out.

He closed his eyes and tried to sing the lullaby, but his voice was stretched and cracked. There was nothing for it but to go out to the kitchen to prepare more milk.

He took the bottles and the milk formula and crept to the kitchen, leaving Dylana crying in his bed. Fritha and Scott were sitting at the table drinking more coffee, both of them smoking. They watched him in silence. A silence dangling with barbed tentacles . . . and the crying of the baby from his room down the hall. Fritha's face taut and pale, bruises of sadness deep in her eyes. Matt stared at her for a second, wanting to tell her he was sorry, but then caught Scott's glare. He turned to the sink, his back bristling with their disapproval. It seemed that they'd survived the little car's journey through the night only to embark on a voyage much more tempestuous. If only they could slip back into that magical moment on the verandah, and start again.

He had to ask for a bowl and a jug. Scott indicated a cupboard with his head, determined not to speak. Matt washed out the bottles. Mixed and boiled and poured. Adding cold water from the tap. Testing droplets on his arm. Taking the two filled bottles and leaving Fritha and Scott. Crying and crying. Dylana howling on behalf of them all.

He sat on the bed and gave her the bottle, and she immediately gulped into a sort of peace. Then he stuffed her unhappy little mouth with the dummy. The amazing dummy. Changed her nappy. Then started walking and walking around the new room, an explorer and his little assistant travelling on and on. Talking to her. Talking to her as they battled through the uncharted continent of Africa, across deserts, splashing through rainforests, thrashing through jungles, paddling up rivers. Walking and walking, past the old wooden dresser with tiny bottles of makeup and perfume and a mirror draped with beads, past the collapsed pram and the jumble of his gear on the floor, past the amplifier and a bass guitar propped in a corner, past the easy chair in the other corner covered loosely with a claret red velvet spread, edged with old-gold tassels.

They hovered under the lightshade fringed by a cylinder of long nylon thread. He wriggled his fingers through the thread, entertaining Dylana with the movement against the light, her own wee fat doll fingers reaching upwards. Until she started to cry again and he had to scramble around the floor for the dummy and then on they travelled: rainforests, wooden dressers, guitars and amplifiers, jungles. Walking and walking, weary and laden, pioneers through the night, through deserts, stopping in big comfortable hotels of velvet easy chairs, the hard bed with the brightly coloured crocheted woollen bed-spread and fresh-smelling sheets and the heavy woollen blankets but still he is cold. He can hear sparrows, and the occasional car, and the stirring of cicadas and the groan of a bus. He can smell cigarette smoke and just a hint of incense. The sunlight casting a lacy patch on the wall.

The wall. His long thin fingers outlining the roses as he lies there in the bed and thank goodness Dylana is still sleeping. He is weighted with something more than tiredness. The wall pink like blood in water, and all he wants to do is lie there. He is so grateful that Dylana is quiet. In fact the whole house is quiet. When he gets up he just might take Dylana and go somewhere, but at this point he is filled with uncertainty.

He remembers the time he ran away from home, and the horror of arriving at the first corner. He could have gone either right or left, or continued down the tunnel of street before him. He had stood there with fury and fear, until, with a sense of retaining dignity more than anything, rather than turn back, he'd turned left, then left, then left again. Around the block. He'd snuck in through the gate, slunk around the house to the bottom of the garden and enticed the cat into his arms before slipping into the cabin of his father's boat. Lay there cramped as night fell, confiding in the cat as he clutched its furry warmth to his breast. Letting the boat drag its anchor and drift out to sea, beyond the headland and through the shimmering sun before it toppled into a vast open nothingness where he didn't have to consider crossroads and streets leading to more of the same.

He'd heard the frantic calling of his name. Through the cabin window he watched the wavering torch beam as his mother looked for him. He'd heard his parents arguing loudly when his father had come out to persuade her to abandon the search, to let him sit it out, wherever he was. The isolation was unbearable. In the end he had to release the squirming cat when it rejected his straitjacket hold to head for a warm kitchen and a plate of food. He'd slouched inside himself, where everybody acted as if nothing had happened. Your dinner's on the table, his mother had said quietly, looking up from television, her eyes swollen from crying.

And now he's ruined everything. Fritha was right to want to leave him behind. He wishes now he had stayed in the bach, just the two of them: Matt looking after Dylana with all the beauty around and just living from day to day. He hadn't imagined that Scott's reception would be so extreme. He thinks of the slamming door last night. The raised voices. Matt thinks of the lingering kiss, their mouths sucking together, their bodies fused in a dervish twirl, and now they are fighting. He thinks of their bodies spinning together in the half-light on the verandah and now they have been flung apart. He knows it is because of him and, worst of all, he knows they are wishing he hadn't come. He can almost hear Fritha saying: I knew he'd be trouble from the start. He's just a little freak. Mucking everything up. You're not his father. Why should you have to look after him?

Probably.

So lucky that Dylana is still asleep. At least *she* is with him, at least he has *her*. Though he suspects now that if he'd been given five minutes to think about it, if he'd known how it was going to turn out, he probably wouldn't have taken Dylana from the truck, chosen or not. But how was he to know that Fritha was rushing to leave the farm after having killed a sheep?

He wonders how she did it. With a knife or screwing its neck? Was there blood? She is so little and yet alarmingly strong and she frightens him a little.

Anyway, all he wants is peace.
    And he has been given this tiny being . . .
    To care for and look after . . .

He must be worthy of her. Whatever Fritha and Scott say, he must care for her.

Lying there, in the bed, his head close to the wall, he listens for her breathing and then turns over and moves to hang his head over the edge of the bed to look at her in her pram and she's not there. Just the animal-nest hollow of where she's been.

He flings back the bedclothes and jumps out of bed, looking wildly around the room to see whether she's managed to clamber out of the pram in the night. But no. She's been stolen. Scott. Fritha. Somebody. They've stolen his baby. He hauls his jeans on, throws the door open, stumbles down the hallway and opens the kitchen door to find Fritha and Scott sitting where he had left them the night before. If he hadn't heard the shouting, the slamming doors, the footsteps up and down the hall, he might have thought they had passed the night like two wax figures waiting for the morning, waiting for his return so that they could all resume their conference of bickering confusion.

But Dylana is sitting on Scott's knee, holding a wet scraped carrot, which she alternately sucks then pulls from her mouth to study intently, making strange contented cooing noises. Matt doesn't know what to say. Such was his despair over the thought of losing Dylana, he'd barged into the kitchen without a thought.

He says, 'Oh, I was wondering where she was. Oh. Is she okay?'

'What does it look like?' says Scott, not unkindly. Matt drags out a chair and sits at the table with them, his hands locked together in his lap.

'She likes you,' says Matt. 'She looks so tiny on your lap.' And she does too. Scott's shirt is unbuttoned and Dylana's pearly silken hair contrasts against the furious dark hairs of his chest. Compared with Matt with his white wispy curls, his pallid complexion, his lanky skinniness, Scott is solid and has that burnished colouring that makes a person think of Greek Islands and laughter. As brothers they couldn't look or be more different.

For a moment Matt thinks that everything is perfect. He has a flash of hope that Scott and Fritha have talked through the night, concluding that they would love to have a little girl around the place. Matt could look after her, and they could pretend Dylana is their own child. They've discussed it and now that Fritha can see that Scott is willing, she is as well. Her main concern was that Scott would not be happy.

Scott says to Matt, 'She was starting to cry. We thought we'd let you sleep. She's had a bottle and we changed her nappy.'

Matt looks at Fritha. 'Not me, boyo. She's nothing to do with me. I leave the baby-minding over to the brothers grim.'

Fritha's hair is wet and she looks worn out, slumping in the chair with her eyes fat and her skin pasty.

She has had a ghastly night, Scott accusing her of 'allowing' Matt to kidnap the baby. Their fighting was fierce, Scott initially with his armour plate of silence, and then fencing with his tongue. Lashing her with his tongue. Biting into her jugular and siphoning the juices from her heart. Their voices at first low then rising to spit and snarl. In the kitchen, his bedroom, the kitchen again. The bathroom. Taking turns to follow each other as they paced. Until finally she took him outside with a torch and unlocked the boot, and as he stood there with his legs apart and his arms folded she unfurled the sheet that covered her quarry. The sweet sharp grassy smell of freshly dried cannabis greeted them as she played torchlight over the heap of squashed plants.

'Holy cow! What the . . .' It had been her turn to stand back and watch, as Scott unravelled his knotted arms and leaned into the boot. He stripped a stem of crackled leaves and broke off a sticky seed-head, pulverising them in his hand.

'Where did you get this lot?' he said, diving his nose into his palm, inhaling loudly. 'Why didn't you tell me?'

'You were yelling your head off. It was going to be a surprise. A nice surprise. For us. I wanted to tell you when everything was right. When we were happy. But you blew your top. You big shit.'

She was overwhelmed by the anticlimax of it all. She spun around and stalked inside, into Jason's old room, and crumpled onto the bed, still in her clothes. She heard the boot slam and later she could smell the distant aroma of cannabis smoke. She slithered into a disappointed sleep, only to wake up soon after to replay in her mind the scenes with Scott. It was so unfair. Her raspberry jelly heart was setting, congealing, hardening within her chest. Then she heard the soft brush of the door against the carpet as it opened. Felt the side of the bed drop with the weight of somebody sitting. A hand on her shoulder. She bristled, holding herself taut against its gentle pull.

'Frith? Fritha, I'm sorry. You're right. It's not your fault. I shouldn't blame you.'

It was her turn to present the armadillo plating.

'Get lost,' she muttered into the pillow. She barely felt the lift of the mattress as he stood up. She lay there wondering whether he had left, hardly breathing, waiting for him to speak again. When she finally lifted her head to inspect the gloom, she thought he might be lingering at the bottom of the bed, but as her eyes strained she saw that the shadow was a coat stand draped with clothes, and that he wasn't there.

An hour or so later she crept to his room and, closing the door, undressed and slipped under the bedclothes to the heat of his body. Her body pressing against his back, his buttocks, her knees tucking under his thighs. Her hands shifting across his skin, her fingers weaving into the hair of his chest, into the long tangled hair of sleep.

She awoke later to discover that he had gone. She found him in the kitchen making toast and tea. I was going to bring it in to you, he said to her, taking her head in his big hands and kissing her on the mouth. They didn't take the toast back to bed but ate instead over the neutral territory of the kitchen table. Scott was just pouring another cup of tea from the big brown teapot when they heard the baby crying. They looked at each other and she started to hate Matt once again. Scott stood up and went down the hall. She waited, wondering what he might be saying to Matt, but he came back in with the baby looking all pink and bewildered, her eyes scanning them and the room for something — anything — familiar.

Scott warmed the second bottle Matt had prepared the night before. He acted so normally and naturally with the baby. For the first time there was a stirring of something within her she might have been able to identify as maternal as she observed him nestling the baby on his lap. She dismissed the feeling with vigour. She pushed away from the table and went to the bathroom. Ran a bath. Collected her things from the bedroom. Sank into the hot soothing water, the reassuring waters. Lying there with her toe on the tap.

Scott came in shortly afterwards with Dylana and filled the basin while she watched him. He placed a towel on the floor and undressed Dylana, wiping her bottom with the nappy and lifting her into the water. Lathering his hands with soap and squishing them over her. Dylana slapping the bubbles on the surface with her open palm. He took tooth-brushes from a cup on the window ledge and dipped the empty cup into the water which he poured over her back. Then he filled it again, this time releasing the water in a single spout which the little girl reached out to grab, confused when her fingers slipped through the water.

'Look,' he said to Fritha. 'I love it when they do that. Isn't she funny? She thinks she's holding something tangible. It looks like it too, doesn't it?'

He pulled out the plug and lifted Dylana while he refilled the basin to rinse her in the fresh water.

Fritha watched.

There was such a feeling of family about this. She closed her eyes and when she opened them again Scott was wrapping Dylana in a towel. He went to the hall cupboard and brought back a collection of things from Jason's early years — nappies, fluffy overpants, a tiny t-shirt and cotton overalls. He placed Dylana upon the towel on the floor again with another cloth beneath her head. Then he spread one of the nappies and started folding it deftly, like a clown making a paper hat.

'You two are amazing,' said Fritha.

'What do you mean?'

'Well. The two of you, you and Matt, you're both so good with her.'

'I've had practice, remember.' A puff of talcum powder under her arms, between her legs. He rubbed her hair dry as she blinked resignedly.

'You're an expert,' said Fritha, somewhat sarcastically.

'Every parent becomes an expert in the end.'

'Yeah, but what about Matt? He's not a parent, even though he might deny that at this moment. What are you going to do?'

'Do?'

'With her. The baby.'

'What am *I* going to do?'

'Well, who else?'

'Look. Things have changed somewhat, with your little surprise in the boot, there. What *can* we do? If we turn up somewhere with a baby . . . ah, look excuse me, we've got this baby here . . . had it a couple of days and we don't want it any

143

more . . . there'll be questions. Such as, *Why* have you held on to it for two days? *Why*? What for?'

'Better two days than three days.'

'And then the place will be swamped with cops. And you've got a bootload of dried dope. Do we hand that in too? And what will they do with Matt? He wouldn't be able to handle it. They'd treat him like some deranged psychopath. They'd question him . . . like he's . . .'

'Not if he went quietly, or even left her somewhere. Anyway, he should have thought of that in the first place.'

'*You* should have thought of that in the first place.' He lifted the little girl from the floor. 'There you are. Pretty as a picture. All sweet-smelling and lovely.' He kissed her on the cheek. She was responding to his assured handling of her.

'She goes or I go.'

He sighed. 'I'll talk to him. Perhaps we can work something out. We need to talk calmly.'

Fritha closed her eyes again. There were many things they had to talk about but her thoughts were melting like butter in the bath as she slipped into sleep. Matt. He was a wishing well with no bottom; he was a mineshaft about to cave in, taking them all with it. Jerking awake as she sank into the water. Two nights with hardly any sleep. She just wanted to turn over and sleep for the rest of the day. She sat up. Scott and Dylana were no longer there. She climbed out and rubbed herself dry.

In the kitchen she had found Scott teaching Dylana to clap.

'Bloody hell,' she said. 'I don't believe this.'

Scott said, 'Be a sweetie and do the next round of toast, will you.' She was livid. 'And while you're up, scrape a carrot for Dylana. There's a pet.'

She did not respond well to soft talk. Geddin behind, and everything would have been okay. She threw on the toast and scraped the carrot which she thrust at Dylana, leaving the scrapings on the bench. Switched on the kettle. But then Matt had come in, his thin pale face awash with fear. She knew the animal look of fear. And the relief when his eyes rested upon Dylana.

✻

'Anyway, Matt,' Scott is saying, 'we are going to have to talk about things.'

'What,' says Matt.

'This little baby here.'

'Well?'

'Well, she belongs to someone else.'

'No, Scott, she's mine now. Her mother is dead.'

'And her father is alive.'

'No . . . well. Yes, but . . . I was chosen . . .'

'Come off it, Matt. What are you talking about?'

'I saved her. I saved her father. He would have drowned and I saved him. And I rescued Dylana.'

'That doesn't mean to say she's yours. Finders keepers does not work with people, Matthew. If you find an old lady lying in the gutter it doesn't mean to say she's your mother. We'll have to take Dylana in, to the authorities. That's all there is to it.'

'No, you can't. She's mine.'

'You'll have to stay somewhere else then.'

'All right then, I will. You're not going to blackmail me. It just shows how much you care. One minute you pretend you're worried about the baby and then you're prepared to throw us both out. Well, we'll go then.'

Scott looks exasperated, pissed off. His knee is jittering like a jigger. Fritha looks cocky: ah ha, so you think it's so easy, don't you? It's over to you, matey. Nothing to do with me, anyway.

Dylana starts grizzling, drops her carrot.

'I'll have to tell Mum and Dad,' says Scott.

'That's okay. We'll run away. We'll live under a bridge. You'll never find us. I should have stayed at the bach.'

'God, Matt. You're pathetic.' Scott stands up. Fritha twiddles with a strand of wet hair, an eyebrow lifted.

Matt jumps up as Scott prepares to leave the room. 'Where are you going?'

Scott looks back at him.

'I'm putting your baby to bed. She needs a sleep.'

Fritha stays in the kitchen while Matt follows Scott down the hallway. She is thinking of Bruce coming back from the airport and finding his plants gone. It serves him right for growing marijuana on her parents' farm. If only they'd known what he was up to — though they probably wouldn't even know what it was. She rests her head on her arms on the table.

Finally the two men return to the kitchen.

'Hey, Frith,' says Scott. 'You okay?' She is too tired to move. She lifts her head an inch, looks at Scott and slithers off the chair to the floor in a faint.

Scott scoops her up and takes her to his bed. To his dark bedroom with the thick red curtains drawn closed and the big double bed and the high ceiling and the air musty and personal, where she curls foetus-like under the blankets on this summer's day. The cicadas sing their muffled song and there's the ancient voice of a baby crying as Fritha finally floats from the groaning half-faint into sleep.

Scott sits on the edge of the bed stroking her head, her tousled head buried in the pillow, until, when he is sure she is truly asleep, he creeps out.

Creeps to the door and opens it so as not to disturb her and there is Matt standing in the hallway, jumping out of the way as if he weren't doing a thing, as if he weren't standing there with his head against the door, listening.

'Oh, I was just going to . . . knock.'

'Yes?'

Scott closes the door and steps past Matt into the hall, his arms crossed and looking at Matt. Matt tries not to lean against the wall. The house sucking the sap from his body, drawing the last colour from his body. Scott staring at him with unspoken questions. We're not up to this again, are we, Matt? Matt's knees collapsing like a blind man's stick, wanting to slip down, to lie face down on the floor, to fold himself away from it all.

'Is Fritha all right?' he manages to ask, as casually as he can.

'Why shouldn't she be?'

'Well, fainting and all that. I thought she might be dead.'

'Listening to see whether she was dead? Listening for breath, eh, Matt?'

'I was, I was just wondering how she was . . . if she was all right.'

Scott relaxes suddenly and sighs. 'Yeah, she's exhausted, that's all. We all are. It was a bit of a tough night.'

'Yeah.'

Matt slinks away to his room, lies on the bed with his arms behind his head. He shouldn't have come. No one likes him. He looks around the room. All the things. Scott's music gear. The band stuff. But the other things — the scarves, the perfume. The little bottles of stuff. They look as though they could be Silvia's, Scott's wife. Ex-wife. Jason's mother. Chilean. Passionate and fiery. Always fighting, the two of them were. And now Fritha, just as passionate but in an earthy kiwi way. But just as fiery.

There is still a presence of Silvia around the place. This is the house they used to live in together. Matt had stayed with them once, in the school holidays when Jason was a baby. He had assisted Silvia with small tasks, helped with the feeding and bathing of the baby. Silvia had touched his cheek with her smooth olive fingers and said, 'One day you will make a wonderful father.'

He doesn't think Scott is good enough for Fritha. Fritha would be better off with him: Fritha and he, together with Dylana.

He looks at the sleeping child. Fat little round cheeks. Her dummy fallen from her mouth. He wonders how babies can think if they don't have words. A head empty of words but filled with pictures. Silent movies, with sound effects added. A head of memory pictures, with no meaning. A book of photographs with no labels. He contemplates his own thoughts. Words. He is thinking in words, illustrated with images. How does she think of her mother, her father, the crashed truck, the journey with him across the river, to the car, to Fritha in the car? If she doesn't have words, every experience must be a new flickering picture. A revelation. Everything is a surprise and nothing is a surprise. There is nothing to understand. Everything is fresh. The crash, the dead mother, could possibly be seen as an event that is just part of life. The unfolding patterns of life. As long as she feels cherished now, currently, that is all she needs. And he does love her.

More even, it is possible, than her parents ever did.

More than his parents ever loved him.

She doesn't seem particularly distressed. She has accepted the situation. She does not yet have the words to question or wonder, just as he does not yet have the words to explain to her. Once she has words, he will tell her things. So that she knows she belongs to him.

She has merely moved from one set of images to another, without her other parents. It is no different from travelling in a truck, with a continuum of life passing by the windows. But she is still loved and has food and warmth, and that is all that is necessary.

Yes.

Everything is all right.

He is doing no harm.

He is alerted to a noise outside. He kneels on the squabs and looks from the bay windows, peering along the verandah to the driveway where he can see Scott. The car is hidden by the house, but he can see Scott, bending over, seemingly fiddling with the boot of the car.

Matt stands up, goes out into the hallway, out the front door, and stands on the verandah. He saunters over to the railing and looks down at Scott.

'What are you doing?'

'Are you following me around or what?' He looks up at Matt with a foxy eye.

'What are you doing with Fritha's car?'

'I'm minding my own business, Matt, me old mate.' He is holding Fritha's keys, jingling them impatiently. He mimics Matt, a higher whining tone rising from his own gravelly voice. 'What are you doing with Fritha's car?'

Matt feels compelled to protect Fritha against his brother's prying. It is obvious Scott doesn't know that Fritha keeps the boot key apart, so he is here without her blessing. She possibly would rather he didn't know about the sheep. *I don't feel that great about it, okay?*

He repeats more confidently, 'What are you doing breaking into Fritha's car?'

'Come off it, mate, I was just getting something from the boot.'

'Like what?'

'Like never you mind.'

'There's nothing for you to get from the boot. It's private. It's *secret*. I'll go and wake Fritha.'

'Look, Matt, matey.' He scratches his back under his shirt with the keys, then shakes his head and sighs. 'Look, Matt. It's none of your business. I know what's in the boot. Okay? We're in this together, Fritha and I. Like *this*, Matt.' He crosses his fingers and jabs them into the air. Two bodies intertwined. Matt feels a lonely stab in his diaphragm. 'So you can calm down, Matt boy. I didn't realise that you knew but I can see you're the guard dog. With all the fuss last night, we didn't have much time to talk. I was just looking to check, in the daylight. She showed me last night in the dark, by torchlight.'

He walks from the driveway to the path, up the steps to the verandah.

Matt doesn't want to admit that he hasn't actually seen the sheep.

'What are you going to do with it?'

'Good question,' Scott says mockingly, his fingers running over the dark stubble of his chin. 'Smoke it. That's an option of course.' He laughs gruffly.

'Like fish?'

'Ha ha. Very funny, Matt. No, I've got contacts. There's plenty of people I know who'll want a bag. So, don't you worry your little self about it.' He slaps his hand over Matt's shoulder. Matt is aware of his own boniness under his brother's fleshy hand.

'Aren't you worried about it going off?'

'Yeah. I'll say. With a bang. I hope.'

'What about the smell?'

'Never you mind about the smell. That's not a new problem. Don't worry, we'll be careful.' They start to walk back inside. 'No need to tell Fritha I was having another look. You know how she is. Jumps at anything. Let's keep the peace. You know.' He gives Matt another slow crafty look. 'You know what she's like.'

As they approach the house Matt hears Dylana starting to cry.

Scott stops and turns to him. 'I wonder what Mum and Dad are going to think of all this?'

'What do you mean?'

'You know, new grand-daughter? All of a sudden? Out of the blue?'

150

They stand at the door. Scott leans a hand on the doorway, above Matt's head.

'Mum rang last night to see if you'd arrived safely. She'll be ringing again tonight, I'd say. What are you going to tell her? Have you thought of that, matey?'

'We could . . . we could say it was Fritha's.'

'Oh great. And where do I come into this? And anyway, Fritha picked you up on the way up here, remember? I suppose Mum stood on the footpath waving her Mummy's boy goodbye. She might have noticed if there'd been a baby screaming in the car.'

'What about . . . yours and Silvia's?'

Scott snorts. There's a growing unease in Matt's stomach. They are out to spoil things, to persecute him.

'Anyway, we don't have to tell them anything. They needn't know. Don't tell them, Scott.'

'Why don't you hand her over while you can. Leave her somewhere safe. In a church or somewhere. Where someone will find her. Before it's too late. Before it's messy.'

'You don't understand.'

'You're right there.' Scott lets his hand slide down the doorway, shrugs and turns inside the dark hallway.

Fritha is just stumbling out of the bedroom, her fingers rubbing her head.

'Anyone going to pick up the fucking baby?' she says.

✳

Quentin wakes struggling to swallow, his throat parched in the dry hospital air. He lifts his head but sees nothing beyond the dusty road winding before him. He collapses into the pillow and closes his eyes once more.

She watches him in the dark, his neck arched, his mouth open, weeping silently in his sleep. Far above him, a hawk drifts with a slow wheel of leaves in a wind. The whole world is motionless except for the hawk and the leaves and the steady movement of his tears, the widening stain spreading over the crisp white linen behind his head.

She leaves him to join the hawk, to join the swirling leaves circling his bed, rising higher until she is an indistinguishable speck twisting in the sky.

Matt takes pillows and props them around Dylana on the bed. She seems to like that, as she does in the bath, sitting up almost by herself. He walks around the room, looking for little objects for her to play with. A makeup bottle. Bright red nail varnish. A pottery bird. A box of matches. She reaches for the varnish bottle, looks at it, puts it in her mouth. He rattles the matches in front of her nose. She takes them from him. Goes to put them in her mouth but he takes them back and she starts to cry. He rattles the box. Opens it. Takes a match and strikes it. The flame immediately quietens her. He blows it out. Takes another. She reaches out to touch the fire. No No! Hot, hot hot. Burn! He blows it out. Takes another. Lights it. She looks at him. For the first time, he thinks she really sees him. There is an openness in her face as she smiles at him. An openness in her eyes as she receives him, accepts his love for her. He laughs with true joy. His legs kicking back behind his knees as he lies on the bed, prostrate in front of her.

✳

PART FIVE

He is cold to his bones, his t-shirt sticking to his ribs, his jeans heavy against his legs. Matt hurries on, licking the fear from his chapped lips with a dry tongue. He lifts a hand behind his head, to feel Dylana's face, to feel the round solidness of her large head. Of course she is still there, joggling against his shoulder blades in Jason's backpack, which he found at the back of the wardrobe in his room. It means he can walk without having to push Dylana in the rattly rusty old pram, its wheels wobbling or locking unpredictably as they go. It means he can change tack on a whim, and cover terrain he wouldn't be able to manage easily in the pram. He drops his hand to his waist and feels behind him to where her plump little leg is hanging from the pack, holding her foot and slipping his fingers between her squirmy toes.

A week now. This time last week he was saying goodbye to his mother. His mother weeping and hugging him tight before his father pulled her away.

A week now since he became a father himself. He hurries along the footpath with bread and milk in a brown paper bag under one arm. From the *good* dairy. Further away than the other, but with the *nice* lady, the kind Indian lady who moves slowly in her red and bright green sari, like something in water, like something growing at the bottom of a pond. Moving in a leisurely dance, her fat arms collecting the things Matt requires from around the cluttered shelves, the sharp smells of curries wafting in from the back. Her eyes soft and faraway, her lips thick and curved in a secret smile, her thoughts fed by the mysterious words that wail from the tape recorder perched among the tins behind her.

He is trying to remember who he was a week ago, what life was like before he met Dylana. He can't believe that there was a time when she was a nothing, when she did not exist.

How complicated his life has become since then. His life which up until then had never seemed simple.

Fritha shouldn't have told him lies. Making him look a fool. They must have thought he was stupid. Fritha telling him that she had killed a sheep. He had wondered at it lying bleeding and decomposing in the boot like that. But he had trusted her. One thing, he is not stupid. They might think so, but he is not.

Like that night, the second night, the Sunday. He knew something was going on. He could see they were trying to get him to bed early. Frith cooking the big dinner — lamb chops and mashed potatoes and frozen peas. He had even asked whether the meat was from the sheep in the boot, and they had laughed and looked at each other and smiled secretively and said again that no, no it wasn't. A joke that excluded him. They did the dishes together, telling him to go and make sure Dylana was settled, because he must be tired after the upheaval. They weren't normally so caring. Not Fritha, anyway. He thought they might have wanted to have sex, and he found the idea of this strangely disturbing.

Fritha and Scott.

He could see they wanted to get rid of him, so he did what they said. Dylana took a while to go to sleep, until he started to sing to her, so softly like a whisper, while he stroked her forehead with his thumb, his hand resting on her pillow, until her eyelids gave up their battle to stay open. Making him feel like a magician. A hypnotist or something like that. A real father.

He turned off the light and got into bed, still clothed, and lay there, the door open onto the hall. Sure enough, Fritha eventually stood at the door and put her head around the corner and waited to make sure all was quiet before shutting the door. A while later he heard footsteps on the verandah, and down the steps to the driveway. He thought they must have been going out. Perhaps they were leaving him, alone in the house with Dylana, like Fritha tried to do in the bach. He flung back the bedclothes and went to the bay window. Fritha was opening the boot. They stood there talking but he was unable to see what they were doing because they were obscured by the house. Then they appeared to be struggling with something large, carrying a large bulky bundle. They were bringing the sheep inside. Matt's stomach twisted. Why was there all this secrecy? Had Fritha killed somebody . . . not a sheep at all, but a person? Fritha was walking backwards and Scott was dealing with the other end. Their cargo appeared big rather than heavy.

He darted back behind the curtains. They went inside the house. He could hear low voices in the hallway outside his bedroom. Then all was quiet. He assumed they'd gone into their bedroom. He stood in the dark and listened. Silence.

He opened his door and crossed the hallway to their bedroom door. Matt was unable to determine what they were talking about, but Scott was obviously excited, his voice fast and animated, while Fritha kept hushing him. Matt went back to his room and sat on his bed for some time, brooding. Dylana was breathing steadily. He stood up again. Fortunately they had left the front door ajar, so he was able go out without making a noise. He crossed the verandah and crept down the path to their window. He climbed up and balanced himself on the front bumper of Frith's car to see in through a crack in the curtains.

His gut churned. The glass was cool against his flaming cheek.

On the floor, on sheets spread out like a big opened parcel, was a heap of bushy plants. They'd covered the bed with another sheet and Fritha, cross-legged against the pillows like a fakir, was stripping the leaves from one of the plants.

Meanwhile Scott was sitting at the desk, which they'd pulled over by the bed. He was taking handfuls of the dried leaves Fritha had already prepared for him, dribbling small amounts from his fingers into a pan as he peered at kitchen scales. He'd tip the quantity into a plastic bag, which he'd fold over several times before securing it with Sellotape. Then he'd repeat the operation, like an old grocer weighing out tea.

After a while Matt slunk back to his room. He undressed and climbed into bed. He lay there, unable to sleep, his mind picking at the scabs of old grievances, seething because they were doing things without him, because they'd excluded him.

He thought of barging in, or knocking on the door and walking in innocently, on the pretext of asking where something for the baby was kept, like medicine. But it wouldn't be worth their anger. The more smoothly things chugged along, the greater chance he would have of keeping Dylana.

He wanted to tell his mother how Scott was being mean to him already, but of course he wouldn't. She had rung that morning, as Scott suggested she might. She had read about the accident in the paper but Matt had told her how they'd left the farm before it happened. She asked about the job in the music shop and he'd told her it had been delayed for a week. He didn't tell her that Fritha was going to take it now, because of Dylana, and his having to look after her. Fritha wasn't particularly keen about this arrangement as it didn't pay much and she was worried about working alongside Scott all day, but under the circumstances it was decided it would be for the best. So the next day both Fritha and Scott would be in the shop.

The next day being Monday. He'd fed and bathed Dylana. For the first time he felt impatient to have this duty out of the way. He took her to Scott and Fritha's bedroom, propping her on their bed against the pillows, while he started to look for the packages. They hadn't pulled the curtains back from the night before so he felt safe, keeping an ear out for Scott's car, just in case.

He opened drawers in a large wooden chest. Clothes. Some little people's clothes, Jason's probably. Shorts, singlets, t-shirts. Fritha had already claimed some of the drawers, her things folded neatly compared with Scott's jumble. Fritha's tiny underwear. He held a soft tank top to his face and breathed deeply, searching for some essential fragrance of her being, until the slamming of a neighbour's door flung him back to his task and he replaced the garment carefully in the drawer.

He stood up. Cooed at Dylana, who was starting an ardent grumble, leaning forward and slapping at the bedspread. He grabbed a handful of objects from the top of the chest and displayed them around her just within reach.

Next, the wardrobe. Scott's jackets, trousers, shirts. Fritha's dresses. Opened a box in the wardrobe. Papers. Music scores. A suitcase. Empty. Fritha's bag. Nothing of interest. Shelves. Under the mattress. Even looked inside Scott's guitar.

Then he went to the kitchen — the fridge, the freezer, cupboards. He took a stool and climbed on the bench to search the higher cupboards. Suddenly he heard a wail, a different desperate cry, from down the hallway. He rushed to the bedroom. Dylana was lying on her back on the floor, screaming, her arms wavering, her face a shiny nut of fury and hurt. He scooped her up, consoling, apologetic, fluttering kisses over her tight cheeks. I didn't know, he told her, I didn't know you could move. What a clever baby . . . moving all by yourself. Oh . . . oh, the poor little bubba.

The carpet was soft and she'd fallen onto a sheepskin on top of it. She didn't appear to be badly hurt but she wouldn't stop crying. Stop it, he said, stop crying now it's all right stop it now. It wasn't my fault, I didn't know you could move. Stop it, now. STOP.

He rushed up the hallway. To the bathroom. Ran the tap and held her face over the basin, swishing handfuls of cold water at her face. She gasped but only cried more loudly, her body rigid in his arms. He held her tightly. Too tightly. No, Dylana, don't cry. He went to the kitchen fridge for an iceblock, let it slip over her forehead. She shoved his hand away. He ran down the hallway again to his bedroom and dumped her on the bed.

The matches.

He knelt beside the bed and lit a match. She continued to cry but he could see she was interested. The glint of curiosity among her tears. He blew out the flame. Another match. She stopped, shuddered, blinking, and her chubby fingers reached out to touch. He forced a loud laugh. 'No — hot. Burn,' he said. 'Burnie.' She started to wind up again and he lit another. The fire like a switch, turning her down. He was exhausted. He threw his arms against the bed and flopped. Whew. This was dangerous. He had to have plans for this sort of behaviour. He grabbed her foot and blew a loud raspberry into the sole and she giggled, her foot squirming. Her eyes were full of tears but they were leftovers, puddles after the rain. Another squall was over.

This was a warning. His priorities were wrong. His commitment was to Dylana. Let Scott and Fritha carry on with their own business, while he looked after Dylana.

'It's all over now, Baby Blue,' he murmured, chewing her toenail. 'You didn't tell me you could move, you little sneak.

As soon as my back is turned. What else can you do? Speak? Speak to me.'

But *how* did she move? Could she crawl? He realised he had no idea. He would have to be careful.

He played with her until she seemed to lose interest. She started to grizzle and yawn so he gave her a banana and a bottle, then put her to bed on the mattress Scott had organised for him on the floor. He shut the door of his room then stood in the doorway of Scott's room. It had the appearance of having been attacked by the SIS. Drawers half opened, things pulled out or tucked in where they shouldn't have been. He set to tidying up. How stupid he had been. What if Fritha had come home unexpectedly? He gathered Dylana's playthings and rearranged them on the chest, then smoothed the bedspread and plumped up the pillows.

The pillows.

One felt . . . strange somehow. He pressed his fingers into the stuffing. Plasticky and lumpy. Yanking the pillowcase away, he found another underneath, and under that, another. Under that one, a black plastic bag and inside that, lots and lots of little packets of dried herbs. He had stopped searching and had discovered them. He was *meant* to find them.

He removed a packet and then started to put everything back as he had found it, though faced with the three pillowcases he realised he couldn't remember their order. Was the floral one on the outside or was that the blue one? He hesitated. Would they know? He was pretty sure it was the floral one, but the other pillow was blue, another shade of blue, with a design around the edge. Wouldn't they have chosen a closer match of colours? He would have. He would have selected the two pillows as near to matching as possible, though there was every likelihood they would not have been thinking of such trivialities at the time. He put the blue one on the outside and stepped back. No, he was pretty sure, now he looked at them together, that they had been different. He changed them around again. Or had they?

Then it also occurred to him that Scott and Fritha might have counted the packets. He was starting to tremble. He removed all the pillowcases again, and spread one of Fritha's scarves on the bed. Then he tipped all the packets from the bag onto the bed, and took a little, just a pinch, from each of the bags, until he'd gathered quite a pile of the dried leaf on the scarf. There was nothing wrong with that. He remembered when he was a kid, lounging around and watching as Scott did exactly the same thing in their parents' drink cabinet, pouring a little of this and a little of that into a Coke bottle. What are you doing? Matt had asked. I'm making a lethal brew so you shut up about it, he'd told him. So, what was the difference? He folded up the scarf and put everything back again. This time he opted for the blue pillowcase to match the other. He stepped back from the room, surveying it as he went. As far as he could see, all was back in place.

Unless the pillowcase should be floral . . .

He was sure it was drugs. Grass. The same stuff he saw Grant Billings and a group of other kids smoking under the trees at lunchtime at school, fallen walnuts around them, some still in their green casings. He was sitting there reading dreamily, but had looked up, alerted by their mirth. What are you staring at, do you want to try some? Grant had called over to him, and the others had laughed. Here, come on, it won't hurt you, he'd said, buoyed by the others' mumbling comments, encouraged by Matt's turning away of the head, turning a page of his book.

They were passing a roll-your-own cigarette around, five of them, giggling and sniggering playfully. Their offering him a smoke was more alienating than if they had ignored him completely. They knew he would refuse, though if he *had* accepted, he would have been an object of amusement. He knew it. He didn't even present himself as a threat. In class that afternoon they had been hilarious, taunting the teacher in an undefinably smart-arse way that set the whole class in fits. They were the 'in' boys. They were enjoying themselves. They were cool dudes. They were having fun.

He checked Dylana, her face glowing with sleep. He checked Scott's bedroom again. Everything seemed normal, as before, as long as the pillowcase was right. He decided that if they noticed anything out of order he could say he had used the pillow as a prop for Dylana in the sitting room. If he did that, at least he'd be justified in having made the discovery. And this was true. He *had* used it for Dylana. And then he could say that she had spilled something over it, that she had been sick over it.

He transferred his stash from Fritha's scarf into one of his clean cotton socks, and put the scarf back over the rung in their wardrobe. There.

Papers. He was certain Scott would have some spares somewhere. Eventually he found some in a bits-and-pieces drawer in the kitchen. Just a few papers left but all he needed. He wasn't very good at rolling cigarettes. He used to pester Scott to let him roll his — big clumsy lumpy things, like an old man's arthritic finger. Scott had explained to him that if he spliced two papers together it was easier. But now his sweating hands, his fingers trembling with nervousness and excitement, didn't help at all. He stuck the two delicate papers together and spread them out on the dining table, then rolled over the ribbing neck of his sock, sitting it on the table like a miniature wool bale, with its produce heaped to the brim. He was delighted at his choice of hiding place for the dope . . . the sock was perfect.

He delved into the stash with his thumb and finger, and sprinkled the leaves over one end of the paper. A good lot, sticky bits with seeds. He didn't know whether the fat pearly seeds would be any good or not but he put them in anyway. Then he rolled the joint, tucking it up tight. It reminded him of rolling up his togs with his towel into a tight worm. There was a knack to it, to get it just right.

It was as thick as a jumbo crayon. He put it in his mouth. Pulled the cool air through the packed herbs . . . pretending to puff out a long stream of smoke. There could be no harm if he lit it. Those other boys had been in such good spirits, so happy. He stood up. Matches. He thrust his hand in his pocket and pulled out the box he'd used to entertain Dylana.

He took a tentative drag as the end flared and the seeds popped like little firecrackers. Letting out a small mouthful of smoke, he examined his inner state. Nothing. He felt just the same. Again he inhaled, this time sucking in the searing smoke in long gulps, until his chest was almost tucked under his chin. Then he exploded. That captured breath escaped in a spluttering attack of wheezing and choking, leaving him gasping for air, and water. He rushed to the sink and poured himself a glass, drinking desperately to soothe his scorched membranes. He leaned back against the wall, panting.

But how did he *feel*? Just the same. Nothing was happening. He wanted to feel happy. It was suddenly vitally important that he should feel happy. Joyous. He dragged again, more cautiously this time, now prepared for the coughing as his throat revolted against this assault. More water, another drag.

He looked around at the kitchen, its sharp white walls, its pink cupboards with handles like small neat mushrooms. A banana drooping over a bowl of apples on the fridge, a frypan soaking in flat grey bubbles on the bench. Salt and pepper shakers standing together like an old married couple with saggy stomachs, just touching shoulders. Everything was normal. Next time he inhaled he forced himself to hold the smoke for a few long seconds while his lungs and throat spasmed painfully, finally bursting into coughing again, his heart whamming violently. His heart a small animal caught in a snare.

But still nothing had altered. The walls bright as light, the cupboards little-girl pink; so much pink in this house. Flesh pink. But everything so rigid, so vertical or horizontal, lines and angles, except for the apples snuggling together in the bowl with the comforting arm of the banana around them. The stainless steel bench a hazy mirror, with his face an indistinct blur peering through fog. He leaned closer, showing his teeth, opening his mouth into a scream, like that painting of the scream on the bridge. Anybody's mouth. A hollow black tunnel of agony. Anybody's ghostly scream locked in the ether. He drew closer still so that his nose was almost touching the bench, to find the image of his own white locks, his chin, his mouth mimicking his puckered lips, now his bared teeth, now his tongue meeting his cold steely tongue, and his forced silly grin.

He stood up. Back in the kitchen. His feet cold on the lino. Dark red lino, swirling galaxies of smoky black whirls among the colour, the end of the world on the kitchen floor, his feet looking pale and long and skeletal against it. So white and clean. He took another drag. He still felt absolutely normal except for his heart beating fast from the coughing fit. Perhaps it was only mixed herbs he was smoking; perhaps Scott and Fritha were doing some deal with a restaurant. He found himself chuckling at the lunacy of the thought. Still, he took another lungful of smoke, holding it as long as he could. He let it go and shuddered, suddenly feeling queasy.

He had nearly finished it all and he decided not to have any more. He shuddered again and dipped the butt in the frypan before mashing it down the plughole. He put both taps on full until the last of it had gone. There. That frypan was disgusting, though, a fermenting stagnant pond. A fly was caught upside down in the fatty lather. He leaned on the bench and watched it spinning in crafty little manoeuvres, like an ice skater showing off its virtuosity. Dipping his finger beneath the creature, Matt lifted it out and eased it onto its feet. With wings hanging forlornly, it hauled itself along his hand then stopped to clean up, sweeping its hind legs nimbly over its wings, then with the front, wiping its nobbly head as if washing its face with little stick arms. Then, quite abruptly, it was still. Motionless. Matt coaxed it along with his finger, then blew insistently upon the bedraggled fly, but it was dead. He couldn't understand it. Why had it died so suddenly? How could life be extinguished so unexpectedly? Was it something he had done?

He was alerted to a sudden excited twittering through the window, a congregation of sparrows jumping like fleas on the lawn around a loaf of bread that seemed to have been detonated in the back yard. Someone must have thrown sodden bread over the fence. Somebody, throwing bread leftover from lunch onto their lawn.

Lunch.

He washed the fly down the sink then opened the fridge and gazed inside. Eggs. Bacon. Bread. Meat. Carrots, tomatoes. He could have eggs on toast. Poached eggs on toast with tomato sauce. Or fried bacon and eggs, and baked beans. There were baked beans in the cupboard, he knew that. But he felt like something sweet. And now. Something to make up for the disappointment of the dried leaves not making him happy. Not having any effect.

He went down the hallway to where Dylana was still sleeping. He considered leaving her while he popped out, but after the fright that morning he decided it would be safer to take her. How hungry he was! He fetched the backpack and dusted it down, propping it against the easy chair in his bedroom. He held it upright with his foot as he picked Dylana from the bedclothes. With luck she wouldn't wake up. He felt as though he were repeating the episode with the fly and the frypan, her little wings still dripping with sleep, her fists digging into her eyes. She was building up for a grizzle, for a good cry, as he tried to stuff her into the backpack, her legs missing the holes and getting crushed beneath her.

He forced his arm alongside her to direct her legs into the openings until they hung there like two fat maggots escaping from an apple. Her face barely came above the top rung. He remembered the banana in the kitchen, so he cradled the pack with Dylana in it, and raced down the hallway, singing bloodle bluebell bliddlydee, grabbing the banana, and peeling it — a magician — revealing a surprise. Voilà, a banana! He broke off half, gave it to her, and ate the rest himself. Now off we go, tiddlypo. He hitched her onto his back. The banana keeping her quiet. Food, drink, matches and the dummy. The list of pacifiers.

He sat on the floor and put on his shoes and socks. Out out out. We're going out, he told her. It was essential that they got out now. Left the house and got out now. The house with its high ceilings where the dark lurked in corners like stuff. And outside the sun shining. And along the street, roses sprawling along a fence, roses so red and smelling of roses, petals as soft as fur. A curtain moved when he picked the second one, as he stripped the thorns from their stems.

In the shop, the corner dairy, two blocks away. That woman. And that man, the grocer.

Matt stood in the shop waiting, while the man attended a lady who looked like his mother, cradling a tiny long-haired dog in her arms. Matt stared at her as she passed, and at the dog with its big blinky hairy eyes, and she looked back at him and Dylana. They were like two people in a doctor's surgery, each wondering what was wrong with the other.

And then it was his turn to be served. He felt strangely nervous, jittery. The man leaning on the counter, his arms stiff like posts, the skin of his hands grey and wrinkled, like the surface of cold porridge tipped up. The fingers like lizards defending a fort. Under the glass there was a display of sweets. Some of those and those and those, he said, feeling suddenly self-conscious about holding the roses. He placed them on the counter. Spearmint chews, pineapple chunks, a chocolate-covered toffee bar, spearmint leaves, snifters. Four yellow eskimos. Two red jelly babies.

The man gawked at the roses lying alongside each other, then he looked at Matt, feigning disbelief. His little white paper bag was bulging with lollies. He selected a large brown bag and tipped in the contents of the smaller one, as if he were really put out.

'Anything else?' His voice was tinged with sarcasm.

'Oh . . . and two chocolate fish, and a bounty bar.'

A packet of chippies. And a king-sized block of dark almond chocolate.

'Look, why don't I just give you one of every sort of sweet in the shop?'

Matt gaped at him. Was he serious?

'I don't *like* everything,' he told the man earnestly. 'I don't like aniseed balls. For example.'

The man vigorously scratched his head.

'Taking your little brother for a walk?' he asked in a flat voice. Dylana was cooing behind Matt. He could feel the sharp but caressing tug as she pulled at his hair at the back of his neck.

'No. She's mine. I mean, she's not my brother. She's . . . she's . . . a girl.' He was stuttering now. 'I'm her father.'

At that point the man's wife burst through a curtain opening from a hallway to the rest of the house. Matt was certain she had been standing there listening. She looked like a spy — thin, with what looked like a wig of bleached straw, her eyebrows painted in constant disdain above wine-gum eyes. Her lips painted fainting-pale apricot, and makeup thick on her face. These two bathed in porridge, he decided.

'This young man's the father,' the man said to his wife. 'They get younger and younger these days.' He turned back to Matt. 'I knew she was related somehow. She's the image of you. Aren't cha, tuppence? Just like your Dad?'

The wife lifted a panel on the counter and came through, her face like a drawing on the front of a boat.

'Yes, yes,' said Matt. 'Yeah, everyone says that.' A likeness. See. Once again it was meant. God choosing him.

'It's the hair, too,' said the man. 'Baby fine and white.'

Matt was aware of the woman. She hadn't said anything yet, but she was moving towards him, around his back, to inspect Dylana.

'I'll have a paper too,' he said. 'And that's all.' Out. He had to get out. She was doing something at his back, she was behind him pulling at the pack to look closely at Dylana.

'You're a little sweetie, arn choo? A real little sweetie. And where's your Mummy today? Hmmmm?' Matt paid and ignored the question. She wasn't talking to him. He didn't have to answer. He clutched the top of the bag of sweets, folded the paper under his arm and put his hand out for the change. The change, man, the change! The man was mucking around in the till. The woman was saying, 'Have you had your little nappy changed today, at *all*?' She was moving from Dylana to face Matt. 'Her nappy is absolutely soaking. The wet's coming through the canvas. Sopping. The poor little mite.'

Matt took the change and walked out of the shop, his pulse nightmare-fast, his mouth dry as pumice. He should have answered her. She was trouble. He looked back. Yes yes. She was standing outside the shop, her hands on her hips, staring at him. Watching him. Watching to see where he lived. She knew something. She was going to follow him. He quickened his pace. His heart, his heart. Racing. He turned a corner, checking for the woman but she had gone. Hiding maybe, behind a bush, that big camellia bush behind the shop.

He hurried around the block. A cat skulked away from him then lowered itself under a hedge, pressing itself into the twiggy undergrowth, its witch-yellow eyes holding him as he passed.

At the corner he made sure there was no sign of the woman before he turned into the street and almost ran to the house, the pack joggling at his back. It was only when he arrived at the bottom of the steps that he saw the front door was open. He stopped, thinking at first that Fritha or Scott had returned, but the car wasn't there. That woman, the shop-keeper's wife. The woman was inside the house, ransacking the house for evidence.

He crept up to the verandah and peeped around the door, listening for sound. The afternoon was aclangle with noise: cicadas, sparrows, other birds, the distant clack clack clack of someone cutting a hedge, the rumble of traffic, the shutting of a car door somewhere, a horn. A barking dog. But from inside, nothing. He peered through the windows into his bedroom. Then he cautiously entered the house. He flung open Scott and Fritha's door so that it banged and juddered against the wall.

After checking every room in the house he accepted there was no one there. Perhaps . . . he couldn't believe he had left the door open himself, but when he thought about it, he couldn't remember shutting it. And there was the evidence, the keys still hanging from the door inside.

He locked the door, looping the chain across the door. Slipped the backpack from his shoulders and propped it on the easy chair while he pulled Dylana like a little case moth from her cocoon. It was true; she was soaking, mainly be-cause he hadn't put on the fluffy overpants which would have soaked up the worst of the damp. She was enemy territory, that woman. Why couldn't people mind their own business? She treated him as if he didn't even care. What if he started to tell her she had too much makeup, that her eyebrows were like a kid's drawing, that she was ugly as uglee. What if he'd said, I'm sorry but your husband needs a haircut. She was horrible.

In the bathroom, he unpinned Dylana's nappy, reeling at the fumes of ammonia. Then he knelt on the floor, holding her upright while the cold tap roared into the bath. The water cascaded in a furious surf which he swished around her bottom, her legs, her stomach. She gasped and yelled until he picked her up and wrapped her in a towel, carrying her back again to her mattress where he plonked her among a fort of cushions and pillows. He grabbed his bag of sweets and the paper, tore off his shoes and socks, and sat next to Dylana, leaning against the wall.

Peering into the bag, he chose a yellow eskimo and gave it to Dylana. She clutched it eagerly and put it straight into her mouth, sucking at the sugary sweetness before pulling it out again to scrutinise her prey. She looked up at him and smiled.

'Ah ger,' she said.

'Exactly,' he replied. He chose an eskimo for himself as well and popped it into his mouth. He felt like a kid. He puckered his face at the little girl, grinning as he chewed. 'Yummmmm,' he said.

Matt unfolded the paper to read but it seemed an impossible task. So many words about so many things, in such an overwhelmingly huge world. Where did he fit into it all? He and Dylana. She was totally absorbed in sucking her eskimo now, her fingers wrapped tightly around it as she might take an old man's thumb. Old and young. Children, the means of marking time, time which was only something people had labelled anyway, in divisions of days and minutes and seconds. Allotments of periods of continuation. But continuation to where and of what? Maybe everyone was living in a stopped moment and travelling over it? Maybe time was fixed and everyone was moving, instead of being fixed to changing time?

He needed a pen and paper. He would find a pen and paper and write this down. In a minute. Whatever a minute was. And where did God fit into the scheme of things? Perhaps God was at the point where time ended and time began, a force to pass through as time revolved. This would explain why God knew everything, because all living things passed through him in a recycling sort of way, like a filtration plant in a swimming pool. Just the pure essence passing through. Maybe that happened every night. Maybe everyone had their own personal God. Maybe dreaming was a part of that process. The residue of the day, the complexities of the day clogging the strainer, for closer examination.

He shoved his bag of sweets behind the mattress and closed his eyes, the back of his head thudding against the wall. The room slithered upwards and over and he tipped his head further, as the void behind his eyes started to lift beyond his head, encapsulating his mind and thoughts, to take them flying from the room from the house and oh God he was going to be sick. He opened his eyes again and the room slapped back into place, the light from the window blasting into his vision. He had to stand up, get out, find a bowl or a bucket. Dylana was still preoccupied with demolishing her eskimo, strings of sticky saliva hanging from her fist. He forced himself to stand up and managed to get to the chair, where he stumbled and sank into its depths, his hands flopping onto each arm of the chair, his soft hands on the rich dark velvet, the red of liver. The red of the insides of closed eyelids in sunshine. It was here he would die. He knew what death was, he had witnessed the end of life and the near end of a life over the past few days. It was the slipping away of the breath, of the soul, from the body. It was a departure and he could sense that he was going to leave his own body; he was aware that he was lifting away and once again his heart was hammering his chest.

The seesawing notes of a single cicada had stuck on a seee and was hanging in a particular tangible spot in his head. If he closed his eyes he could locate it, now, where the cicada was hovering in the chasm within his head. He opened his eyes briefly, closed them again to the realisation. Maybe, whatever was in the pillowcase shouldn't be smoked, or so much. Maybe he was allergic to it, maybe he was being punished. It was not marijuana in the bags inside the pillow. It was not grass he had smoked. It was some terrible poison. Like rat poison. He was going to sleep, slipping away now, nodding off. He was such a fool, that was true, such a fool.

He felt as though he were on a plane, a dangerous little plane preparing for take-off. Taking off now. He pressed his body into the back of the chair. Soaring backwards to flip and dive and dangle with the cicada in the void, letting out a groan as he plunged. He could hear his breath escaping in short laboured gasps from the back of his throat, like the sound of someone sweeping leaves from a path. Then the void behind his closed eyes started to fill with an inkjet of darkness. It was like the thing in the car. It was coming for him, coming to inject his heart with black. It lunged for his throat, it was coiling like a python around his throat, tighter and tighter and he couldn't breathe. He cried out, bellowed in fear, his knees kicking under his chin, his bare feet scuffling on the seat and his arms flailing over his head.

And then it was over and he was cold and trembling, crying uncontrollably. It frightened him; he never cried. Ripples of fear were charging through his body, a buzz of intense shivering. And then gradually another sound penetrated his

172

own suffering. A snuffling, gurgling sound, the noise of a sink draining through a blocked plughole. He looked up.

Dylana. Dylana was lying on her side twitching like an insect, her face purple. He jumped up. Her eyes were bulging. She was choking. Choking. He forced his fingers into her mouth where the stump of the eskimo protruded from the back of her throat. Whipped her upside down, thumping her hollow little back.

His fingers pushing through her gummy mouth and scrabbling at her throat again. Another firm whack against her back. Suddenly she vomited. The soggy lump of eskimo landed on the carpet. She whooped great gulps of air, choking and crying and farting. He rushed her to the kitchen, a sticky gooey mess of saliva and sick, grabbed a bottle from the fridge and jammed the teat in her mouth. Drink, drink. She took a couple of desperate sucks and bawled again. He held her across his shoulder, rubbing her back, patting her dimply bare bottom, crying with her. The two of them bawling together from utter confusion, fear and relief.

He couldn't do it any more. He couldn't stand it. He would hand her back. He would ring the police and hand her over. Then he could work in the music shop with Scott, as they had planned, and Frith could look for a job she wanted. Dylana could go back to her father. His stomach twisted at the thought but he went to the hall where the phone sat on a little table outside the bathroom. He eased himself down onto the chair. Dylana was still crying. This wasn't an emergency now; there was no need to ring 111. He would explain calmly that he had been caring for her and that he hadn't realised they were looking for her. He looked up the police number and picked up the phone. He put it down again and studied Dylana. Her dribble-splotched t-shirt was scrunched above her fat little paunch and bare bottom. Her red face shiny with tears and goo. Bawling her little eyes out. Better not to ring while she was crying like this; they would be around with sirens wailing. Better to give her a bottle and settle her; better to bath and dress her. They would think that he had deliberately hurt her; they'd think he didn't know how to care for her.

Taking the bottle he was still holding, he placed it in a bowl of hot water to warm while he ran another bath. Then he dumped her in the hallway while he knelt on the toilet floor, as sick as a dog.

The evening meal had been brewingly silent, Dylana sitting on Matt's knee as he fed her spoonfuls of mashed potatoes and gravy dotted with pulped peas, the insides of which he had carefully squeezed from their tiny casings. Dylana seemed unscathed by her escapade that afternoon. She had finally slept, and after he had cleared up the mess he too had lain down on his bed. Before he dozed he called blearily across the room, telling her that he loved her and always would, and that he was sorry he had considered giving her away but he wouldn't again, and everything would be all right. The two of them together, for always.

Fritha suddenly waved a chicken drumstick at the air and said, 'Well, fuck it, Matt, if you're so intent on playing housewives and Mummies, you're going to have to start cooking for us while we're at work. There's no way I'm going to come home after working all day to cook a meal for you and your brother.'

Matt said, 'Okay then. I don't mind. But you'll have to tell me what to cook. You'll have to show me how.'

'Show you how! It's a prerequisite for having babies, Matt. Knowing how to cook. That and a few other things, but we won't mention those in front of the children.'

Scott scowled and put a warning hand over hers.

'No, bugger it, Scott. This is not turning out the way it was supposed to at all.'

'I *can* cook,' said Matt. 'But not very many things.'

'There's a few of Silvia's recipe books in that drawer down there.' Scott nodded towards a set of drawers under the bench.

'Great. And give him one of Silvia's aprons and you won't need me at all.' Frith splashed the drumstick down in the gravy and sat back in the chair, wiping her fingers with a serviette. 'Anyway, I don't care, it just gives me the creeps. Honestly, I can't stand it, I'm sorry, Scott, just sitting here watching this fiasco. He's going to have to hand the baby in. It's too weird for me. We're involved too, you know, we're in it as well now, letting it happen. We're just as culpable. Letting it all go on. It's not right.'

She glared at Matt then, her dislike like a painting spread across her face. He pulled Dylana towards him, tucking her into his body.

'I can't let her go,' he told her. 'She's my baby now. She's happy with me. Look. She's really happy.'

Dylana was holding her mouth open as the spoon wavered in front of her face. She placed her hand on his arm to draw the food closer.

'Look, isn't she cute?' he said, kissing the top of her snowy head.

Fritha turned to Scott. 'You don't care, do you? You think it's all right.'

'Hey, come on, don't blame me. I wasn't even *there*, remember? *Remember?* It was *you* who arrived on my doorstep *avec* the baby. Remember? My only crime was opening the door to let you in. God almighty, we've been through all this before. I'm sick of it.'

Frith clawed her hand through her hair. 'Well, me too. I've had enough. The baby has to go.'

Matt's stomach churning with horror.

'It's impossible,' he told them. 'If you make me give up Dylana, I'll tell the police about your drugs.'

He had not intended to reveal that he knew about their cache. That was going to be the white rabbit pulled from the hat, the very final last card. But it had come to that. Frith and Scott spun their heads to confront each other with accusation, each preparing to challenge the other. But they could see that neither was at fault. So they turned to Matt. Finally, belatedly, Scott said, 'What drugs?'

'The dead sheep,' Matt replied haughtily.

Fritha threw the crushed ball of her serviette into the centre of the table and stood up, the chair screeching across the floor. Her shoulders were high around her neck as she clattered bad-temperedly at the bench.

'And may I ask,' said Scott, his gravel voice rattling with razor splint stones, 'may I ask just where you might have found this dead sheep?'

Matt could only feel relief that he had prepared himself for this moment, though he wouldn't have guessed that he would have had to use his excuse in these circumstances. That his exposure would have been his own doing.

'Well . . .'

'We're waiting . . . We're bloody well waiting, boyo . . .'

'Well, I was wanting to prop up Dylana in the sitting room. She can sit up but sometimes she falls over a bit. So . . . so I went around the house looking for pillows and cushions. And I grabbed the pillows off your bed. We were in there and she was sitting there and I . . . I gave her a banana to eat and she got stuff over the pillowcase and I took it off to wipe it, wash it, and then I . . . then I . . . then I found those bags inside.'

Scott sighed, a long slow deep sigh, shaking his head and chewing the inner flesh at the corner of his mouth. Fritha had turned around, was standing with her back to the bench with her arms folded. Both stared at him. It obviously sounded totally feasible and he felt that they might have believed him. Scott looked exasperated but Fritha looked coldly furious. He hated the way she was so angry with him. A fist of fear turned in his gut. He cuddled Dylana, absorbing her love to give him strength.

He shrugged. 'They *are* drugs, aren't they?'

Neither said anything. Fritha continued to stare at him, almost as if he weren't there, as if he were invisible or transparent, and she had found a smudge of grease behind him on the wall and was wondering how it had found its way there. He picked up the spoon and dipped into the stodge of mashed potato, but Dylana pushed his hand away and started to wriggle.

'Well,' said Scott eventually, digging into his pocket. 'Well. That's that, then.' He pulled out his tobacco, started to prepare a cigarette.

'That's bloody that, all right. That's bloody that, I'll say, you've hit the nail on the head there.' Fritha dragged her fingers through her hair. 'I should have known. A couple of bloody hillbillies. Huh!' Her face was sallow, her lips taut. 'Well, it serves me right, I suppose. I shouldn't have done it. I just thought it would give us a fresh start. Give us a bit of a boost, you know, financially, something that we were in together. A little project. Give us a bit of a bounce off the conveyer belt of domestic grind while we were setting up house. Huh! I made a mistake, a big mistake. I hadn't accounted for this fucking *time bomb* in the equation of things. This weird . . .' She was beginning to splutter as she searched in vain for the words. 'This absolute and totally weird mummy oxymoron. This creeping gherkin. This . . . *creep*!'

Scott stood up beside her and squeezed her arm gently. She flung him off. Matt was fighting the tears he could feel welling behind his eyes. His newly found tears. He breathed deeply from Dylana's head. Tried to concentrate on all the fresh and sweet and wonderful things about her. Fritha didn't mean these things. She was just upset. She liked him, loved him, really. If Scott wasn't here, she would choose him, he knew that. They both knew that. It was understandable that she was upset.

'We'll sort something out,' said Scott, picking the scrappy tufts from the ends of his cigarette, sprinkling them on his plate. His expression was serious. Concern, now, more than anger.

'I'll say we bloody will, mate. I'm leaving, that's what I'm going to do. Leaving you to it. It's all yours, the whole bloody lot. The whole bloody domestic bliss. I've got my own life to lead, thank you very much.'

'No, Fritha, no, you can't leave, Fritha,' Matt said. Pathetically. He could hear it in his voice, the pathetic tone. He was standing up then, pacing a little, Dylana whimpering over his shoulder as he strummed her back. He was trying to keep his voice calm, to keep from breaking.

'Try and stop me, matey.'

'But you're the *mother*.'

'*Huh*? Oh . . . so . . . I'm the mother, am I? Oh god. Oh god oh god.' She slapped the heel of her palm at her forehead. Half laughing, mirthlessly.

'Yes. You are.'

'That's a beauty. It truly is.' She looked daggers at Scott. 'Nothing to say on this one, sweetie pie? Okay by you?'

'No, of course it's not okay by me. We've got a lot of sorting out to do.'

'*You've* got a lot of sorting out to do. Nothing to do with me any more. As I said.'

'Don't be silly, Fritha.'

She swept past them, knocking Matt's arm brutally as she passed. Her long hair down her back like the final curtain.

The house shuddering as the door to their bedroom slammed shut, then again as Scott followed her. The kitchen light starting to sway as if a gentle but poisonous breeze had found its way from a distant wasteland strewn with rubbish and rotting corpses. Strewn with all the bad things of the world.

All the bad and filthy evil things.

✳

That night again the arguing across the hallway as he paced the bed-room with the crying Dylana. Finally she slept as he lay on the floor alongside the mattress, stroking her back and singing the lullaby over and over again. Silence. He realised with relief that the muffled shouting he had caused had silenced as well. The house had yielded to the night. He got up to go to the toilet, his bare feet padding down the wooden hallway, his fingers lightly brushing their way along the wallpaper in the orange-hued darkness. Then he heard that indeed the house was not quiet. He heard them. He heard Fritha's soft moaning and the thick grunts of an animal. He stood there, his blood swelling with horror. Fritha and Scott. Scott like his father. Like an animal. He stood there, his breath caught like a clump of hair in his throat, as her voice rose in small cries and then higher in a long squeal of pain. Of agony. He pushed at his pyjamas, punched at the heat in his pyjamas. How could she do that with his brother? He was an animal. *He* would never do that. He would love her without that, he would never do that to her, he would never, he would never never never . . .

he would never . . .

do that

✳

The sound of soft cooing.

He emerged from a dream-threaded net of sleep, like a man scrambling from a straitjacket of woollen yarn. Morning, finally morning. And the sweet stink of pooey nappies. He peeped over his bed to see Dylana lying on her stomach with her upper body propped by her elbows, as if she were on a Sunday picnic. Somehow, in that secret way she had of moving, she had hauled herself from the mattress and was studying a piece of fluff from the carpet, rubbing it between finger and thumb, before putting it in her mouth.

'Dirty,' he said.

She jumped, her reverie broken. She lifted her head like a drunk. Then her intent expression collapsed and reconstructed itself into a smile, a beaming smile for him. It was mysterious, the way she could dissolve his bleak moods with the touch of a glance. A magic wand that pinged away the evil. Hanging his arm over the bed, he clicked his fingers and called her, as he might call his cat. Here, Dylana. Here. Over here. But the distance across the room was vast, and besides, moving was a private activity. She was a rabbit checking for farmer Brown before she raided the carrots. She was a young ballet dancer unsure of her first awkward steps. Her performance needed practice, needed perfecting. It occurred to him that she might be planning an escape, that these unobserved forays across her terrain might be calculated attempts to leave him. He would have to watch her, just in case. The little monkey.

They both looked up to a gentle tapping on the bedroom door. Matt lurched upright, yanking an armful of blankets around his stomach.

'What?' he croaked.

The door opened. Scott and Fritha. Them. Together. Scott first, in jeans and bare chest. Fritha dragging behind, wrapped in a great red dressing gown, tied roughly at her waist, looking like a rough parcel that had started to unravel in the post.

Matt glanced at Dylana, prepared for trouble. He pulled the blankets higher, clenching them tightly at his middle, examining their faces for clues.

'What?' he muttered again.

Scott sat at the end of the bed, cupping his hands under his armpits, as if self-conscious in his nakedness. Fritha stood there, her arms also crossed, her lips pursed.

'We've been thinking,' said Scott.

'What?'

'It's the best thing. It's the only thing.'

'What?'

'We've talked this over and we've decided the only acceptable answer is for you to go back to the bach. We'll both drive you down in the weekend, possibly on Friday, after work. We'll set you up with food and money. You'll be safe there. No one goes there.'

'But . . .'

A strip of sunlight fed the colours in the crocheted blanket, glistening among the hairs on Scott's chest, striking his arm as he raised a warning hand.

'No buts. The alternative is to give up the baby. Georgia.'

'Dylana. It's Dylana. Don't call her Georgia.'

'The alternative is to give up the baby. If you want to tell them about the dope, that's just how it will have to be. We'll take the risk but anyway they won't believe you. We'll absolutely deny it. If they find anything, we'll say it must be yours. They just won't believe you. You're a kidnapper. A babynapper. A kid babynipper.'

'Very funny,' mumbled Matt, knitting a finger through the crocheted holes of the peggy squares. Up and over, up and over, in and out of the holes in the patterns.

Fritha went over to the baby and crouched beside her, waggling the red tail of the dressing gown belt. Then slowly, with care, she lifted Dylana from the carpet, embracing the child as she might hold a large urn. Matt bristled. It was unfair to do this to him. It was unfair to gang up on him when he was feeling so vulnerable, his flesh goosy as he sat there so absolutely and totally freaked out, watching Fritha with his baby.

'So?'

'You're going to leave me? By myself?'

'It's the only way we can do it, mate. Think about it. It's the perfect solution. You'd be isolated but within range if you need help, if you want to buy things, if you need people. We need some time here, some space while we sort a few things out.'

'You mean I can come back?'

'Of course you can, mate. Of course. Look. We're not so good for you here either . . . imagine, if we were caught with our little secret here, you'd be a sitting duck. A few questions asked and you'd be sprung. So it's in your best interests as well. Just for a while, and then . . .'

'And then I can come back?'

'As I said, of course. Promise.'

'So what will you tell Mum? If she phones and I'm not here?'

'We don't need to tell her anything,' said Frith, rocking with the baby from foot to foot. 'If you write to her from time to time, send the letter to us and we'll post it from here. And you can ring her. As long as she hears from you, she won't worry.'

Matt glared at her, shrugging. They had him. It was blackmail. 'Have I got any choice?'

'No, you don't, boyo, sorry.'

'Well?' said Scott.

'Well what?'

'It's a deal?'

'How long for?'

'Let's play it by ear. A couple of months possibly?'

'*Months*?'

'Or thereabouts, yes.'

'Why months?'

'Because we'll need about that long. Okay?'

'I have to think about it.'

'No thinking about it, sorry.' Fritha was sidling towards the door, still holding his eye. With Dylana, who was wriggling in her arms.

'All right, all right. But give me Dylana.' He held his arms wide.

'So, it's a deal?'

'I suppose so.'

'Great, fantastic. Good lad.' Scott thumped his fist into his palm. Fritha came to the bed and dumped the baby into his flailing arms.

'You're like a bloody cow with a calf,' she said as she turned to leave the room. 'Anyway, she stinks.'

Scott stood up and ruffled Matt's hair. 'It's the best thing, matey,' he said, and followed her out.

✳

He is cold to his bones, his t-shirt sticking to his ribs, his jeans heavy against his legs. It is the women he has to fear, the older women. They are the foe. It is they who would pluck Dylana from him if they could. He sees the menace in their outstretched arms, the lurking peril in their eyes. Even now he notices a palm pressed against a front window, like the underside of a slug, her face a dark fuzz in the room behind. A curtain dropping as he pauses.

It is the women who approach him with their sickly voices, their softhard eyes, their all-knowing unctuous smiles, their masks of universal maternal affection which seems to give them licence to interfere. Their fingers greedy to touch, even with a swift sweep across her cheek as they hold their cheeks to their shoulders in that way.

Matt hurries on, licking the fear from his chapped lips with a dry tongue. He lifts a hand behind his head, to feel Dylana's face, feel the round solidness of her large head under the hood of the coat. Of course she is still there, joggling against his shoulder blades in Jason's backpack.

This morning a woman had come to the house. Dylana was inside sleeping, and Matt was sitting on the back porch throwing crusts onto the lawn, watching the nervous sparrows flit from the window sills to the bread, fluffing their feathers in the soft rain.

He was alerted by the confident crunching of footsteps on the gravel before she appeared from around the corner bush. He saw the red nylon scarf tied tightly under a long chin, a face severe and harassed, emerging from hair pulled back in long blackgrey streaks. A wicker laundry basket heaped with wet clothes bumped against her thighs as she walked. She dumped the basket on the path, one hand pressing into the small of her back, the other wiping the rain from her cheeks.

'I've come to use the dryer,' she said, wearily. As if she had met him a million times before, as if she knew him.

'There isn't one,' he told her instinctively, thinking of the bucket of soaking nappies. Thinking of a house full of secrets.

'Yes there is.' She nodded towards the wooden door at the end of the porch. 'Scott lets me use it all the time.'

'Yes, but it's broken,' he said.

'Are you sure? It was all right a few days ago. Let me have a look. You mightn't know how to use it properly. I've been using it for years. Sometimes if you don't turn the thing far enough . . .'

She started to edge past him on the steps, into the wash-house behind him. He put his arm out to prevent her passing. The calf of her leg mottled and lumpy alongside him.

'It's broken, I said.' He shoved his elbow in irritation, catching her shin, and she stumbled backwards, falling, yelping as she grabbed the handrail to prevent herself crashing onto the path.

'What's wrong with you? You're mad,' she said, breathing heavily and eyeing him contemptuously as she readjusted the red scarf. 'You're absolutely mad. I could've killed myself.' She was panting with fright, her voice rising. 'Scott *always* lets me use it. And Silvia, when she's here. They always have. Look.' She delved a hand into her skirt pocket and brought out a long grey key. Her hand was trembling. 'See? The key. To the wash-house.' And then she snarled at him, 'You're not fit to look after that poor little baby. I've seen you. Not fit.' She twirled around, scooping up the washing basket. Matt watched the defiant curve of her back as she disappeared around the side of the house.

It wasn't his fault. He hadn't meant to make her fall. She'd looked at him as if he'd done it deliberately. She'd given him a fright, that was all. Why hadn't Scott told him about her? *He* wasn't to know whether a stranger could use their dryer or not. Did she have a key to the rest of the house?

He stood up and went inside. He climbed on a chair to look from the small high side window in the kitchen, in time to see her scrambling over a rickety part of the fence into the section next door.

She'd seen him, she said. Had she been spying on him? Perhaps Scott had been right about his going away until everything had settled down, with neighbours like this. He felt a growing agitation. A feeling that something was going to happen. Something that wasn't good. He had that horrible tight feeling boring into his diaphragm and he rubbed his fist deeply into the soft flesh, to try to locate it, to ease it. The house was suddenly dark. The whole day sprawled in front of him. The whole long day. What would he do? All day. Waiting for Scott and Frith to come home. Waiting for Dylana to wake up.

His mother.

She was only ever a phone call away, she had told him. A voice like a bird drifting through smoke.

He went into Scott's room and looked through Jason's things, found a little coat with a hood on it. It was far too big but it would keep Dylana warm and dry.

He laid everything out on the bed, ready to dress her when she woke up.

Her nappy, neatly folded. He would make sure to change her nappy, in case some woman complained again. He was good at changing nappies now, folding them like origami and putting them on so that they stayed intact. He was lucky that Scott had kept Jason's baby things; that they had planned to have another child before they split up. He had everything he needed. They'd only had to buy the bleach powder to soak the nappies in, and a few disposable nappies.

He went down the hallway to the kitchen window again. The woman was hanging her washing out, in the rain. *She* was the mad one. She looked up suddenly and caught him observing her, and even from that distance he could see her curling her lip at him.

He should ring his mother to say hello. He needn't tell her anything. Daytime, peak time, the most expensive time but she did say . . . And she would assure him that everything was all right. That was all he wanted to hear.

Unexpectedly though, his father answered. His father. What was his father doing at home? He slammed the phone down. Had something happened? Something had happened to his mother. He'd had a *feeling* something was wrong. Why wasn't his father at work? He looked at the clock on the wall. Quarter past twelve. Lunchtime. Lunchtime!

He'd thought it was still morning. The day halfway over. His father would be home for lunch, as he was occasionally.

Panicking. He shouldn't be panicking. He had to pull himself together. He tried to make himself think of pleasant things. The nice and lovely beautiful things. Not the bad things. Not the bad things. The good things. God.

He went to his room. Threw himself to his knees with his elbows on his bed and buried his face in his hands. God. Please, God. Calm me down. Thank you for giving me beautiful Dylana and please don't ever take her away from me. Don't let anything happen to Mum. Or me. Don't let anything happen to me. Please don't make Fritha hate me. Please make Fritha love me. Give me beautiful things. Beauty. Love. Thank you, God. God. God, help me to be good. A good person. Please, God. Amen.

And now he is walking. He has been walking all afternoon. In the rain. His arm aching and his fingers stiff from holding the umbrella over Dylana's head.

He'd found himself in Karangahape Road where for a while he was joined by a man in a long coat dragging a trundler behind him. He didn't speak to Matt but chuckled at Dylana, his tongue a slab of old meat flapping around toothless gums. He lifted filthy swollen fingers to touch her cheek. Matt increased his pace and the man wheezed alongside him, the wheels of the trundler whirring and jumping along the footpath like an eager pet. Matt stopped abruptly, walked back the way he had come then, as the man turned to follow, Matt made another u-turn and trotted onwards. The man started to cough and Matt didn't look back, allowing the rasping hacks to become more distant until he could hear them no longer.

After that he'd headed away from town, his shoes pinching his feet, pausing for a while to stare from a bridge to the river of traffic pouring far below until, feeling vulnerable, he strode out again, his head whirling at the space between himself and the road. He passed shops boarded over with plywood, entranceways stinking of urine and decay. Two girls sat huddled in a doorway, shivering and giggling, their knees under their chins. Cars had splashed past, throbbing at the lights. He made towards the hill dominating the skyline.

Now he is trudging up the road to the top of the crater. A jogger is running towards him, his expression distorted with the effort, his hair flattened by a cascade of rain pouring down his face. Looking straight at Matt as they pass each other, his face a wretched canvas of agony. Looking straight at Matt so that Matt receives the full blast of his pain, like the veiled threat of a chain letter, as if he is offering it to him like a gift, so that the twisting anxiety in Matt's stomach which has been lurking there, which he has been fighting to shove away, comes screaming back. His heart, which had been slogging over the hill climb, fires into a frenzy, the terrible frenzy. His heart is

188

going to burst and he can't breathe. He can't stand it. He is being punished for doing nothing. It is unfair.

He sees a park bench under a tree and moves towards it, slipping the backpack from his shoulders. Pulls Dylana out of the pack and holds her. Sitting rocking on the bench, holding her tight.

'It's all right, my darling,' he murmurs, cradling her head against his shoulder, fluttering little fish-mouth kisses on her cool cheek. 'It's all right. Nothing is going to happen to us. I am here to save you.'

She is uncomfortable, wriggling, gazing about her, starting to cry. Shhhsh. He presses the bundle of her little body close to his. Making him feel better. Shush. As if her purpose is to fill the chasm of emptiness inside him. The hollow which, if he thinks about it, if he shuts his eyes and looks within, is infinite. As if he is gazing into the sky at night. As if he is thinking about the end of the world, or how the world was first made and who made the world and who made God. As if he is thinking of unfathomable darkness. But it is tolerable now, because Dylana is here, and she is here to fill that hole with her love. Like a wound healing. And in a different way Fritha, but she has turned against him now. She has betrayed him.

Think of good things good things good things. Think of good things happy things beautiful things. The good colours. Blue. Deep sea on a summer's day out in the boat blue. And the pure yellow of sunshine and daffodils. And soothing calming peacock green.

The good colours within his soul, filling the darkness with the good colours and Dylana's love. Breathe deeply. The living smells. Fresh cool smells of cows, and wet grass, and nature, and Dylana.

Opening his eyes, he releases Dylana and turns her around to face the view. They watch a cow tugging at grass and a bird flitting across the branches above them. The rain has eased. He places her beside him on the seat and stands up to pee against the tree, holding his back to her modestly. Then he loops the pack and umbrella over his shoulder and scoops Dylana from the bench, his hands feeling her solid plumpness under the coat. He perches her upon his bony hip, his arm supporting her back, and moves on.

Towards the top the sky is a pink and bruisy turbulence of cloud. Sprawled below, houses, everywhere houses, spread like mould on bread. Houses merging into houses, into sea and islands, into formless smudge as the day prepares for night. And the people. All the invisible people inhabiting the earth. All the busy people, like insects scurrying under a scabby crust. This is the symbol of his isolation, he thinks, as he gazes at it from above.

'Look, Dylana,' he says. 'Look at all this. This is your world, our world. And it goes on and on, over the curves of the sea and then, beyond the sea, there's still more. More people, and they all think they are something but they're nothing.

'I will tell you things, Dylana. I will tell you about all the good things. I'll be gentle with you. I'll keep all the bad and ugly things away from you. You will be the perfect person that you are now, for ever.'

He makes his way over to the rim of the crater, a great throat leading nowhere. Down the funnel into the centre of the world. Near the bottom there is a makeshift heart, constructed with large stones. Somebody has written *I love B* in rocks, within a wobbly heart.

Somebody has 'B', and he has Dylana.

It has always been a mystery to him as to why he exists at all. He's always felt that his being on earth is as meaningless as a raindrop on a window pane, either evaporating on contact or dribbling into a gutter to join a seaward torrent . . . to eventually become a component of another raindrop. Part of the cycle of condensation and evaporation. Or, he thinks, as he notices another cow, like a clump of grass. Whether it lives through the full cycle — sprouting, seeding and dying to add nutrients for the next round — or is torn off mid-flourish and processed in the belly of the cow; it all ends up the same. Composition and decomposition. The endless cycle. Something emerging from the earth and then feeding it again. Breathing in, breathing out. Day night, summer winter. Mechanical, almost. Why is he, or anyone else, any different? He's had a persistent notion that perhaps the answer might be revealed to him, that his mission in life would become clear, his reason for living. And now he knows. The essential ingredient is love.

Gazing over the plains again he says out loud, 'Thank you, God.' He must remember to be eternally grateful. To never take her for granted. To always appreciate the miracle of her.

He puts his nose against her cheek. Her sweet cool scent seeps into the air around them, and again is exhaled through his breath, to shift in a breeze across the earth below, to infiltrate the dreams of restless souls tossing in their beds. Yes, it is the goodness of her, feeding the very source of life. A beacon of benevolence and love, radiating into the air.

Turning away from the vastness of it all, he picks his way down the hillside again.

His arms are almost breaking when he arrives at the house, still carrying Dylana, the empty backpack slung over his shoulder. Fritha and Scott are home. The car is in the driveway and the front door is open. He pads up the steps and goes straight to his bedroom. Once he puts her on the mattress, Dylana immediately grizzles and holds out her arms to him. He loves the way she does that.

But she's building up a noise. He'll have to go to the kitchen, to intrude upon their togetherness, which holds him apart like a veil.

He's so pissed off with them. He's in a real brood. He feels betrayed by them, especially Fritha. And going back to the lake. Sending him off to the bach like that. They have him. He can't do anything else. And to make matters worse, he can see their logic. Really. It makes sense. But on the other hand, he knows they're doing it to get rid of him.

In the kitchen he takes a prepared bottle from the fridge.

'Sulky pulky,' sings Fritha. 'Look at you, your mouth pulled tight like a drawstring purse.'

'Quit it, Fritha,' says Scott. There is a bottle of wine open on the table. They're celebrating. Celebrating that he's going. Fritha's glass is on the bench in front of her cooking. Scott is sitting on a chair holding his, smoking a cigarette.

'You're out late,' he says. 'Had a good day?'

As if he cares. 'Okay,' says Matt.

'Had a bit of trouble with Mavis Thomson, I believe.'

'Who?'

'Next door.'

'Oh, her. Well, how was I to know that she used your dryer? You didn't tell me.'

'Pushing her down the steps.'

'I did not. I did not. She fell. She was trying to barge past me and she fell. She's lying.'

'And picking her roses the other day, I believe.'

'I knew she was spying.'

'Anyway, she wasn't very happy.'

'So what? She's horrible.'

'We had to tell her that the baby is a family scandal. An unmarried mother. A girl still at school. A cousin. See — already the lies have started.'

'You didn't have to tell her anything.'

'Better to have people like that on our side, Matt. Better friends than enemies. Think of that. The thing is, it doesn't help anyone if you alienate people. You don't want to do anything to attract attention.'

'I wasn't. It wasn't my fault.'

'Anyway, Matt, there's a small change of plan.'

'What?'

'I'd forgotten, with all the fuss, that this is my weekend for having Jason. And also I discovered today the band's got a gig on Saturday night. So I can't go to Taupo.'

'That's okay. I don't mind.'

'No — Fritha's going to take you down as planned. On Saturday. Okay?'

'Sure,' he mumbles, not looking at either of them, trying hard, so hard, not to show his agitation and relief.

✳

The high river of tinnitus flowing above his head. The chicker chicker of a machine somewhere. He is aware of the breath of slippers shuffling across the hospital floor and elsewhere the uneven rasp of waves lapping on a stony shore. He doesn't bother to open his eyes. Day and night are the same to him now. The darkness which is not darkness but an infusion of light from the long busy corridor outside the ward. Through the window the moon sears a hole through the thick racing clouds, piercing his soul with ice. He is a frozen thing, he is encapsulated in a moment between one heartbeat and another.

✳

PART SIX

Matt jerks awake, the car shuddering to a stop.

'Okay, boyo, that's it. Mission accomplished. You're here.'

'We're all here.'

'And I've had enough. I'm going for a walk. You know where the key is.'

'But you'll be back?'

'Of course I'll be bloody back, I'm just going for a bloody walk, that's all. I'm not leaving you with the car, am I? See if you can get the car unpacked before your baby wakes up.'

But it is too late, she's already stirring, farting and stretching, unhappy in the confines of the pram.

'She's already awake.'

'Oh well. You'll manage. You're about to find out what it's like to be a mummy and a housewife all on your own. Like a war bride. Dinner will be ready when I get back, will it, sweetheart? See ya.'

She leans back into the car and pulls out a towel. 'Might even go for a swim.'

She's gone, running almost, her hair flying behind her like washing on a line.

He looks around the car, jammed packed with boxes and supermarket bags, and the pram base with Dylana in the middle. Dylana awake and wriggling for his attention. Could he leave her there while he opened the bach and unpacked the car? It would be easier and quicker. Fritha was so mean leaving him to do it all by himself. So mean. She'd been mean to him the whole journey. And he'd been looking forward to it too, the two of them together, without Scott.

But no . . . he's learnt his lesson. Things can happen so quickly. You never know what they can do, babies.

He thinks of that puzzle about the man and the boat, with the goat, the wolf and the cabbage, trying to get to the other side of the river. The man could take only one thing over at a time. He had to chose the right combination, knowing that the goat would eat the cabbage or the wolf would eat the goat if they were left alone together. In the same way, he has to sort out the combination with Dylana. He'll leave her in the car while he opens the bach. There's no harm here now because she's so jammed in. He'll take the heavier boxes and then he'll put her inside, prop her up with pillows on the floor. He can talk to her while he works.

He watches anxiously for Fritha, for her return. A chicken is cooking in the oven. Potatoes peeled and soaking in water ready for boiling, and tinned peas in another pot. He's stacked the boxes in the spare room . . . enough cans and porridge and sugar and milk powder for a winter at the South Pole. Dylana has been fed and there are two more bottles prepared in the fridge. He bathed her in boiled water in the basin. She is now fresh and glowing, embedded in the easy chair, with a barricade of cushions around her, ready for bed.

He is proud that he has met the challenge of unpacking, proving that he is able to set up house by himself. Fritha will be pleased with him. He has wandered through the bach, room by room, imagining them all living there together, he and Fritha and Dylana, as a family. He imagines them all deep inside a story, some crazy ancient story about an ugly but kind monkey who rescues a human baby from a pit in a dark dense forest, carrying the baby back to his shelter, to his childless wife. The two of them care for it tenderly, hidden from the dangers of the world and the people who might steal the baby back from them.

He picks Dylana up from among the cushions and lifts her effortlessly above his head, as if she is a trophy. She gapes down at him, spilling with giggles. She is so light that he feels he could throw her into the air and she would float away, out of the door and away on a breeze to bring her magic into the lives of others. But not tonight. He swoops her down and whees her up again, high above his head, wiggling upon his outstretched arms, her eyes bulgy and her face red. Trusting him as he gurgles at her. He doesn't hear Fritha until she is there. It is just on dark; they have suddenly shifted to a deeper, murkier place in the day. She is lurking behind him in the shadows.

And even then, he senses her presence rather than hears her. He spins around and she is leaning against the wall, against the wall with the spreading water stain. For a second he is pleased and relieved to see her. A vestige of his fantasy lingers, in which he greets her as she walks in remarking on how cosily he has arranged the place, how tantalising are the smells of the cooking chicken, how she admires him as she can see that after all he has surprised her, he is able to cope. Like a hawk lifting a wing to expose tender skin and a sigh of down stirring, that moment is over before the sweeping shadow of it passes overhead. Before it dives. As he takes Dylana down from the air. As he notes Fritha's face. As he sees the beak open and the shiny red of her tongue and hears the thrashing pounding of wings in his ears as the moment passes and is airborne again.

His head buried against Dylana's stomach, her body shielding his head. Cowering and holding her body like a pillow over his head. He is using Dylana to shield himself. Only for an instant but he looks up, ashamed. Fritha still standing there, her hair wet and dripping lost rivers onto the towel around her shoulders. Her arms twisted like her lips, in a pact with themselves against him.

'Hi. Hi,' he says. Then, hopefully, 'Dinner's ready.'

But he knows already. She is not going to eat with him.

'We were wondering where you were.'

Still she says nothing. He sits down, holding Dylana on his knee. 'Dylana's eaten. She's all ready for bed. She's going to bed soon. And then we can eat. I just have to cook the potatoes and the peas. Everything's ready. The chicken. The chicken's cooking in the oven.'

He can't conceal his pride but still she stares at him, or doesn't stare at him. He shuffles his bottom to the back of the seat, lifts his feet to the edge of the chair. His knees to his chin. Dylana nestled within his limbs, her wobbly legs scrabbling over his lap, her tiny round hands clutching his knees. Her soft noises like the chatting of an oblivious bystander during a play. The last light lifting from the lake and the sky, drifting in to settle across Fritha's face, playing across her ashen face.

'What?' he says eventually, his stomach contracting. 'What, Frith? What's wrong?'

But she turns then and goes to her room, closing the door. Closing the door. He scrambles from the chair. His body fizzing, and again that sharp tightness in his diaphragm. He kisses Dylana on the cheek.

'Beddie byes, sweety pies,' he says flatly.

Her bed is laid out on the floor; he has pulled the mattress from the bottom bunk, in a similar arrangement to the one they had in Auckland, so that if she tumbles from bed, it is a mere roll onto the floor, a bump on a curving road through a dream into an awakening.

He puts her down and when she cries he rubs her back and sings a strangled lullaby. The words jam in his throat like fish in a net, but he continues. Dylana cries on and on too, writhing as if in agony, perhaps remembering that this is the place where it all happened, the beginning of the time when her parents weren't there any more. Remembering that there were other people who loved her too, a mother with breasts of sweet milk and the smells that were of her own flesh, her own pumping rhythm, her own voice which was taken away like a cup of water from the ocean, like a drop of sweat from a brow, her own from the first instant of her life.

He lies alongside her in the plunging darkness telling her sssh, telling her sssssh because the lullaby has died in his throat. And finally she is asleep and he lifts his fingers from her back so carefully, so that the stroking becomes lighter and lighter until the movement is a hovering dragonfly above the contour of her body, and higher until his hand is reclaimed. He creeps from the room. Opens the door and into the hallway into darkness and silence and the acrid smell of burning chicken. He could tear out his hair with disappointment. The chicken is black, a charred and cringing thing from a dream. The roasting dish a tarry mess of sludge.

He boils the kettle and puts on the potatoes and strips the black scab from the chicken to find the white stringy flesh underneath. A slow leakage of transparent juice seeps from somewhere, the last moisture from its life leaving, blood with no substance, a sentence with no meaning.

He stands over the potatoes until they yield readily to the fork. Heats the peas while he mashes the potatoes, adding pepper and salt and butter and a splash of milk. Mashing until they are smooth and as soft as summer clouds. And now everything is ready. The table is set and he dishes the food onto two plates. Salt and pepper on the table and the flowers he has picked from a garden bush in a jar. The food looks bland without gravy but that can't be helped.

How apprehensive he feels as he taps on her door. He is not surprised when there is no reply. He waits in the hallway.

'Fritha,' he calls quietly. 'Fritha. Dinner is ready.'

Silence. It is the silence of no one there. The silence of a waft of fairy down tossing in a blue sky, higher and higher on an eerie wind that is quite separate from the breezes below. Jerking this way and that until it becomes the sky, until it becomes nothing and the eyes ache searching for it against the sunshine.

He turns the door handle. From the light in the hallway he can see the lump on the bed, the huddled lump turned against him to the wall.

'Fritha,' he whispers into the room. 'Dinner's ready.'

She is still. She is dead. She is dead like the mother in the tree. Dead.

He creeps over and reaches to touch her shoulder. Just an uncertain prod on her shoulder but she whirls around, a wild and spitting animal, roaring at him from the back of her throat.

'What the *fuck* do you think you're trying to do?'

She has thrown him against the wall with her anger; he's sidling along the wall to the doorway and out.

'I was just telling you that our dinner is getting cold.'

'I don't want any dinner.'

'But I've cooked it specially.'

'I don't give a fuck what you've done. I'm not hungry.'

'But you said . . .'

'I don't care what I said. I'm not going to eat your fucking dinner so get out and leave me alone.'

See. He knew. He just knew she wasn't going to eat his dinner after all that trouble he went to. After all those times of her going on about him being useless, when he proves he's not, she won't eat his food anyway.

At the table he picks up the plates and squashes them together, potato kissing potato, and the chicken trapped in a useless dangle, while the peas are skittering away like scared children in a playground, escaping across the table and onto the floor, only to stop, stunned, caught in the headlights of his despair.

He drops the plates to the table and leans his full force upon them with the heel of his hand. He knew. He knew she wouldn't eat his food. The top plate crunches into three pieces, potato oozing from the side like the innards of a bug.

He tried to be nice to her. He tried. He *loves* her. No one could say he didn't try. Her anger is unfair, unjustified. Whatever has he done to her? She'll leave in the morning and he hasn't had a chance.

The idea of her leaving is intolerable. He should take in a coffee. A drink — the ancient offering of peace and a means to communication. He throws the broken plate in the rubbish bin, scrapes the food from the other. She doesn't understand how he would be willing to care for her. He would cook and clean and look after her. They could be so happy. The three of them. A family.

Standing at the cluttered bench, he picks a filament of flesh from the chicken. He holds the morsel between his front teeth in a nibble, then chews reluctantly, for although he has not eaten since they left Auckland, he is not hungry. The meat doesn't feel like food in his mouth. He takes out the chewed wad and stuffs it down the sink, then idly tears another stringy piece from the carcass, like a thread from a jersey. The first thread from an unravelling jersey, the first sod pulled from an archaeological site, and another and another as he carefully peels away the sinuous fabric of a lifetime, looking for the spirit beyond the flesh, to find the architecture of the skeleton, the finely arched bones of the temple. He pulls aside a curtain of membrane, snaps a rib: a brick pulled away. He stares into an empty tomb. No relics from the past. No heart, no soul, no fossilised evidence of a beating force.

He stuffs his finger through the slit, probing the cavern, the palate of a mouth, his father's fingers slithering around his mouth forced open over the hard basin digging into his chin. Washing his mouth out with soap and water. His father's nicotine-reeking rough-skinned hairy fingers roaming around his mouth, spreading the soapy slime around his gums as he desperately tried to keep his tongue from touching the fingers raping his retching throat. All for lying when he didn't lie, when it wasn't his fault. When it wasn't even his fault. He hadn't done anything. He was only protecting his mother. It was his mother. His mother, sobbing in the hall. His mother's fault, for not owning up. For not saying that she had been the one going through his father's jacket pockets — she, not him. He had seen her as he watched through the slit in the door. Desperately going through every pocket.

Now he slams his fist in a surge of exasperation, through the fragile bones, so the carcass hangs heavily, a boxing glove from a limp wrist. He wrenches his hand away and suddenly sees the mess he has made: the smashed corpse with the gaping wound in its side, the pile of shredded chicken on the bench. He holds his mucky hands under the running tap, rubbing them together like an old man he saw once crying outside a church, wringing his hands over and over. Finally he stops, slides to the floor and sits against the wall, his face locked within its dark casing of dripping cold fingers.

Some time later he hears a noise. The tinny slam of a car door. He jumps up and hurries outside, clattering down the wooden porch into the dark and towards the car, into a thud across his shins which sends him sprawling onto the path and grass. His chin hitting the path. He is lying there struggling to breathe when a thump lands between his shoulder blades and stays there, squeezing the remaining breath from his lungs. It has all happened so abruptly. He can taste the dry must of dirt. He spits grit from his lips, heaving his head up against the weight on his back. He thinks of thugs and burglars and ghosts and he shoves his shoulder upwards but can't turn over; the pressure upon his back clamps him to the ground. Then a fumbling grip twists his hand up his back to his neck, pumping from him a yell that is flattened by the earth around his face.

'What do you want? What are you doing?'

'What have you done to the car, you little shit?'

'Nothing.'

His hand yanked higher. The farmer's daughter dealing with a runaway sheep. He yells again. 'Nothing, I haven't done anything. Ow. Nothing. Ow. I just took the battery out.' She releases the hold, still clutching his hand at his waist.

'So where is it?'

'Inside.'

'Where?'

'Inside.' Tighter.

'Where inside?'

'In the spare room.'

'Where?'

'In a box. In one of the boxes.'

'Get up.'

He lies there.

He pushes at the grainy alien stones with his tongue; licking at his numb lips as if tasting blood from a plum.

'Get up, I said.'

He tries to scramble to his feet. 'I can't with you holding me. Why are you holding me? What are you going to do?'

'Your guess, boyo.'

'What's wrong with you . . . why are you suddenly like this with me? What have I done?'

'Huh! What have *you done?* That's a little beauty.'

She frogmarches him through the dark to the bach. His arm hurting like hell — why does she have to *hurt* him like this? He can't stand it any longer. He swiftly flips his leg behind hers and trips her over, so astonishingly easily, her feet flicked from under her. They are on the ground, she tiny and clawing at his face, snarling at him, so strong. He pushes his hand into her chin. Her head hits the path and she is suddenly limp.

'Fritha,' he calls, groping for her, the lifeless form in the dark, fumbling across the panic to lift her, to pick her up in his arms. Like a cat with a bird he runs one way towards the bach, and then swerves into the bushes where he sits on the soil tucked among the branches of a bush, with Fritha's head on his lap, stroking her head and saying, 'I'm sorry, Fritha, I'm sorry. I didn't want to hurt you.' She groans softly. 'Fritha. I love you, I love you,' and he is crying, sniffing, blubbering. 'I always have and I always will. I'll always look after you. Everything is going to be all right, Fritha. Truly.'

And then he is aware that she is conscious.

There is that barely perceptible stiffening, that subtle change in the breathing. She is still . . . she is listening, waiting.

He feels self-conscious now, his recital overheard as the spectator slinks from the streets into the darkened auditorium, witnessing the dress rehearsal, before time.

He sniffs in the silence.

'Ever since I met you . . . when Scott brought you around after he'd split up with Silvia the first time. You were different, somehow. I always remember that time you talked to me. Sitting by the fire and Mum and Dad had gone to bed and Scott was out when you called in and you decided you'd wait for him. And I knew he was starting up with Silvia again. You must have thought I was just a kid. Playing chess with me to fill in time. You were the black and I was the white. I was pleased you won. I thought you were so beautiful and sad, like a princess. I didn't want the night to end. I didn't want you to go. In the end you stared into the fire, your face sort of alive with the flames flickering, and then you stood up and smiled at me, and said, "Well, check matey." I still remember that. After you left, I moved my hand over the carpet where you'd been sitting, feeling the heat of your body. Then I lay with my cheek absorbing your warmth from the carpet. Breathing in the warmth of your body so that it became a part of me. Watching the fire go out. I slept there all night. I knew even then he wasn't good enough for you. That was just before he went back to Silvia and they moved up to Auckland. So I was right.'

He feels her tensing further, as a cat might in preparation to leave his lap, selecting the conditions to leap . . . to catch him unaware. He is ready to grasp her if she tries to flee. One hand loosely around the top of her arm, poised to tighten the grip.

'You are so precious,' he says awkwardly. He wishes he could find the words to tell her just how precious. This is the occasion for poetry. 'As precious as . . .' Now the time has come, he realises he has no words to describe his feeling for her without sounding corny, without sounding dumb. You are like a jewel in an antelope's ear. Wandering lonely as a cloud doesn't seem to fit here either. Fragments of poetry learnt at school flutter through his mind. Water water everywhere and all the birds did shriek. Something about warbling magpies. The black bat night has flown. Wherefore art thou, Fritha. Wherefore art thou, my darling Fritha. My darling one. In my arms.

If only he had the words to somehow explain to her the *depth* of the feeling he has for her. Something that is so much more than anything physical, something more profound, something purer, higher, than *that.*

'I love you, Fritha,' he says.

A morepork cries across the night. Insects clicking like women knitting at the guillotine.

He is starting to tremble; he feels so stupid knowing that she will feel him trembling as if he is terrified. As he is.

She will think he has never held a girl before. As he has not.

A girl in his arms. To love.

He lifts his hand and puts it on her hair, which is still damp and cold. Her hair, which is tangled. Her hair, which does not flow like a river down her back, but has captured the clotted twigs that fly along beaches in the wind. He touches her forehead and her cheek with the tips of his shivering fingers. Like a blind man might discover a loved one, for the first time. He is not prepared for the sudden strangling grabbing of his testicles as she twists them like a beggar yanking grapes from a vine. As he crumples, she tears herself from his grasp. She's ungrappled herself from his clutches and he hears the rush of her steps across the lawn, up the wooden path into the bach as he crumples in agony, an excruciating spasm invading his whole body, his whole psyche in anguish as his humiliation intermodulates with pain. Breath-sucking pain.

He manages to drag himself to his feet, staggering to the house.

Fritha is already in the spare room hauling cartons aside. Tins, jars, packets are tossed across the room in a fury.

A jar of raspberry jam shatters, a lethal mixture of oozing red shards on the floor.

'Get out,' she says without even looking up.

'You hurt me.'

'Good,' she says without hesitating, as she comes to the bottom of one box and moves into the next.

'You *really* hurt me.'

'Even better.'

'Stop,' he says. 'I'll show you.'

'Get out,' she mutters. 'Get out get out.'

'You'll wake Dylana.'

'Stiff.' Her shoulders working as she throws things around the room. Her jersey tight across her back. The side of her neck. The long muscles in her neck. He can see them. Tight. As he stands there.

'Frith.'

'Shuddup. Get out. Geddout.'

'Frith.'

'Piss *off.*'

'It's not here.'

She stops. Stands up. Glares at him with eyes. With eyes like sticks. With eyes like hatred.

'Well, where the fuck is it then, Matt?'

'It's . . .'

Oh God, she is coming towards him with her hands on her hips and she despises him so much.

She does not like him one bit.

After all the things he told her, and the cooking and everything.

'It's . . .'

'Yes?'

'Um . . .'

'Matt, where the fuck is the fucking battery?'

'It's in the lake. Frith don't go. Please don't go.'

'If you are right, Matt. If you have done something to the car to prevent me going, I'm going to take Dylana and throw *her* in the lake, okay? I wouldn't think twice about it, boyo. Then I'd ring the police and say that you'd done it. Okay? So . . . are you sure? Sure you've thrown the battery in the lake? I don't believe you actually. You wouldn't dare. Little wimp. Mummy's darling. You've ruined everything for me. I hope you're happy knowing that. So, do I throw Dylana in the lake or do you tell me?'

'It's in the car.'

'Where in the car?'

'Where it should be. I didn't touch your stupid battery.'

'Christ. I might have known. You wouldn't even know how to open the bonnet, let alone have any idea what the battery looked like.'

Every opportunity. Every opportunity to tell him how ridiculous and horrible she thinks he is.

'So what have you done to the car?'

'Nothing. I haven't done anything. You were hurting me so I just said the first thing.'

She closes her eyes and rubs her forehead as if she is trying to think of the name of the longest river in Africa.

'I had everything packed away in order.' Even he is aware of the petulant whine in his voice. Everything is disintegrating. The chicken burning, the fight outside, and now this mess. His testicles are throbbing, the ache spreading throughout his whole body. He feels sick. At least Dylana is sleeping through it all.

Dylana.

'So why won't the car go?'

Dylana. If she has done anything to Dylana . . .

'How would I know?' he mutters as he turns away and rushes to the bunkroom, dropping to his knees and patting and fumbling in the half-light for her sleeping form, her warmth and aliveness. She squirms under his touch but thankfully does not wake. He gets up, his heart still beating anxiously from the fright, and closes the door.

Fritha is heading for the kitchen and he follows her, ready for her next attack. He knows he should keep out of her way, just let her be, but he can't help himself.

'What the hell has happened here?'

Matt watches her sheepishly as she shrugs at the chaos around the sink, shaking her head in disbelief. He can taste blood in his mouth, and he runs his top teeth over his bulbous lip. He dabs at it gingerly and his fingers come away red. Fritha fills the kettle, shoves her sleeves up to her elbows and starts picking into the mess, piling dishes and pots into order to create some space on the small bench. She casts a questioning glance towards Matt, then looks at him again.

'God, if you could see yourself.' She throws several spoonfuls of tea in the teapot and fills it with boiling water. Then she carries it over to the table with a couple of mugs.

Matt hangs back, his hands behind his back, feeling for the wall behind him.

'Bring over the milk and sugar,' she says. He fetches them obediently but still lingers, unsure of what he is expected to do. She pours the tea and pushes one cup in his direction.

'Well, don't just stand there, for heaven's sake.'

He moves to the table and sits on the edge of a chair, reaching forward to scoop three large heaps of sugar into the cup.

He doesn't look at her. Sips his tea, slurping, his swollen lip making drinking awkward. He's going to get it for slurping. Just wait. But no. He glances over at her. She's staring at him over the top of her cup as she drinks. He hates the way she stares at him like that. He never knows how she is going to be with him; one minute she's so horrible and the next she's offering a cup of tea. Perhaps she has drugged his drink. She had mentioned something about him doing it last time they were at the bach and he himself had considered the idea fleetingly as he made the dinner tonight, just as an idle thought, a fantasy about picking her up in his arms as she dreamily woozily smiled at him, as he tended to her, stroked her forehead. Having her in his arms all to himself without any struggles or fighting. Just to look at and talk to. But now she, she is probably plotting to make him sleep so she can escape without problems, possibly taking Dylana with her. He won't drink the tea, it's as simple as that.

He puts the cup down. Clutches the sides of the chair, scratching underneath the seat.

'Don't do that, it's annoying.'

'Sorry.' He puts his hands in his lap.

'What's wrong?'

'Nothing.'

'Why aren't you drinking your tea?'

'I am.'

'No you're not.'

'I am.' He picks up the mug and makes a display of pretending to take a bubbly sip. 'It's too hot. It hurts my lip.'

She puts her cup down. 'Look Matt, for heaven's bloody sake, I'm sorry I was so rough with you, okay? I hope I haven't done you any permanent damage but you asked for it, boyo. Really. But I shouldn't take it out on you. I was at the end of my tether. I was really upset.'

'Why, what did I do?'

'Apart from all the obvious things — nothing.'

'You seemed to be really mad with me.'

'Well. It's just . . . well, it's just that I rang Scott when I went for my walk. Before. Who should answer but bloody Silvia. I tried to make a collect call. She wouldn't accept it. She had no right to do that. I don't know what she was doing there . . . maybe she'd just brought Jason around. I don't know. But why did she answer the phone, and why didn't she let my call through? That's what I'd like to know. I rang a bit later and the same thing happened. So. I've been walking and thinking, walking and thinking. I blamed you a lot, you know, but perhaps that's not fair.'

'Well . . .'

She put her hand up, her small tough hand.

'But anyway. As I said, I've been chewing it all over. I've had enough. It wasn't going to work out anyway. If everything had been normal it might have been okay for a while. But . . . no. I've gone through everything. I've had enough.'

'What do you mean?'

'The problem's not only you. I'm not going back. I've decided. That's it. There are other things I want to do. Travel. Whatever. Probably end up back on the farm for a while, who knows. There's worse things. I love the farm, actually. Certainly better than working in a music shop alongside my boyfriend all day. My ex-boyfriend.'

'But that was just until he found someone else. To replace me . . .'

'Yeah, but . . . it's everything else too.'

'So . . . you'll stay here? You'll stay with us?'

In the bach, the silence of the night gathers tightly around them, the silence of the panting crickets, the tumbling moon, his waiting heart. The question is a stone which has left his raised hand, and it rises to hang high in the air. It is a stone seemingly selected at random, and yet it is the same stone he has been keeping warm in his pocket, incubating in his hand . . . turning over and over until the edges are smooth, until it almost has a pulse of its own. As it flies through the air and lands to be swallowed in a clean plop, to disappear within a soft waver of ripples through the black oily lake of night.

She rolls her eyes, purses her lips.

'Come on, Matt. Out of the question. Sorry about that. But no.'

'But why? Why not? Now. If you're not going back?'

'Because I have to start making my own life all over again. I have to start reconstructing my own life.'

'But . . . I'll look after you.'

'The thing is, Matt, I don't need looking after. I'm a free spirit. Like everyone else. Free. People don't live in jars. They're not things to be kept.'

'Well. Can we come with you? Just for a while.' His heart is a tiny flickering bird in an empty sky.

Leaning her head into her fingers. 'I shouldn't have even told you. It was just . . . just . . . the things you said out there. I felt guilty for being rotten to you. Felt sorry for you. But I don't even know where I'm going. I could go home just for now but Mum and Dad are still away and Bruce will be on the warpath with his precious crop gone.'

She looks up at him again, her face pasty, her eyes like stones. 'Sorry, boyo. I'll head off in the morning, like we planned, but back to Wellington instead. Probably.' Then she thumped her head. 'Oh no . . . I was forgetting the car.'

'There you are. It's a *sign*. A sign that you should stay. Please, Fritha. Just try . . . just try being with us for a while. To see what it's like.'

'Oh yes . . . and I suppose you're wanting to sleep with me. To have *sex* with me. Into the bargain.'

Her words like a wet fish whacked across his face. He reels with humiliation, embarrassment, shame.

'No. No not at all. Nothing like *that!*'

'Sex. And after that a kiss on the lips.'

'No!'

'And then . . . and then to go the whole way, you might want to *hold hands!* And after that . . . oh my God . . . a little *conversation*: Hello, what's your name? Do you come here often? I seem to know your face. Something familiar about it. Do you want to come to the movies with me? First the baby, and now the sex. We're advancing well.'

'No. No, stop it. Stop it. It's not like that at all.'

'Well, thank bloody goodness for that then!' she says. But she peers at him quizzically. 'But why ever not, anyway?'

'Don't be stupid.'

'No, I'm curious. What's wrong with sex, Matt?'

'Forgeddit,' he mumbles.

She takes the cups and gets up from the table.

'I'll have to look into what's wrong with the car.' She stands at the bench and turns the tap on. The water pounding the tinny sink. 'I suppose I *could* stay around for a few days.' She fills a cup with a surge of bubbles, which she tips back into the sink, then holds the cup to be filled once more. Filled and overflowing as she thinks. Until she empties the cup and places it upside down on the bench against a saucer. 'I suppose there's no harm in that. I guess it will give me time to think about things. Sort a few things out. All right?' She washes the next cup, spraying Matt with pinprick droplets. 'So will that make you feel better? But. *But*. If I find out that you've done anything to the car, or if I discover you're doing anything at any time to try and stop me leaving, that's it. Okay?'

'Yeah,' he mutters, afraid to catch her eye. He studies the dark indentations of his teeth marks in his finger. Where he has been gnawing at his flesh. Chewing at his knuckles like a gummy old dog.

She moves from the bench and he is aware of her standing behind his chair. Feels her fingers through his curls, her nails through the back of his head, then a sharp tug at the sensitive baby hair in the hollow of his neck.

'Ow,' he shrieks, slapping the stinging skin. 'Why'd you do that?'

'G'night, boyo. Sleep well. Don't forget the dishes.'

'Fritha?'

'What?'

'Promise. Promise you won't leave, you won't leave in the night.'

'Another word about it and I'm off, out of here, car or no car. So.'

'We could go for a drive, we could go somewhere for a picnic tomorrow.'

'Hmmm. We'll see. Maybe.'

'Really?'

'Maybe, I said. We'll have to see about the car, anyway. We mightn't be going anywhere.'

'How long will you stay?'

'I don't know. A day, a few days. Who knows. No one ever knows these things, Matt, whatever the situation. You might *think* for ever, and then it's over. But everything is for ever, it's just that circumstances change within. Floundering around in

212

the river of infinity. And all that. All that bullshit.' She peels herself away from the wall. 'Anyway, I'm tired and I'm going to bed. I've got a helluva headache. Throwing me on the path like that.' She runs her fingers over her scalp and winces.

'It wasn't my fault. I . . .'

'Shush.'

'Have you eaten?'

'I had a couple of chocolate bars.'

'I cooked dinner specially.'

'Another time, okay? Now. This time goodnight.'

That night after clearing up his mess and washing the dishes, he'd hung around the hallway, listening for her deep and even breathing. When he was certain she was asleep he'd crept outside, clutching the bag of rubbish as a ready excuse, should Fritha catch him. Wincing with every step. Cringing at the tinny crunching of the handle as he opened the door to release the hood. The pop of the bonnet a detonation. Every sound a clanger in the silence. His torch a glaring searchlight over the deserted city of grease-metal and wires. Searching for the cable he'd pulled out that afternoon, lying like a bent street lamp. This one, No that one. And it went here, no there, or perhaps here. Finally, still unsure, he slipped the lead back onto the distributor.

He eased the bonnet closed, navigated his way around the back to throw the rubbish in the bin, and returned inside.

The trembling lake, the pearly skin of the lake trembling. And the clouds, rippling in a rough and fluffy way, mirroring the tremble — the face of a poodle looking into the face of an old lady. Across the lake, small pockets of sunshine glowing in the far hills. And a lone seagull flapping its tired wings. One bird. One for sorrow, his mother would say, one for sorrow, two for joy.

But he is joyous. He would be proud for his mother to see how happy he is; he can hardly allow himself to feel so happy. They could be any married couple with a child.

He, Fritha and Dylana are sitting on a rug spread over the narrow pumicey beach between the lake and the bank behind them, above the straggly line of debris, the collection of old weed, sticks, tangled fishing lines and the junk belched up from past storms.

Dylana is nestled between his legs with a bleached bone, a ball of pumice, a headless doll and a rubber monkey he has gathered from among the stranded flotsam. She likes the monkey, which squeaks rusty spittle when it is squeezed. She holds up each article for inspection. Studying form and detail. Taste and smell. The parade of new things. Everything fresh, untainted by experience. Everything in its nowness. Here and now.

And yet, he is thinking about the future. Tomorrow. He would like to talk about Dylana going to school. He'd like to talk about frilly dresses he has seen other small girls wearing, as they toddle with their arms pulled high by the hands of their mothers and fathers. Their feet scuffing the ground, dog-paddling in the air. He'd like to discuss where they're going to live, and what Fritha wants to do, and how they're going to manage for money. That's all. He has no wish to do anything else with his future. Dylana is a perfectly exquisite gift sent to occupy the fullness of his time.

Earlier he'd removed his shoes and socks, turned up his jeans to his knees and suspended her above the water, his hands cupped under her armpits as he immersed her feet and legs in the icy water. She sucked in her breath, pulling her legs high like a fat frog. Skimming her feet above the surface of the water, and the lake bottom with its round stones, like carefully laid eggs, sloshing around like jelly. His white hairs clinging to his legs, like eyelashes. The water clear, the clarity of ice. Of sharp memory. Of reflection. Almost like an invisible but tangible manifestation of cold, wrapped in a membrane of skin.

This morning he'd hovered by the window, watching through the curtains as Fritha went outside to try the car, which had started with no further trouble. When she returned inside she had glowered at him, but neither of them made further reference to it. Fritha made sandwiches from the remains of the chicken, and a thermos of tea. She is softer with him today. Kinder. She even entertained Dylana while he had his shower . . . when he emerged from the bathroom he found them on the floor together. He'd hung around, rubbing his hair with a towel. Fritha sat cross-legged, distractedly twirling an apple on the floor like a top, while Dylana leaned forward to try to catch it.

Sandflies rise from the water's edge to look for prey, like hunchback crows dipping into the white skin around his ankles, dancing before his eyes as he prevents them from alighting upon Dylana's fine skin. He brushes them aside and watches as one settles onto a nail to dip into the soft quick beneath. There's another on his wrist. He holds his skin taut while it drinks, so that it can't escape and its body becomes swollen and red, translucent with blood. In the end it squirts an ejection of liquid from its back passage. Its abdomen tight and rigid, so fat, as it struggles, twitching, in an effort to escape. Finally he releases his fingers from his arm to allow it to fly away ponderously, like a helicopter with too large a load.

He, too, this morning, eating to excess. They had breakfast at the table together, he finally able to wolf down several poached eggs on toast after the day before of virtual fasting.

He feels less anxious when he eats but when he is anxious he isn't hungry. A vicious cycle. But now he is happy. He has tried to talk to Fritha about this but she diverted him; she didn't feel like talking about *anything*, she told him, so he left it. He wants to do everything right. Everything. He wants Fritha to see that he is not like Scott.

She is lying alongside them, on her towel, one arm folded behind her head, the other flopped over her closed eyes. Her head tied up in arms. She's wearing jeans too, and the same fitting green jersey she was wearing the day before. Her waist tight and her breasts — as far as he can make out — with no bra, as rounded as the hills across the lake. He watches a tiny spider scrambling across her middle, picking its way awkwardly over the fibres of her jersey. He lifts his hand tentatively. He feels like a god hovering over this creature, capable of snuffing it into a smear between his fingers or alternatively rescuing it from the grassy terrain of the fabric. Like God flicking that truck off the road.

He holds his finger out, his nail barely touching the fuzz of fabric to allow the spider to clamber aboard. But Fritha opens her eyes, whacks his hand aside, sits upright.

'What the bloody hell are you doing, Matt? Can't I trust you for a minute? What are you on about, groping me as soon as my eyes are closed?'

'I wasn't, I wasn't groping you. There was a spider, a spider on your jersey. I was just getting it off.'

She looks down at her clothes. 'Where? What spider?'

But it has gone, thrown off in the upheaval.

'Truly.'

'Well, leave me to deal with my own spiders, okay?'

He holds Dylana closer, kisses her on the head.

216

'Honestly, Fritha. I wasn't touching you.'

Fritha lies down again, turning over with her back curled against them. There is so much to learn. He spies the spider skittering across a pebble by a tassel on her towel. Smudges it into the smooth white stone like the first hesitant brushstroke of a painting.

'I wasn't.'

There is a bird singing nearby. Practising the theme over and over. A note here, a phrase there. An attempt at that one, this one. The liquid whistle of a tui. It seems as though those birds can never get it right.

❋

While Dylana had an afternoon sleep at the bach, Fritha drove into town to buy another chicken so that Matt had another chance to show her he could cook. On her return she insisted on taking the baby for a walk. He watched from the sitting-room window as she lifted the loop at the gate and walked out across the grass and down the track to the lake once more. Dylana's hat bobbing behind her in the backpack. He clutched the vegetable peeler in one hand, and in the other, a potato naked of its skin. His eyes upon them until they vanished behind bushy shrubs, to appear again as a hazy unit, distant and indistinct, while in his mind the silvery crunch of Fritha's footsteps made their way over the pumice, away from him.

When he heard her feet clomping on the porch again, he hurried out to greet them. 'Safely home,' he cooed with relief, smiling widely, though the baby was miserable, her face snotty and pink.

'She's getting a tooth,' said Fritha as he helped to take Dylana from the pack. 'Look, one side, one cheek is hot. It's hotter than the other side.'

He took her in his arms, wiped her nose with a tissue. 'She might have been sleeping against the frame of the pack.'

'You need to buy a book. Dr Spock. That will tell you everything you need to know.'

But now, later, Dylana is asleep. Fritha had uncharacteristically offered to give her a bath. She washed and dressed her as Matt fussed over the dinner. He insisted on putting her down to bed but she was more restless than usual. Flushed and grizzling. Maybe she had too much sun. He, too, is feeling this. His fair skin prickling. Although the weather had been cool and the sky cloudy by the lake, the reflected glare from the water must have caught them. Unless she was unnerved because she had been parted from him. Missing him.

He paces around the kitchen, opening the oven door, basting the chicken, pricking roasting kumara. He is determined that this time the dinner will not spoil. Tonight he is enjoying the cooking. He is doing virtually the same as the evening before but with a lighter heart. The comparison is revealing. The process repeated but with the difference in feeling. Like the day after recovery from an illness. Only then, when cured, would he be able to judge how bad he'd felt at the time.

He realises with a shock that he hasn't been aware of Fritha for a while. He rushes to the window but the little car is there. She must be in her room. Why is the door shut? He hangs about in the hallway outside her room, listening. Is she in there? He knocks. Fritha?

'What?'

'Um, oh, um, I just wanted to say dinner will be ready in half an hour, is that okay?'

'Yeah, sure. Fine,' she calls.

Faith. Trust.

Relax.

He checks Dylana, who is still unsettled. He is wishing they hadn't left the dummy behind in Auckland, though she'd been needing it less and less. But already tonight she has woken once and he hears her again now, brewing up for a cry which fizzles out.

The chicken is looking perfect and the kumara are softening and brown, all sizzling tantalisingly as he pokes and prods. The potatoes are just on to boil as he sets the table. Knife and fork on either side of a hard floral mat. Everything looking great. Geraniums crammed into a jar, deep purple and lolly pink. And soon he will put on the frozen peas that Frith brought back with the chicken.

Last night was a dress rehearsal. A practice run. Tonight is the night.

With improvements. She will see that he is not useless. That he is perfectly capable.

Will he call her before he puts the food out or after?

'Fritha?' His ear against the door. 'Frith?'

'What?'

'Just putting the dinner out now.'

'Okay,' she says.

It is almost difficult to believe. She is still there and coming to eat the dinner he has cooked, willingly. Of her own free will.

He tears a leg from the chicken. One for her. And the other for him. The kumara yielding easily to the fork, and the mashed potatoes without a lump — peppery and creamy. He spoons a careful dollop onto each plate.

Drains the peas. The peas tastefully arranged around the potato. In a ring around the potato. Like a necklace around a thick throat. Ha ha. He picks up two of the peas and pokes them in the potato, for eyes. Well. The kumara could be the nose. A big bulgy nose. There! A nose in each one. And the mouth. What about the mouth? He cuts two slithers of kumara which he arranges in a line under both noses. Bending over the job intently.

'What the fuck are you doing, dabbling in my dinner?'

He bolts upright, spins around, his hands pressed against the bench behind his back. Guilty guilty guilty.

'Nothing. I'm doing nothing.'

'What were you messing around with the dinner for?'

Mea culpa mea culpa.

'Nothing, nothing, I was just . . .'

She stands beside him, staring at his animated dinners, scratching her head. One of the kumara is gradually fainting from its post. The vegetable grin now looks hard and thin, a mean mocking smirk.

'I was just . . .'

'Okay. For heaven's bloody sake, I just asked. Which is mine?'

'That one,' he says.

'Okay, I'll have the other one,' she says, whipping the plate from the bench and going to the table.

'That's fine, they're both the same.'

'That one's cross-eyed.' She smiles at him as he drags a chair to the table.

'Righteo. Can I start? Oops. No gravy?'

He slumps.

'Ah, I wasn't sure . . . no, I er . . . didn't make gravy.'

'Oh well . . .'

He watches as she lifts her knife and fork. She looks up at him.

'God, Matt, are you going to monitor my every chew?'

'No. No, I'm sorry.'

He picks up his own eating utensils and together they eat. In silence. Fritha eating at first warily, and then hungrily.

Eventually he stops, his fork poised above his plate.

'Well?'

'What?'

'Do you *like* it?'

'Yep. Yep. It's very nice, Matt. Thank you. Sorry. I was thinking. Lost in thought. Yes, no, it's *very* nice. Well done.'

'What were you thinking about?'

'I don't know . . . just musing.'

'What about?'

'I don't know what about. Just thinking, that's all. Stop being so bloody serious about everything, Matt. Hang free.'

His stomach tightens again. 'Is . . . is everything all right?'

'Oh yes, yes, sure. Just a life to sort out, that's all.'

'A life?'

'Never mind, Matt. Great potato. Lots of pepper. I like lots of pepper. And the chicken's like butter.'

'Thanks, Frith. But what do you mean you've got a life to sort out?'

'Quit it, Matt. I just meant I've got to think about what I'm going to do.'

'But you can stay here.'

'Sure, sure, I know.'

'So?'

'So what?'

'So what's the problem?'

'There's no problem, Matt. I was just eating my dinner. Don't spoil it. It's delicious.'

'But you said . . .'

'*Matt*!'

He pierces a pea with his fork. Buries it in the potato. Stabs another pea and buries that one too. Soon all the peas are hidden under the mound of potato. All safely buried.

'And stop bloody well sulking. You're spoiling things.'

'I'm not sulking.'

'Eat your dinner. I finally got hold of Scott today.'

'Oh.' He places the fork by his plate and looks at her carefully. He realises her eyes are bruised and sad. He hates to see her looking so sad when she is with him. 'Did you tell him . . . about me?'

'About *you*?'

'I mean staying here . . . I mean, what did you tell him?'

'Just that I'm not going back. I think he was relieved, really. He didn't even ask why.' She sighs wistfully. 'Can you believe that? So it's for the best. If that's his attitude. Bastard.' She picks up the bone from her plate and nibbles at a strip of meat. 'It's always a bit of a blow when things don't work out. Like planting a garden to have a pig root it up. But I guess it's better than discovering you're growing a crop of poisonous weeds.'

'Yes.' He would like to put his hand on hers but she is waggling the bone in the air. It would be like catching a bird and not knowing what to do with it afterwards.

'Which reminds me.'

'What?'

'It's weird, isn't it? All that trouble. If I hadn't gone back to take Bruce's crop, you wouldn't have discovered the baby. We would have missed the accident altogether. Down the road and not even knowing about it. We'd be up there now, you working in the shop, and me free to find my own job. We might have had a chance. Huh. Twisting fingers of fate. Though if Silvia's hanging around, it's better to know now . . . I don't know. But the irony of it all is that I haven't got a leaf of it myself. I mean, he can keep it for all I care. I don't want it. He can make his thousands and think of me. I don't care. It was just an adventure. I thought it might help things. The stupid thing is, my parents would give me money any time I needed it. But I thought it would be fun to do something exciting together. To set us up. A joint project . . . Ha. But as I said, it's ironic, isn't it? After all that trouble, not having any myself. Not even one smoke, for the memory. Never mind.' She drops

222

the bone onto the plate. 'Better off without it. Not so good for the memory, anyway.'

Matt pushes his dinner away and stands up.

'Just a sec,' he says.

He returns with his hands behind his back, deliberately coy.

'Which hand?' he sings. She chooses. 'Nope, sorry. One more guess. Hey, you got it right!' He leans across the table, his hands cupped into a little igloo in front of Frith. 'Close your eyes, now. Are you ready? *Close* your eyes, I said.' He lifts his hands in the air. 'Ta-daaaah!'

'God, Matt! That's fantastic! An old sock, out of mid-air. One sock! Just what I wanted! You should be a magician. Does it smell into the bargain?'

'Touch it if you dare!'

She gives him a wry glance, then pokes her finger at the sock and yelps. 'Yuk! It's soft and hairy.'

Matt crosses his arms with delight. 'Go on. Have a look. Pick it up. It's for you from me.'

She picks up the sock gingerly. Presses into it, and, feeling its bulkiness, curls the ribbing down and peers inside. Then gapes at Matt.

'From you to me?'

'Yes.'

'Or from me to you to me?'

He shrugs. 'Whatever. From Bruce to you to me to you. It's yours now.'

She sighs, shaking her head. 'Oh well. You're a little beauty, you are. Really.'

'Aren't you pleased?' He isn't sure. Is she mad with him?

'Oh well, we may as well have one. I see you're armed with papers here as well. Do you want a smoke, Matt?'

He thinks of the boys laughing under the walnut tree at school. He thinks of kneeling on the floor in Scott's toilet, his stomach turning inside out. 'I don't know.'

'Have you tried it before?'

'Once. But I was sick.'

'Oh, that's normal the first time. Well, it happens often anyway. That's just to get a few cobwebs out of the way. Clearing away the old pipes of your inhibitions.' She is already preparing one, deftly, on the table. Licking the paper and smoothing it sealed. A much slimmer version of the one he had rolled.

And then she's standing up, slapping her jeans pockets, sliding her fingers along shelves, opening drawers. She goes down the hall and he hears the back door sticking on the lino. As always he stiffens when she leaves the bach. He hears the car door. He jumps from the table and peers from the side of the curtain into the twilight outside. She's leaning into the car like the witch with her head in the oven. Then the car door slams and when she comes back again he is holding exactly the same stance as when she left. As if he hadn't moved. Even his hands in the same awkward position on the table. She rattles a box of matches at him.

'You can never find them when you want them.'

She lights the joint, inhales and passes it to him. He is feeling self-conscious now. Remembering the coughing. He takes a small puff, holds the smoke in his mouth, blows out a steam-train cloud. She takes it from him. Dragging deeply. Pacing around the room. 'Pity,' she says as she takes small inward puffs, 'pity we (suck) don't (suck) have music.'

Passing it back to him. His next draw is a braver one, making him choke, the smoke scorching his throat. He lurches to the sink for water and takes a glass with him, ready for the next onslaught. Neither of them speaks as they continue to smoke. Once again, the shadows billowing around the bach. Small lights appear across the bay. Frith settles into the easy chair, watching him as he inhales, chuckling knowingly when he coughs again. Her mockery feels harmless, even friendly, but as he passes the joint over he is suddenly scared. Night has descended too rapidly. A shadow flaps across the window, a thing leaving from under the eaves of the roof.

'What was that?' What else was lurking there, hunched and waiting? The night full of things. Unfathomable things. Fritha is knocking his hand gently, handing him the joint.

'A bird,' she says.

'At night?'

'Don't waste it,' she says.

'Does this stuff make you happy?'

'Usually,' she tells him. She is grinning. Frith is grinning at him. With a mercury glint of smiling eyes. A sepia photo of a child smiling.

'What's so funny?' The burning glow creeps dangerously close to his lips.

'Everything.' She sighs and slinks around into the easy chair, her feet flopped over the arm. Clicking her fingers for the joint back again.

'It's nearly finished.' In the dimming light, their fingers scramble to exchange the damp and flattening butt. Frith takes a couple of sharp hisses, then flicks it onto a plate. 'Yep, that's done. What a pity we don't have music.'

She is a lump of shadow.

'I'll turn on the light.'

'No, no . . . this is so mellow.' Her voice is husky. He goes over and kneels on the divan at the window, clutching the curtain as he gazes into the darkness, searching for solidarity and form within the void. Feeling the furious spluttering of his heart.

'My heart is beating so fast,' he says. His tongue has been grafted onto his palate. In that short time it has been melded there. His mouth dissolving into itself, becoming an amorphous mass of flesh. He is incapable of speech. Though he has just spoken. His last words. *My heart is beating so fast.* His last words. In his whole life. His long, unbearably long life. There is nowhere to go. He is lost. Lost in the central vortex of his life.

'That's normal.' Fritha's voice is reassuring, the willowy guide, beckoning him along the mountain path. 'Have another drink of water. Listen to the sounds. Find your inner calm. You've got to relax. It's so peaceful. The little clicky whirry sounds of the night. Sit down, Matt. You seem nervous.'

'Fritha? I'm going to die. I'm going to die. I know it. I've got this feeling I'm going to die.'

'We're all going to die, Matt.'

'What do you mean? What do you mean, Frith?'

'Well, he who isn't busy being born is busy dying. Bob Dylan said that. Or something like that.'

'Be serious.'

'I am. Let go of that curtain and sit down.'

'I can't. I can't let go.'

'God, Matt, you idiot.'

The lump of darkness that is Fritha rises and floats to the wall and the room is thrown into light. Lasers stabbing his brain. He screws his eyes closed, tying the curtain around his head. He is aware now of her hand on his shoulder.

'Matt. Grow *up*. You are acting like a *child*. Pull yourself together. Everything is okay. What's wrong with you?'

He ignores the drawn, frightened face he sees at the window when he opens his eyes again as Fritha unwraps his head from the curtain like a parcel. She's kneeling alongside him.

'Matt.'

He ignores the face.

'Matt,' says Fritha.

He ignores the face, pressed against the window, the eyes pleading with him, imploring him. He will not look, he does not see the face at the window. The face with begging eyes, with eyes that scream at him across the dreaming night.

'Matt!' says Fritha. Her hands on his shoulders, forcing him away from the window where the face, where the face does not exist. From where there is nothing but the soft batting of moths against the glass, from where the light in the room sails into the darkness to reach the twinkling light of the stars, like a streamer from a departing ship linking the souls left behind on shore. From the face against the window.

Fritha is shaking his head. Each hand is gripping one of his ears. 'Matt, for heaven's sake, Matt. We are safe. Read my lips. Say it after me. I. Am. Safe.'

'I . . .'

'Good. Now. Look at me. Say it again. I am . . .'

'I am . . .'

'I am safe.'

'I am . . . safe.'

'Good lad. I'm proud of you. Now breathe. A deep breath. Say it again.'

'I am safe.'

'Thank bloody goodness for that.'

'Frith. There was a face. I saw a face.'

'Matt! Stop it!'

She is holding his hand now, as she might lead a child. Tugging him away from the divan. He is unfurling his lanky bleached foal legs from underneath his body as she releases him and leaps onto the divan, scrutinising the dark before battling to haul the curtains along the rusty coiled wire. To close the curtains as if to signify the end of a play.

He looks around at the bach. All the normal things. The shiny lino on the floor, the walls with the wide stains like maps. The barometer stuck on cloudy. The green formica table with Fritha's empty plate and his food abandoned. The pink and purple flowers in the jar. He stands at the bookcase and looks at the tattered books. His finger bumping along the spines. *Doctor at Large. Argosy. The Wind Cannot Read.* The Bible. *On the Beach.* Words and thoughts captured in books like bait. He realises books are traps. The reader lured into the writer's mind. The writer reaching through a fog and pulling a stranger at random into his or her fantasy.

'Okay now?'

'I was just thinking — all these books. You've got to be careful with what you read, really. When you think about it.'

'I'll say. Thinking's pretty dangerous too. When you think about it.'

'No . . . really.'

'No really.'

'I mean, these books are other people's selected *thoughts*. Like Pandora's boxes.'

'Imeanthesebooksareotherpeople'sselectedthoughts-blahblahblah.'

'Frith.'

'Frith.'

'Stop *doing* that.'

'Stop *doing* that.'

'Fritha, I really love you.'

'God look at these bloody dishes, come and help me with these dishes, will you?'

'You saved my life just then.'

'Oh good, now I'll put you in a jar and feed you for ever.' She hands him the plates. He stands there as she gathers the salt, pepper, knives and forks.

'You are so funny.'

'Come on, Matt, get going, and stop goggling at me. Lighten up, for heaven's bloody sake.'

'You're beautiful, Frith. I love your smooth olivey skin and your little beaky nose. And the way you move. I love the way you move.'

Frith is bustling at the bench now, wiping, stacking and rinsing. 'Come on, Matt, bring those plates. Don't just stand there. Help me.'

'I love the shape of your neck and shoulders.'

She comes and takes the plates from his hands. He releases them passively and takes the tea-towel she thrusts at him. 'If I could paint I would paint you. If I could write poetry, I'd write about you.'

Her hands in the sink filling with steamy frothy water. Stirring the cutlery and plates in a rumble. Grabbing the dishmop with its plastic frightened spikes and attacking each plate with vigour. The sink is a fury of volcanic turbulence. Bubbles climbing up her arms.

'So, ah . . . Tell me something, Matt.' Scraping the bristles against the plate.

'What?'

'What are you interested in? What are your hobbies, interests, dreams?'

'What do you mean?'

'Well, if you had to fill in a form, say, an application form for something, what would you put in the place for hobbies and interests?'

'I dunno.'

'Consider it, then. What do you think about? What do you like doing most? If you had all the money in the world and you could do whatever you wanted, what would you do?'

'I dunno. I've got everything I want now. With you, and Dylana.'

'Come on now . . .' She pulls out a plate in a ferment of lather and thrusts it into the tea-towel hanging from his hand. '*Before* all this happened, then. If you had your choice what would you do with your life, your time?'

'I dunno.'

'What was your favourite subject at school?'

'Biology. I really liked biology.'

'What did you like about it?'

'Studying things. Frogs and eyes and amoebas. Looking at things, and how they worked.'

'Did you think of getting a job in that area?'

'No, not really. When Scott suggested I could work with him in the music shop I thought that would be okay. Mum and Dad thought it would be okay.'

'Do you like music?'

'Yeah. I do.'

'Can you play anything?'

'No, not really. Scott's the musician. I started to play the guitar and the piano and I really enjoyed it but Mum and Dad said it was a waste of time. They didn't want another one like Scott in the family. I used to write the words for songs but they were dumb.'

'What about? What were the songs about?'

'Aw, stupid stuff about being lonely and all that stuff. And love.'

'Are you lonely?'

'I dunno. Isn't everyone? But anyway, I'm not now.'

'What's the most important thing to you? What do you want most in the whole world?'

'Love.' He surprises himself; the word comes without a thought. But he knows it's true. 'Love and beauty and . . . God. Are all the same. One and the same. If you love somebody, you are whole. Humans are only half things without love. They are like stars without anyone on earth to look at them. Bees without a hive. Like butterflies, fluttering endlessly, with nothing to land on. Like rivers without water . . . Like . . .'

'Okay, okay, I get the picture. I take it sex doesn't come into it.'

He can feel himself blushing, an ugly uncomfortable surge. He puts the plate away and takes another one.

'*Pure* love, I meant. But what about you? What do *you* think about? What do *you* want to do?'

He has never thought about this before. It is a scary question. A question that is leading dangerously into areas that he might not be able to accept. What if her ideas don't include him?

230

'I think about my family, the people I know and like. I like to read. I think about the farm. Now that I've got my degree, I feel happy at the idea of working on the farm. Not yet but one day. I love the land and the free air. The smells and the country people. The hard work. I didn't want to go there straight from school though, and I'm glad I didn't. I want to experience other things, and travel as well. India and Nepal. Anywhere. I want to discover things about life.'

'So what's *your* most important thing?'

'Hmmm . . . Freedom. Yes, above all I like to feel free. To deal with life as it comes. Live and let live.'

He is still drying the same plate. The tea-towel wiping round and round like a satellite picture of a slow gale. He wouldn't mind living on the farm. That would suit them.

'Oh, and another thing I strongly believe.'

'What?'

'That you can't truly love someone unless you are whole. That you have to be able to live by yourself alone *contentedly* before you can live with someone else. You have to feel comfortable with your own person. Otherwise love becomes parasitic. You feed off each other's needs and deficiencies.'

'What's wrong with that, needing each other?'

'It's not good, that's all.'

Fritha pulls the plug and sponges down the roasting dish, sliding it into the oven to dry. The dishrack a jumble of crockery and cutlery. She slickly and efficiently wipes the bench, in the corners, along the ledge. A wet flick over his nose.

'Well. That's me done. Bedtime then.'

'Bedtime?'

'Yep.'

'Oh, I haven't finished doing the dishes.'

'That's okay. But I have.'

'Fritha . . .'

'What.'

'Um . . . Can I . . . I ask a favour?'

'Go ahead. All ears, boyo.'

'Can I brush your hair?'

The sink gargling in a final strangled gasp.

'Whatever bloodywell for?'

'It's just . . . it's just . . . it's just something I'd really, really like to do.'

'I don't think so, Matt. Honestly . . .'

'What would be the harm in it?'

'No harm but it seems . . . Golly, Matt, you're not backward in coming forwards, are you?'

'Please, Fritha, don't go to bed yet. I don't want to be alone. I'm frightened.'

'I'm in the room over the hall. Dylana's in your room. And this is probably the most peaceful haven in the whole country. There's nothing to hurt you.'

'No, but . . . sometimes I feel frightened. A feeling of something else out there. Something terrifying. A presence. It's stupid, I know. But I can't help it.'

'So, how would brushing my hair help that?'

'It'd be nice. Soothing. I dunno. I've always wanted to. Your long hair. Your lovely long hair. Please.'

She rolls her eyes but takes his tea-towel and grabs a handful of cutlery.

'My brush is in the bathroom.'

Matt pauses for a second of disbelief, feathers bursting in his chest as he turns to skip down the narrow hallway to the bathroom. Her brush is sitting on a ledge, like a hedgehog with swirls of escaping hair. He catches his reflection in the mirror, pausing to study the wild-eyed clown with white down around red lips, above the sharp line of his jaw. A swollen blue vein snakes up his neck, ticking like a clock.

What does she think of him? He grabs the brush and returns to the room.

He is impressed first by the colour of the bright blue t-shirt, and her hair tumbling in disarray across her shoulders, under the hanging cone of light. Fritha has positioned herself on a chair in the centre of the room, her back straight, her bare feet square on the floor. Her crumpled jersey lies alongside, discarded like the skin of a caterpillar. She doesn't move when he walks in. Matt hesitates, overwhelmed with shyness, before taking a few paces towards her. It's as though he has been away, as if he is returning from a long journey. She seems thinner. Smaller. Remote. He lifts the brush to her hair but the movement has a quality of brutality about it, as if he is about to commit an assault. He circles around her, creeping like an intruder, his skin burning and his fingers already aching from clutching the brush handle so tightly. She has transformed herself into a statue. Her eyes are closed and her face is empty. And her lips . . . her lips are perfectly formed and defined. They seem relaxed and rest slightly apart except for a point where they appear to be stuck together, a Siamese union joined by a shared membrane. He bends to see the suggested glisten of her teeth. He is not thinking as he places his lips in a whisper touch upon hers. That butterfly resting for a weary second on a summer's day leaf. He notes a quick warm whiff of her breath, the crack of a whip through his body as she jumps like a startled chook, her eyes opening with the full blast of accusation in their glare.

He stumbles backward, crashing onto the divan.

'I'm sorry,' he says, whacking his forehead repeatedly with the bristles of the brush. 'I'm sorry, Frith. I didn't mean to. I'm really sorry.'

He is cowering, waiting for her thrashing words.

But she is standing in front of him, her hand firmly grasping his, to still the frenzied beating against his brow.

'Don't do that, Matt,' she says, unfurling his fingers from the brush handle. 'You could hurt yourself.' He wipes his eyes roughly and looks up to the blue of her t-shirt, the small roundness of her breasts so close to his face. She starts to brush his hair. He holds his hands together on his lap, where they clasp and unclasp in an agitation beyond his control, like a sea creature caught in a swift current. He is biting at his lips, and sniffs until his chest is bursting with stale air which then floods from him in a long shudder. Her arms work around his head, an elbow cracking, and a hot drifting of her scent from under her arms. Tugging at his curls. He would like to bury his head against her breasts. He could drop his face a little and he would be there. To do no more than to lay his head across her breasts and listen to her beating heart, and to smell the heat from her body.

From a forgotten tuck in the night, a nocturnal animal calls. A single wail, whose sound brings into relief the rich throb of silence, the short sweeps of the brush at his hair, the gentle rustle of Fritha's shifting movements around his head.

Then the cry comes again, more distant, as if a delayed echo from the first. From the bush in a mountain valley, across the lake, a creature detached and isolated from its kind, signalling distress. A small animal flattening itself upon its stomach, a small animal he knows nothing of, which has nothing to do with him at all.

Dylana.

Frith continues to brush his hair and the cry rises in tempo. He sits there, screwing his hands together, daring not to breathe, daring not to be a living thing in this moment, daring not to have a voice, or legs which will take him away from this intimacy, daring not to remove his face from the proximity of her, in case she goes away. His head tugged and pulled in such a restful way, as though battered by a surf pounding onto a hard stony shore, his mind detached from his body, being taken further and further out to the ocean, to drown in turquoise depths, to drift on and on and on for ever.

But eventually she stops. She tosses the brush to the divan beside him, and stoops to kiss him firmly on the forehead. 'Off you go, then. Duty calls.'

He scrambles to his feet, trudging along the hallway to where Dylana has bunched herself up into the end of the mattress, locked against the corner of the walls as if thwarted in an attempt to burrow her way to freedom.

He scoops his hands beneath her. She's hot and wet with fury, her nappy sodden. He carries her to the sitting room.

She refuses the bottle of milk he warms for her. She takes a few gulps then spits it out, to cry once more. She is inconsolable.

It's a different cry, a different tone of cry. She's angry with him for ignoring her while Fritha brushed his hair. Fritha moves from where she has flopped on the divan, her feet crossed over the arm. She tugs at the neck of Dylana's towelling nightclothes. 'Hmmm, she's not very happy tonight, is she?'

Even Fritha recognises the difference. He looks at Frith, feeling a surge of tenderness towards her. Dylana is tossing her head against his shirt, as she might to ease a deep itch.

He sits down and once more prods the rubbery teat between her lips, but she shoves her head aside, pushing the bottle away. She's crying again, pulling her knees up to her stomach. Suddenly she vomits, a tide of pungent mess over her front, his hand, his shirt.

'Oh no, she's sick,' he cries unnecessarily to Fritha, his hand holding a puddle of molten goo. 'She's sick. What's wrong with her?'

'Babies get sick all the time,' says Fritha. 'It's quite normal. My brother's children were always spewing when they were babies. When they eat too much. Or drink too much. Or when they're upset.' She grabs a box of tissues, dabbing at the mess.

'Can you please hold her?' he says to Frith. 'I'll give her a bath. She always likes a bath.'

'She's hot,' says Fritha as she takes the baby, first of all warily, at arm's length, then holding her closer as she feels her skin. 'She's burning. She must have had too much sun. Has she got too much on? You feel her, she's a little furnace.'

'But she's hot all over.'

'Babies are delicate.' Fritha sits in the easy chair, cradling Dylana in her arms.

'I know that,' says Matt, a little pipped at her being the one who thinks she knows everything all of a sudden.

Matt goes to the bathroom and runs the bath, stirring the water with wide swooshes. When he returns, Frith has already undressed Dylana, wrapping her incongruously in a bright red and green beach towel.

'Her nappy was disgusting,' she says. 'What have you been feeding her?'

'Nothing different; just the same.'

Dylana seems to be soothed by the bathwater, watching passively as he slaps his hand on the water's surface. His knees hurt on the hard floor, and the rim of the bath cuts into his chest. He thinks he has won. That the battle is over. When she is dressed and fragrant again, he lowers her into the bed. But she cries once more, in that relentless way. Pushing her body up like a cobra, looking for him in the dark. He sits on the edge of her mattress and strokes her back, talking soothingly to her. Then he remembers the game they had in Auckland with the matches. Even better, he remembers the candles he has seen here in a cupboard under the sink. Boxes of them.

Matt goes out to the kitchen. The matches they used after dinner are still on the table and he melts the base of a candle onto a saucer. Fritha doesn't look up, lying back on the divan again, reading determinedly.

'There we are,' he says as he returns to the bedroom with the candle. The flame throws the shadows into a drunken dance. Dylana stares, the intensity of her crying easing. 'There we are.'

She drops her head to the sheet. He can see the candlelight burning in her eye as she looks. The candle is for him as well. He places the saucer on the floor by her mattress. 'This is a beacon,' he tells her. 'This is a beacon leading you through the night.' He grabs a pillow from his bunk and lies on the floor, telling her of the places he will take her to, and the things they'll do together. He'll take her out in a little boat and sail to the centre of the world. He tells her that a boat is a thing like a bath except the water is on the outside, as if the plug has been pulled out to let the water spread on and on around them, lifting the bath like a moving thing that drifts into places where dreams are made, where all things begin. And they'll sail to the centre, with water all around and below, with the sky above, and the land so far away that it's just a distant lumpy rim. And everything they need will be in the boat, all the good things . . . like the kernel of a nut feeding a tree. A walnut tree. And they'll live there happily, Dylana and Matt and Frith, where no one can touch them . . .

He is wakened by the splattering candle extinguishing in its own juices. His hip aches and he is cold. His eyes open in time to see the sparking strobe of the room, the bulge of Dylana's head above the bedclothes, before a descent into space-black silence. Except for her breathing, a soft little machine chigger, fast and short.

He pulls himself stiffly to his feet. The bach is in darkness. He fumbles his way to the sitting room, where he kneels over the divan to peer through the curtains, checking that the car is still there, a shape hunched alongside the bach. An empty capsule, prepared for take-off, to take off and leave without them.

He moves around the bach gravely, his hand sweeping the walls. Thinking that he must learn to trust, that he must resist the temptation to sneak outside into the cool night to release air from the tyre, in a sharp exhalation, like a long whistle from the throat of a sleeping man.

✳

Matt. Waking up. The sun is streaming though the bach window, through the yellow cotton curtains with blue flowers floating as if someone has thrown them into the air to fall like feathers through sunshine. He is on the top bunk looking down at Dylana, who seems far away, and growing smaller and smaller before his very eyes, as if she is drifting away from him, as if the room has become an elongating bubble that could snap off, and slide away, leaving him alone, alone again.

He blinks and rubs his head, then clambers from the bunk. Dylana is whimpering as she sleeps. He kneels down to study her. Beads of perspiration leak from her nose and across her cheek, like dew on a rose. Her hair clings to her head in yellow tails around her face.

'Matt?'

He jumps.

Fritha is standing at the doorway, that old rigid expression back again.

'What?'

'It was you, wasn't it?'

'What?'

'Come on, Matt. What did I warn you? About the car?'

'What are you talking about?'

'We've got a flat tyre. A very flat tyre.'

'So? Why look at me? Every time something goes wrong, you blame me.'

'It was perfectly all right last night.'

'So what? It wasn't me. Anyway, where are you going?'

'Outside. To change the wheel.'

'No. Where were you going? Before that.'

'Nowhere. I was just going to get a paper.'

He stands up. Looks at her. Looks at her with her hair all tousled and her face still moulded into the soft crinkles of sleep.

'Don't go, Frith.'

'For heaven's bloody sake, Matt, I'm going to have to go and get this tyre fixed, so calm down.'

'Nothing'll be open yet.'

'I don't mean right now.'

'Well, why did you go out to the car then?'

'I was passing, going for a walk.'

'But you said you were going to get a paper.'

'*Jesus!*'

She turns to go but stops. 'Is Dylana okay? Not like her to sleep on through the noise.'

'She's hot.'

Fritha ventures closer, crouches alongside the mattress. Rests her hand on Dylana's forehead. The two peer over her, examining her.

'She's got a temperature. She's not well.'

'What should I do?'

'Take her to a doctor.'

'She's not *that* sick.' There was that time when Jason came to stay, sleeping in his room, when he had the measles. The windows closed to shut out the light. Jason feverish and mottled, Silvia sitting on his bed stroking his head, cooing around him with concern as the little boy battled with delirium. He thinks of his own childhood illnesses, with roaring sore throats and aching limbs, as kind of tortured journeys through convoluted forests, battling demons and strangling vines, and eventually waking up to find that it was over, that he had somehow arrived. These things had to take their own natural course.

'Well, you asked me, that's all. That's what I'd do. Just to be sure. Now, I'm going to change this tyre.'

She's two people, Fritha. She's back into the daytime one, the defensive one. The brittle one that keeps him away.

Later, she calls him for breakfast and they sit at the table together, drinking tea and eating toast. His awkwardness towards her after the night before is alleviated by the constantly whimpering Dylana, bobbing on his knee. She vomited again, just a little, on the sheet as she woke up, and refused to take any milk. She is a third force, a focus away from each other. Matt cringes with embarrassment as he remembers the things he told Fritha, his lightly kissing her lips, his terror-stricken obsession with the face at the window. Had he imagined this? The new day changes the perspective, though he is not sure whether his announcements have helped the situation or turned Fritha away. He should not have let the tyre down, he knows that. What made him do that? Those drugs, probably. He was not himself.

'Try giving her water,' suggests Fritha, nodding towards his attempts to jab the teat into the baby's unresponsive lips. And this seems to work for a moment; she drinks a small amount before screwing her face and pushing the bottle away.

He stands and starts to pace around the room in an effort to pacify Dylana, as Fritha clears the table and does the dishes.

'Well, I'm off,' says Fritha as she wipes the bench.

'Where are you going?'

'I told you, to get this tyre fixed. We can't rely on the spare tyre, in case it happens again.'

'We'll come. We'll come too. I'll just get our things.'

'Listen. Settle down, Matt. You can come if you like, that's fine. I don't mind. Why are you so jumpy this morning?'

He rests his cheek against Dylana's, against her burning soft cheek.

'So, are you coming? But you'd better hurry up.'

'Don't hassle me, Fritha.'

'Who's doing the hassling? I just said hurry up, though I wouldn't want to be taking Dylana out as she is. She'd be better in bed, I'd say.'

'What's the hurry?'

'Okay, okay . . . *don't* hurry then.' She flomps in the easy chair and picks a book at random, which she opens, sighing heavily. 'Just let me know when you're ready.'

'Fritha, don't be like that.'

'Like what?'

'Horrible to me.'

'Just get ready and come, Matt.'

He looks out the window. The day, which had promised to be sunny, is now dull. The lake is metallic green, and an ominous bank of clouds is billowing around the hills, obscuring the mountains from view.

He takes Dylana to the bedroom, and sits on the edge of the bottom bunk. Her eyes, usually alert and darting, are glazed. He kisses her forehead, feeling the soaring heat of her body. He thinks of the women in Auckland. Strangers who felt they had the right to criticise him. He thinks of Fritha, her gentleness with him the night before. He has to learn to trust her. There is no reason for her to leave him. She is learning to love him, and Dylana.

He lays Dylana down on the mattress and pulls the covers over her shoulders. He goes out to tell Fritha that they will not be accompanying her to town. She tosses the book aside and stands up, then goes to him.

'Good boy,' she says. 'I knew you'd see sense.'

He follows her outside. Stands on the gate as it swings closed, waving as the car trundles down the road. She waves at him and blows a kiss. He blows one back. He loops the wire around its post and rushes inside, stands at the window, watches the wake of dust rise behind the car as it meanders along the road around the lake. Until there is nothing but the gathering storm clouds. He checks her room. Her bag is still there, a towel hanging on a door handle, the blue t-shirt tossed across the bed. Her red sleeping bag folded loosely at the end of the bed.

PART SEVEN

Matt stops his lumbering through the bush when he comes to a river, retreating into a small dappled clearing nearby. For all he knows, this could be a stream leading off the same river from which he pulled her father. The same waters searchers sieved for her body. There is a fateful intervention here; she was intended for this river all along. He intruded. And now he is putting her back, after a borrowed time with her. Alongside the river of a life she would never have now. A shared life together they would never experience.

He heaves the backpack from his shoulders and props it against a tree. Gingerly, mindful of its precious cargo, her head slumped forward, buried in the canvas, her limbs loose as if asleep. He places his hand on her forehead, once again to determine that she is in fact dead. Her cold hard forehead, void of pulsing warmth.

Dead.

Not the dead of rats abandoned on pathways by cats tired of play; not the dead of splayed hedgehogs and the ooze of intestines upon a shimmering tar road; not the dead of a sheep bloated and cast in a grassy paddock; nor a budgie found at the bottom of a cage in the morning, its little feet like hands curled tightly into a pink knot around an invisible perch. Not the dead of a woman flung into a tree, a woman with long plaits like ropes hanging.

This was Dylana. This is somebody who has gone away. A sense of horror clings at his throat. A scream is stuck there, a wailing lament is stirring in his chest, far below the surface of his being. He is acting now, a robot doing what must be done. He observes his actions as though they are the function of somebody else, as though he is witnessing this event as he might watch a movie. Dylana's body. Not only dead, but gone. Her body, the container of her own cherished self; her body, already useless, which has to be disposed of. But Dylana, that sweet spirit who nurtured his heart, has left him. Voluntarily. She has left him.

He slices the spade into dense moss. Cuts past the leafy humus of the forest floor. He talks to Dylana as he digs, lifting large sods onto a growing ragged heap. His anxiety is on hold, a cage of wild birds muffled under layers of blanket, while above him a fantail dances from branch to branch, squeaking in agitation, flicking its tail feathers coquettishly.

The spade edge cuts into his bare foot as he heaves great chunks of soil from the soggy ground. Tubular roots wind across the hole, intestines of the earth, yellow veins worming towards the stream for succulence. The soil smells dingy, sweet and cold. His fear waits like a skulking wolf, waiting for him to relinquish his grip. Waiting to pounce on the birds flitting in his chest. The earth black, moist, heavy on the spade. The stream nearby chattering incessantly, the gurgling becoming a choir, a choir of high voices singing for Dylana, the high voices of angels.

He has the Bible from the bookcase. He knows nothing from the Bible but he is sure he will find something meaningful.

The hole, this gaping cavity in the earth, reaches up to his thighs now, but still he digs on, stopping only to wrest stones from clinging sockets or to chop at the tendons threading across

244

the underground. Suddenly there is a crack, and the spade, hauled from spiders' webs in a corner of the shed, snaps in two, the grey wood frayed and jagged. He tosses the handle aside and continues to gouge at the side of the pit with the blade, then claws with his nails, scooping handfuls of roots, soil and squirming larvae to dump on the surface. Finally he flops over and throws his head into the crook of his arm, among the dank stench of rotting leaves and the earth's green sap. He can't delay the deed any longer.

A spear of yellow light finds its way through the canopy above. He had left the bach at dawn but the sun is moving high in the sky now. He leans over to reach for the backpack, easing Dylana's body out in a way that has become familiar to him over such a short period. Was it only two weeks? She is dressed in the same pretty pink dress she was wearing when he discovered her. He crumples into the hole, curling around her unbreathing body, and lies there, clutching her to his chest. He listens to the river, the babbling of water over stones. The coldness of the earth seeps into his body. This is how it will be for her, now and for ever. This is how it is, he says to her. We return to the earth, to feed the cycle of life and death. In a thousand years we'll exist as particles in other beings . . . our cells pulsing around other bodies . . . with the memory of you here and now lodged into the sleeping bones of those ones . . . passed through the rivers of mountains into the milk of time . . . while our spirits . . . our spirits . . .

Where is she? Where is her spirit now?

He squeezes his dry eyes closed. God, he says, if you want me to die now, I am ready. Take me now as you took this little child. Take me now, so that I am with her for ever. If you want to punish me, I am here and waiting. Make me die now.

There is a moment of utter stillness, a sensation of time stopping. The bush ceases its relentless rustling and wavering.

Birds are throttled in the frozen air. Every living thing has paused. Matt is approaching a void that is total in its nothingness. He hovers there, on the edge. In his mind, he hands Dylana over, releasing her to tumble over and over into a darkness where there are arms outstretched, catching her as a sportsman might clasp a falling ball, in a definite solid grasp.

He opens his eyes. He is shivering, his teeth clenched and his nerves wired. A root is jabbing his spine, the pain shooting into his back and around his ribs. He scrambles to his feet, and places the body of Dylana on the ground before he scrambles out. He has had the whole night to plan this. The whole night working, cleaning the bach with bucket and mop, washing and dressing Dylana, choosing the things to bring. He unzips Fritha's bag and tips it upside down, selecting from the jumble the pile of nappies, with which he lines the bottom of the pit. Lying on his stomach, he takes Dylana and arranges her on the prepared bedding, on her side, facing the river. She looks like a big grey doll, a child's grubby toy. He packs Jason's clothes around her, using the soft fabric to somehow alleviate the assault of weight that will soon be pressing upon her.

When it comes to her face, though, he is loath to stuff the padding around her closed eyes, the sweet curve of her little nose, her lips so pale. He looks frantically around, scrabbles through the clutter of clothes, bottles, tins heaped in front of him. His own clothes perhaps? His hair? His very own hair. He delves into his jeans pocket for his army knife. Still hanging over the hole, he runs his fingers from the back of his head and scoops a thick topknot of curls, which he saws with the knife blade until a large tuft breaks away in his hand. He drops the hair over her head. This is an essential part of himself, basic elements of his being which will mingle with hers as they reconstruct themselves. Their merging chemistry. He hacks again at another fistful. His hair, although fine and wheaten,

246

seems coarse lying against her own silken down. When he has finished, it is almost as if her face is obscured by the tussled curls of a child tucked up in bed asleep.

He hauls himself to his knees, then selects the baby bottles, the Napisan and the tins of milk formula, which he positions within the grave. He works rapidly now; he just wants the job done. He tosses in the rubber monkey he picked up from the lake shore on that happy day with Fritha and Dylana, the happiest day of all. He pauses when it comes to the backpack and Fritha's bag but in the end places them in too. All the connections. Finally he spreads Fritha's t-shirt over the top, like a tablecloth at a picnic.

Clambering to his feet, he flicks agitatedly through the skin-soft pages of the Bible. Words words words. What can he find to read, of significance? God, he says, his voice sounding puny in the vast silent gabble of the bush. Please help me. He hears a steady hum weaving a weary path across the clearing. It ceases abruptly as a fat blowfly alights in a leafy patch of sunlight. Matt swats at the fly and snaps the book shut. How can he possibly choose? He places the Bible on top of the t-shirt. *Every* word. Every word can disintegrate and flow down to greet Dylana and merge with the residue of her flesh.

On his knees now, he embraces a heap of soil, which he drags into the grave. The first messy clods on the bright blue t-shirt. He rolls over onto his bottom so that he doesn't have to see any more, using his feet to bulldoze mounds of the earth into the hole. As the hole starts to fill, he scrabbles at the dirt with his hands and the blade of the spade, then slices the spade well beneath the surface. He stands up. He tries not to think, tries to shut his mind from Dylana's innocent sweet face, but his stomach twists savagely as he jumps upon the mound, pounding the sticky earth with his feet. I'm sorry, I'm sorry, I'm sorry, he whispers. He knows that if he stops now, he will not be able to continue. He adds more dirt and stamps once more. Afterwards, he replaces the last of the mossy, grassy clumps, each portion a piece of jigsaw placed in position. He scatters a coating of loose leaves and twigs, smoothing them out as someone might make a concrete path. The surplus earth he carries to the river. He stands back to survey the job. After a bit of rain, and time, it should be fine. Dylana has gone. She exists no more. He will never mention her name again, never touch the dank cavity she has left in his heart.

He is filthy. Sweaty smudges of grime and soil stain his skin, a collage of leaves and twigs stuck to his body. Matt makes his way back to the river where the sunshine sparkles and glistens on the water, causing him to flinch from the glare. He hasn't slept all night. All night. He is utterly drained. He removes his t-shirt and squats in the shallows, ladling the cold water to his face with his hands. Then he starts to scrub at his skin and jeans with the shirt, scrubbing at the brown smears, the dirt-filled scratches scored along his arms and hands, his raw, torn knuckles. He searches for a sharp twig which he uses to scrape dirt from every finger and toenail. Sifting his hair through his fingers he discovers, with some surprise, the shortened tufts.

He straightens himself and totters along the stream from stone to stone, using the broken spade handle to balance himself, until he finds a deep swirling green hole. His jeans cling heavily to his legs as he slides with a gasp into the icy water, his back supported by a round submerged boulder, his arms looped around adjoining rocks, like comrades helping him after battle. His body frays away from him, a tattered remnant tugged by the clear gargling waters. He lies there as his flesh turns numb. He lies there listening to the roar of water. He is nobody. He is a snag on life's journey. Above him the sky is a long ragged strip of blue with fragmented puffs of cloud drifting high between the dense foliage on either side of the river. A hawk slips into view and sits there, watching him, until it glides out of sight far across the tree tops. He is nobody. He is merely carrion. Nothing.

✳

It was because of Fritha. If it weren't for Fritha this wouldn't have happened. He is sure this is the case. It is all her fault. He did all he could for Dylana.

After Fritha left that day the clouds that had been gathering around the lake moved in and seemed to fold themselves around the little bach. The dread that lurked within him began to swell as the day grew dark. Dylana continued to cry drowsily and the rain began to spatter in large angry drops against the windows.

The trees and bush wavered and tossed in the wind and Dylana's head wavered and tossed against the sheets or against his chest as he held her in his arms. She had developed a cold. He'd been relieved that he could identify the nature of her illness . . . he had been worried that it might be something serious like food poisoning or something he had never heard of, or would not know how to deal with. But a cold, a little wheezy cough, and her nose running with thick bubbles of green mucous which he wiped away messily with tissues. His mother would have given him lemon and honey for such a thing; he had no lemons but he melted honey in water and tried to force her to take that. She took a few sucks and once more pushed the bottle away, pushed him away as he tried to comfort her, and he caught a glance in her eye that he felt could almost be hatred — her eyes red and her face distorted with the fury of crying until she was exhausted and sank into sleep.

Hatred. It could not be so. He had given her nothing but love. But she'd woken up again and on she cried. Stop it, he told her, as he gazed out the window at the slate grey lake, and the trees like old women in conference, with fingers pointing in disapproval, as if the whole earth had turned against him. Lightning stuttered around the room, followed by the low moody grumble of thunder. And on Dylana cried, oblivious to the storm, oblivious to his concern about Fritha's failure to return, and after some time the noise seemed to be a contagious force that was invading his every cell. He paced the little bach, to the back porch, along the hallway, around the sitting room, and down and up the hallway again, a cry gathering in his belly, pulling strength from the howling wind, the growling thunder, the wailing child. Stop it, he hissed, *stop it*! She just had a cold, a silly cold. Whining on and on. And Fritha out in the storm. The air sighing. The rain splattering.

Enough, enough, he told Dylana. You have to sleep now. You are being a pest.

He dumped her roughly on the mattress, but she vomited again, a small stain of the honey water she had just managed to drink. He scooped her up again, wiping the pungent smelling dribble from her face. I'm sorry, he whispered. I'm sorry. He kissed her on her forehead, staring over her head into the storm, deciding that it might be better not to give her anything more for a while. He put her down again, tenderly this time, tucking the blankets around her chin. She continued to grizzle but he left her there. He remembered Silvia saying that if you leave them to cry they soon find out who's boss, that otherwise they rule your life. And he couldn't tolerate the crying a moment longer.

The storm was lashing the bach. Leafy branches scraping against the windows. The lake was a turmoil of white waves, like the handkerchiefs of drowning men. Occasionally Matt would hear the rumble of a car and he'd rush to the window to see whether it was the little blue car forking upwards towards the bach. He started imagining that the bald spare tyre might have slithered in the wet, skewering the car into the lake.

He hung around the bedroom door and stared at Dylana panting on the mattress, and then wandered back to the window to gaze again at the lake. Finally he went to Fritha's room, creeping in to sit on her bed alongside her overnight bag. He unzipped it. On top was a pillow. He pulled it out.

Nothing. Nothing left. Only a pillow in her bag. One of the hard kapok pillows from the bed.

He ran outside, ran in the beating wind and rain, leaning over the gate to search stupidly down the dirt road, acting in that futile way people do when they are confronted with an indisputable but unacceptable fact.

He scrambled across the gate and strode down to the lake, his t-shirt hanging like an old man's skin from his body, his hair slapping around his head. The empty road wound for some way around the shore before it disappeared behind trees and, much further along, a scattering of other baches. Beside him, a flax bush taller than himself clittered and clacked like a bag of knives. A large boat motored far across the lake, men with yellow raincoats running to and fro, hunched over defensively. He could hear disembodied voices whipped over the choppy water as they yelled to each other, small broken sounds of yelling, like lost birds smashing against a window pane.

Help, he screamed at the air, *Heeeeeeelp*. The sound burst from him in a torrent, a sound he hadn't been aware he harboured. The cry was swallowed by the yowling wind. The boat chugged onwards and Matt wrapped his arms around his sodden shivering body and turned back for the bach.

How many days ago was that? Two or three? Four? That time is a blur, the days and nights melting into each other, into what seems now like one continuous event. The storm subsiding into silence, the day slipping into night, the night slithering into another pearly dawning as Dylana grew hot, and cold, with a persistent drowsy cry. Finally she refused to feed at all. Her skin became cold, clammy to touch. He thought this was a good sign, thinking her temperature must have abated, but her breathing deteriorated into strange grunty gasps. At times he held her, talking soothingly to her. Then he would put her into bed while he crawled into Fritha's sleeping bag, shuffling into the chair in the sitting room. He tucked his padded knees up to his chin and tied the bag over his head, inhaling the essence of Fritha into his body and rocking rocking rocking himself into a journey inward, a journey through the galaxies of his inner space, going over and over the things he had said and done with Fritha, praying that she would come, that she would turn around and come back to them, desperately hunting to find her mind in the wilderness to persuade her, to *make* her come.

But she was unattainable. There was nothing but his own lonely speck of self. He journeyed through his life and the injustice of it all, holding his arms over his ears to block out Dylana's sounds, which reminded him of where he was, and what was happening. Blocking out her raspy breathing, a hedgehog snuffling through the knotted underground of his mind, its snout nudging just below the surface of his consciousness in search of the writhing worms and creamy grubs that squirmed there.

Then he would crawl out of the bag, and sometimes it would be light and sometimes dark, and he would go to her, his stomach tightening further into the steelrock of horror when he found her blue, her skin and flesh blue, the blue of frost, the blue of an arctic cave. The blue of an alien sun. He lay on the floor alongside her, listening to every wheeze, her scratching gasps suddenly transporting him back to a day when he was lying on his bed at home, his father outside on that summer's day, sanding the paint off the weatherboards. Matt could hear the uneven rhythm of the sound come closer and closer, as he lay there, afraid, watching the open window, the net curtains gently swelling in the breeze, like a mist swelling in warning, lying there on that summer's day afraid to move, the constant scraping of his father's sanding, approaching. It stopped. The sanding stopped, and a large hairy arm came in through the open window, yanking the curtain aside.

He sat up. Her eyes were closed in sleep, her mouth open as if in an attempt to form a word she had not yet learnt to say. What would it be? A plea for help, a message of love, a curse? A curse on him for letting this happen to her? He could not deny now that she was very ill, that he must go for help. Fritha was not going to come. He wrapped Dylana in the sleeping bag, and filled a sticky red hot-water bottle he'd found under the bathroom sink, and placed it snugly alongside her. Put a blanket over the top and leaned over her, telling her that it would be all right, that help was close.

He climbed over the gate and walked down the road along the lake shore, thinking of the last time they had walked down this road together, he proudly pushing Dylana in the pushchair, Fritha feisty and sarcastic the way she always was. They had a spring in their step as they hurried, with the sky gathering its colours for the sunset. He thought of how he waited outside the fish n chip shop, watching Fritha chatting to the fat man with his sleeves rolled up, on that first day. That seemed so long ago. That seemed like years ago, when he was a different person. The day was quiet now, still except for a seagull soaring in the sky in that lazy drifty way. He reached the rickety cluster of buildings — the dairy, the fish n chip and motor-mowing repair shops and the red telephone box. These were the only shops for miles, their windows pasted with curling handwritten notices and fading advertisements for icecreams, magazines and cigarettes. But they were closed. He realised he had no idea of the time. He did not know whether he was too early or too late. He stood there in his bare feet, scratching his arm.

He opened the door of the telephone box and let himself in. It smelt smoky and stale, a suggestion of urine and beer and the sweat of frantic conversations through the ether. There was a grubby shiny poster with instructions, and an outline of what to do in emergencies. 111 calls did not require money. He picked up the phone, the dial tone droning in his ear. He decided he could ring his mother first. Then he would ring 111.

He rang the operator and put a collect call through to his mother, praying that his father wouldn't answer the phone. When she answered he had to bite his lip.

'Mum?'

'Matt, Matt, how lovely to hear you.'

It was too much. He couldn't speak.

'Matt? Matt?'

He leaned against the glass of the telephone box, battling to contain the crying that was cracking his body, as he slammed the handset down. He folded his arms over his head and crumpled across the phone, sobs wrenching from his chest, his face pressing into the hard dial. How long did that last, before he pulled himself together and started again?

This time he was prepared.

'Matt, Matt, are you all right? What happened?'

'Yeah, I'm fine. I . . . I dropped . . . something . . . and was trying to pick it up and we must have got cut off.'

'Is everything all right?'

'Yeah, I said.'

'I rang you. Scott said that Fritha had taken you to the bach for a few days, while he sorted things out at the shop.'

'Yeah. Yeah.'

'So is that working out well?'

'Yeah, it's great.'

'I'm really pleased, dear. I'm glad you're happy. I was worried about you.'

'No, I'm fine.'

'And Fritha, is she all right?'

A man was opening the door of the shop. A few lines of hair covered his scalp. He put an OPEN sign out on the footpath and stood there tucking his shirt into his trousers as he had a good look at Matt.

'Yeah, she's fine too. Anyway, I'd better go. She's waiting. I just . . . wanted to say hello.'

'I'm really pleased to hear you. I'm so relieved. I started wondering whether everything was all right. Are you eating well?'

'Yes, I am. Look, I've got to go. Don't worry about me.'

He put the phone down and turned his back to the man, aware that he must look unkempt, scruffy, suspicious. He pulled fingers through his hair and patted at the curls, rubbing his hands over his face. They smelt of sick and metal. The man had a broom now and was sweeping leaves and twigs into the gutter. He couldn't ring emergency while that man was staring at him in such an unfriendly way. He made him feel nervous. And anyway, there was a chance that he was overacting. He pulled the door open and squeezed out, nodding at the man as he went into the shop.

The man followed, propping his broom behind the door. The shelves were cluttered with tins and boxes and packets. Matt moved up and down staring at the blur of merchandise.

'Looks like it's going to be another nice day.'

'Yeah,' Matt replied. What had happened to the storm? He stared at the man leaning on his arm with his knuckles white against the counter, his other hand a tight fist on his hip.

'Anything I can help you with?' His voice was strangled and tense with mistrust.

'Aspirin,' said Matt. 'Have you got any aspirin?'

'Coming out our ears,' said the man, pulling a packet from its place and slapping it on the counter. 'Anything else?'

Matt fished in his pockets for the money. He was twenty cents short. The man picked up the aspirin and put them back on the shelf. Matt turned and sidled out, aware of the shopkeeper's eyes on his head as he walked back along the road.

When he arrived back at the bach, Dylana was dead.

✳

256

Matt has no recollection of when or how he pulled himself from the river. He finds himself sitting at the lake's edge, the broken spade handle still in his hand, as a skinny black dog approaches him along the shore. He sees the weeping sore in its flank, the wariness in its timid swivelling eyes. It stops some distance from him to hold its nose in a high drift of scent, before turning its head across its back, looking in the direction from which it came, as if expecting something or someone to appear.

Matt stares at the waves surging inwards to be sucked into the sand at his torn feet. He gazes out over the immense expanse of water; at the hills, fluorescent blue and razor sharp against the darkening sky; at two black swans bobbing nearby, their necks curling like periscopes. And always the water is moving, a teeming mass of maggots churning under its green-grey skin. Without warning Matt's head jerks as he plunges into sleep, swooping into a momentary nightmare, to peck at a dead thing at the bottom of a well.

He yanks himself upright, blinking, and notices the dog on its haunches still looking steadily over its bony back. He is sure it has crept closer. He is suddenly terrified that the creature is waiting for him to sleep so that it might eat him, devour the flesh from his bones. He scrambles to his feet and the dog turns to glance at him, once more sniffing at the air.

Matt moves on, picking his way through the rubble of squeaking pumice, the chewed and twisted leaves, the twigs like fingers, the white tortured bodies of driftwood with desiccated squinting eyes.

He looks back. The dog is following, pausing as Matt stops, then again turning to stare eerily back along the beach. They are both confined to the path between a steep rise of bushy hillside and the lake. The sweep of the shoreline ahead is interrupted by a straggle of willows dipping into the lake. Matt realises he doesn't know where he is. How long has he been walking? It occurs to him that he must have crossed the stream and is moving away from the bach, for otherwise the area would be more inhabited.

He switches direction and starts to retrace his steps but the dog stands firm in his path, still some distance away. It seems to interpret Matt's change of tack as confrontation. He can hear the low rumbling in its throat as it lifts a lip to reveal ugly teeth.

'Get lost,' he says, his voice cracking with fear. The growl intensifies, the bony legs trembling like a small engine. Matt casts his eye around for a rock or some missile until he remembers he is still clutching the spade handle. He strides into the water, splashing the surface and roaring like an animal. He hurls the handle, which hits the dog's back with a sickening clunk. It spins around and runs yelping, its tail flattened between its legs. Matt lunges from the water and picks up a large stone, but the dog stops and faces him again, now barking resolutely, skittering sideways over the sand, its legs splayed apart.

Matt gives up. He shambles onwards, away from the dog and the bach. There is no need to go back anyway, he tells himself. The bach is little more than a shelter that holds his neatly packed bag. The night before he had spent sweeping and mopping, wiping surfaces, stacking boxes, tidying every object into its place: mattresses to bunks, dishes to cupboards, books to shelves. What does it matter that he doesn't have his toothbrush as he staggers into the unknown, a starving guard-dog at his heels? It would not be an unjust fate if he had to move perpetually around the lake shore. If he had any courage he would succumb to his exhaustion now, crumpling into the sand as an offering to the dog. He drives his body forward in the fading light, scrambling through toppled trees, among flaxes, over logs and through swampy marshlands. He crashes over a protruding root and quickly drags himself up again, scanning the terrain for the dog, which is always there, a cringing shadow keeping well out of reach.

At times he has to wade through the lake to make his way around a rock face or a fallen willow. He turns back to see the determined little face of the dog as it paddles through the ever-moving waves.

Pushing through a thick clump of flax he finds himself in a clearing where a middle-aged man in shorts and gumboots is struggling to winch a boat onto a trailer. He straightens up slowly as Matt appears, his palm rubbing the small of his back, his face contorted.

'G'day,' says the man.

Matt hesitates, jolted by this unexpected human contact. He is not prepared for company.

'Er, g'day,' says the man again.

Matt sidles around the boat, but the man calls over to him.

'Do us a favour, will you?'

Matt stops.

'I've got a bit of a bung leg . . . back trouble. It goes out on me when I least expect it. And when I least need it. Could you give me a hand getting this boat up?'

Matt stands there looking at the man.

A bunch of keys bulge from his belt. He lifts a woollen hat and wipes his hand over a smooth head before replacing the hat. He takes a step forward. Matt backs away.

'I'm not going to hurt you. I'm just asking you to give me a hand here. Look, over here. Can you speak English?' He starts to speak slowly and loudly. 'Can you help me steady the boat here . . . Please.'

Matt goes over, tentatively.

'At last,' says the man. 'Thank you.'

Matt helps secure the boat onto its rollers, while the man yanks at the winch, sucking in breath as he does so. He instructs Matt to lift the trailer onto the tow-bar of the ute, while he backs the vehicle down the track.

There. It is done.

He is free to walk on. He is compelled to walk on. But the man is calling to him again from the ute, his tanned arm resting out the window.

'You couldn't have turned up at a better time.'

'That's okay,' mumbles Matt. He can feel the man's eyes assessing him. He nods towards his bleeding feet. 'Where are you off to now? Are you wanting a ride somewhere?'

Suddenly Matt is aching all over. The light is fading in the sky. It will be night soon.

'G'awn. Hop in.'

'It's . . . a long way. I think.' He tells the man the name of the bay. The man slips his hand under his hat and scratches his head.

'Er, yeah, a bit of a drive. Tell you what, come with me and I'll drop the boat and take you back after. In you get.'

Matt passes around the side of the ute and climbs in.

'So what are you doing around these parts anyway? You look as if you've been in the wars.' Matt hears the man distantly, as if his voice is from a television in another room of a large strange house. Something unconnected to him. Matt clutches the seat, watching a spider swaying in a web woven across the corner of the cab.

The man repeats his question, lifting his voice.

The effort is to find the door to the room with the television, to switch it off. But he finds himself answering, explaining that he was going to work with his brother in Auckland but there'd been girlfriend trouble and the whole thing had fallen through.

'So what have you been up to, then?' the man persists.

'We've been staying in the bach. But that didn't work out either.'

'We?'

'Fritha.'

'Fritha?'

'Yes. And me.'

The images. The images of the past few days flashing through his mind.

Twisting at his chest. He rests his head against the cool glass of the ute window.

'So what next? Looking for other work?'

'Yeah. Yeah, I guess.'

Outside, the bush and trees passing.

'Well, blow me down,' the man is saying. 'You wouldn't read about it. Heck. It was this morning, this morning I was saying to the wife, over breakfast. I hadn't had such a good night. And I was saying that when we go back to the farm, we're going to have to think about taking someone else on.' He looks across his arm and studies Matt. 'We'll need to feed you up a bit, though.'

'What?' says Matt.

'You're a gift from above. You've been sent to me.'

Matt stares at him, his mouth open.

'So whaddaya think of that, then?' The man's voice has become sharp, insistent, excited. He adds, 'I *said*.'

'Whaa?'

'As I said you're a gift from above.'

'Above?'

'Are you *deaf*?' he shouts, darting glances across the steering wheel. 'Well, are you looking for work or not? It's up to you. You'll be all right. With a bit of meat on your bones, of course. We'll soon fatten you up.'

The bush pushing past, a crowd of stampeding phantoms.

'I know what. Come and have dinner with us tonight. Don't mind the wife, I'd better warn you she's a bit sharp but don't take any notice and she's all right. We're heading back to the farm tomorrow. You can sleep on it. We'll collect your things in the morning and, if you want, you can set off with us. Mind you, it's a bit isolated. Not much in the way of girls.' He gives Matt a sly glance.

And the leaves fold layer upon layer over each other, like fingers over a face, but beyond them, through the foliage, beneath the canopy and among the trees, he knows the air is dank and dark and fantails flit from branch to branch. There is a certain silence there. The leaves are moist on the ground and below the leaves and twigs and moss, the earth is black and rich, with sinuous roots and creamy grubs and . . .

'And we wouldn't be able to pay you much. But we'd feed you, and toughen you up. It'd be good for you. Plenty of work, so you wouldn't be bored. The place is a bit run down but it's not too big.'

And far below, deep at the core is a centre of molten red, a rumbling boiling sea of red. Within caves of glowing embers. Fire. The red of fire restrained . . .

His head jerks painfully as he dips briefly into sleep. He forces his eyes open. He has no choice. As the man says, the encounter was meant. This is his fate. This is God telling him where to go. This is his punishment.

'Nice sunset,' says the man.

Matt swivels his head around and sees through the back window the sun dipping behind the hills, a fan of golden spikes weaving through the clouds. Then he notices the little black dog, teetering against the fishing gear stacked on the tray of the ute, its tongue escaping as if its mouth is being shredded by the wind, flying around its head like a leather strap. Its hair and ears are pulled back from its face. Its eye catches Matt's and locks in there, a beady eye across the distance, this constant distance between them, as they hurtle over the bumpy road, a fixed but moving time and space between them, between their terrified eyes.

✳

Matt can tell without even opening his eyes that the day is sunny. There's something about the intensity of the twittering of the sparrows and the light over his face. He can smell bacon and eggs and over the dull chatter of the radio he can hear his mother bustling about in the kitchen.

He has an uneasy sense of having been awakened after a bad dream that is still crouching, unwilling to leave, in a corner of his consciousness. He turns over heavily, to doze further, but is aware of someone walking into the room. Someone grabbing his shoulder roughly. His father.

'Matt. Hey, Matt. Wake up.' His shoulder shaken again, this time more roughly.

He spins around. A bald unshaven man is peering at him, his face red from bending over.

'Whaa . . .?' Matt gapes around the room. It is empty, except for the bed he is lying on, and a wooden chair in the corner. There is a small framed picture on the wall, of a haloed Jesus with hands at his chin, closed in prayer. Matt stares at the bald man.

'Breakfast is ready, and then we're off to pick up your things. We have to get going. Haven't got all day.'

Matt sits up and rubs his eyes. He is still fully clothed. There are no sheets on the mattress and he is covered by an eiderdown.

He drops his feet to the wooden floor. They are dirty, scratched and swollen. One of the cuts is inflamed and throbbing.

'My shoes . . . ? I . . .'

'You weren't wearing shoes. Come on, you'd better eat. You went to bed without eating last night. You were buggered.'

263

Matt hobbles to his feet and follows the man out of the room. He feels like vomiting, in a strange empty way, as if there is something within him, a part of his own self, that needs to be purged.

A scrawny woman in a floral shift is wiping her hands on a tea-towel, chewing a mouthful of food. She swallows and greets him, before turning to do the dishes. There are two plates of bacon and eggs on the table, readymade toast in a rack.

'Get that into you and you'll feel better,' says the man, pulling out a chair.

The dream shuffles forwards a little, still on its haunches.

Matt sits down and picks up a fork.

'Eat,' says the man.

Matt starts to shovel the food into his mouth. He butters the toast and lifts an egg onto each piece. He cuts up the bacon and crams it into his mouth. He is stuffing a straw thing, thrusting padding into a guy made for a bonfire. He swallows almost without chewing, his eyes watering as he gulps.

The man looks up from cutting the rind from his bacon.

'Hungry?' he says.

The dream. The dream is edging closer.

There's a glass of milk in front of him. He hates milk normally. He picks it up and drinks in deep gulps, gasping as he puts it down again. He wipes the drips from around his lips, then slumps in the chair. Then he wipes the eggy juice from his plate with a piece of toast. Matt looks out the window. The lawn is dry and brown and there's a corrugated iron fence around the yard. Tied to the clothesline is a little black dog, chewing at something on its leg.

He remembers the dream. He remembers the dream in all its horror and knows that it is not a dream.

✳

The same morning Fritha is pulling up at the bach in her little blue car. The day is sunny and the lake is blue and she is beginning to feel that she has some control over her life again. She has booked her tickets for her overseas trip. Perhaps this is why she is calling in on the way back through, on the way to see her parents on the farm, though she is unsure of her actual motive. She could tell herself that she needs to collect her bag and sleeping bag. She'll pick up the rubbish too, just to keep things in order. But she knows there are other reasons, perhaps not altogether rational. She has to admit to feeling a pang of guilt at leaving Matt with the baby after he was beginning to trust her. On the other hand, there was nothing else she could do, without causing a scene. But she finds that she is haunted by thoughts of him: something about his dedication to her; she knows it is no more than flattery but she is affected all the same. It is certainly not love but she feels a warmth towards him, weird though he may be. She owes it to him to say goodbye, to check that everything is all right.

The door is open and she walks in.

The little bach smells freshly of disinfectant. She knows immediately that they are not there. It is a strangely deserted house, a house of ghosts. The tinned and packaged food is stacked tidily in the cupboards and the jar on the table has been emptied of its flowers and placed back under the sink. She moves from room to room until she comes to her bedroom. Her bag isn't there but his suitcase is, and his shoes and socks placed neatly on the floor. She clicks open the bag. His clothes and belongings neatly packed.

Nothing of the baby's. Nothing. She closes it again. She doesn't want to think about what might have happened to them. Either of them. She doesn't want to know. It is nothing to do with her, nothing to do with her at all, but nevertheless she is gripped by a sense of dread. She wanders out to the back shed. There is the pram, propped up in the corner, where she'd found it a couple of weeks ago. She calls, once, into the morning. Matt?

For a while she sits on the grass, the sun hot on her neck, thinking of his long white soft feet. He couldn't be far, without his shoes. No . . . everything must be fine. They've probably just had a wander down to the beach, the baby in the backpack. It is a beautiful day, after all. She could go and look for them but she feels they are better left. Everything seems to be in control. Sleeping dogs and all that.

She scrabbles around in the car for a notebook and pen, writes him a quick note, then returns inside and curls it into his shoe. She bolts the back door with the long black key, then opens the fuse box in the porch and clunks off the power switch. Down the rickety old steps and around the back of the fibrolite bach, scrabbling under leaves, until she finds the round damp wooden lid over the slug-strewn drain. She takes the tobacco tin from its place on the grating, places the key inside, puts it back and closes the lid. Then she throws the rubbish in the car, climbs in and drives away.

PART EIGHT

Matt's boots squeak as he trudges on his daily rounds to a paddock further up the valley.

This is the first winter it has snowed in the three years he's been here, and it is a source of concern as the ewes are lambing. He hasn't seen snow before. There is a special quality about the silence of the landscape, the stillness of the earth, the purity in the stark whiteness against the bare outcrops of rock, and the stands of manuka dusted so lightly.

The sky hangs heavily with low grey cloud, as if the world is closing in, moving in to reduce his territory even further.

He has been banished to this wasteland; he has been cast out from the rich circus of the human spirit; this is his deserved fate. He has no doubt about that.

Jock and Delma haven't paid him properly yet but he has no need of money. His boots and warm clothes are hand-me-downs from Jock. After the day's work and a feed at night he goes to his room and plays with an old guitar he has found in the house, or writes poetry which he burns in the coal range in the mornings. He rarely answers the letters that arrive from his mother. His room in the house is bare, at the end of a dark hall, and these last nights he has been cold, waking up shivering before dawn, lying there listening to the magpies gargling with the early light.

He makes his way up to the saddle, checking sheep he knows are near to giving birth. He stops and looks back over the scene, the evidence of his breath hanging before him. Nestled below is the farm-house with its wonky red roof and the thick fuzz of smoke rising to join the cloud. He can see the distant figure of Jock appearing, blowing into his bare hands, untying his dogs from the kennels under the trees. They bounce around him and their barking clatters around the hills, along with the lonely bleating of sheep.

At the top Matt comes to a sheep in difficulty. He noticed this one yesterday. She has somehow become cast, on a grassy patch shielded from the snow, froth at her mouth, her eyes swivelling, her woolly mass throbbing heavily. The sheep snorts softly, as if scoffing. Matt pushes his sleeves up and kneels in the snow between the sheep's legs, plunging his hand into the birth canal, searching among the slithery heat, through the hot wet shapes, feeling for the position of the body, for the cord, for legs. The limbs are like a snare preventing the easy flow of birth. He has the sense of desperately grasping for a hand buried in mud. He grips two legs and eases them through, then the head and shoulders and the rest arriving with a relieved swoosh. The thing lies there unbreathing, with swollen slitted eyelids, the slimy yellow grotesquerie of birth. The mother is exhausted. The lamb looks dead. He wipes the mucous from its muzzle with his jersey, then slaps its face sharply, splattering the soggy wool pressed over its body. He picks up the lamb, then breathes into its mouth. He squeezes its chest. Puffs into the mouth. He continues to do this until there is a shudder. And another shudder. A wobbly breath and a convulsion of life through its body to its tail.

Matt places the animal on the ground, then he turns his attention to the mother, seizing great handfuls of wool to hoist her over onto her feet again. She flops into a sitting position. He wipes the lamb against the nose of the ewe, a trick he has learnt from Jock to seduce an uninterested mother to start

268

licking, to encourage circulation. But the birth process has been too long; she is too exhausted and too weak to respond. He runs his fingers over the lamb, then rubs it briskly all over with the sleeve of his jersey. At last it starts to shake its head, then to struggle onto its feet.

It totters there, bleating uncertainly. The mother lifts her nose and drops it again.

Matt takes off his jersey and wraps the bundle of lamb inside and hurries down the valley. Jock is just walking up as he comes. They stop as Matt reports on his rounds, and Jock, his face purple, curses the inopportune timing of the snow.

'Anyway, you'd better get inside with that lamb and get another jersey on. You'll catch your death.'

Already his footprints in the snow are mucky. He holds the lamb close, grateful for its warmth.

The kitchen as usual is warm and fuggy from the ever-burning coal range. Delma turns around from mixing something in a bowl as Matt enters. He's collected the cardboard box from the laundry on the way in, and now he sets it down in front of the range, lining it with an old towel, placing the lamb inside. He kneels over the box, fussing with the towel, to make sure the lamb is comfortable. He strokes it between the eyes, under its chin.

'I'll make up a bottle in a minute,' says Delma.

He was going to tell Delma that he saved this one, that it was dead and he saved its life, but he stops himself.

He looks at the lamb again, then stands up reluctantly, pulling a clean jersey from the clothes rack hanging beneath the ceiling. He goes out to the laundry and scrubs his hands and arms in the steaming water, building up a thick sweet-smelling lather of soap suds in the concrete tub. He rubs himself dry with a towel and puts on the jersey.

On the porch he pauses for a moment to slide his hand into his back pocket, carefully pulling out a ragged piece of paper, torn from a notebook. *Hope you're okay. See ya*, it says. *Love from Frith*. He folds it again along the worn creases and puts it away, then steps out into the snow and continues on his rounds once more.

Again it has happened. Again.

He parks the car wildly, between trees, nearly clipping a cyclist who topples to a stop and whams the palm of his hand against the boot in fright.

Quentin climbs out, muttering apologies to the cyclist, and negotiates his way through traffic to cross the road. He'd spotted them at the lights, crossing the intersection. She was flaxen-haired, a long plait twisted up in a clip behind her head. She was pushing a child in a pushchair. Quentin knows how old Georgia is, how old she would be if she were still with him. He has observed little girls around him growing up, read about their development in psychology books. He used to stand outside the wire fence at the crèche and watch the children there, until he was forbidden near the place any more.

But this child. As they passed, he noticed something in the child's open happy expression, caught in a particular light as they crossed the road, something familiar that filled him with absolute certainty. This time.

The woman was chatting to the child as she walked. The little girl was responding. Joy was mirrored in their faces.

He runs to catch up with them as she walks up the city street. She's wearing a long blue Indian cotton dress, and sandals. Her neck and arms are tanned and relaxed; her head is swaying a little as she talks to the child. As he approaches he hesitates, a rational hunch holds him in check for an instant, but he is unable to restrain himself.

'Excuse me,' he calls, touching her lightly on the shoulder. He's panting. He can feel perspiration dripping from his face. He runs his hand over his cheeks and forehead.

She stops and looks up at him. Her skin is clear and glowing, and she has a smattering of freckles across her nose.

'Excuse me . . . I thought . . . I thought I recognised the child . . .'

'Oh . . . do you?'

'Yes I do. I know this child.'

'Do you know this man, Sammie?'

The little girl puckers her lips and shakes her head firmly in confirmation of her mother's doubt.

'No, she . . . wouldn't recognise me. Would you mind if I held her? I'm sure she'd recognise me if I held her. You'd see,' he blurts.

The young woman senses his anguish, does not understand but is kind. Kind but wary.

'Oh. Oh . . . I don't think so. It would be a pity to disturb her. She gets terribly upset with strangers.'

'Strangers! Do you . . . do you know her father?'

The woman's face clouds. 'Of course I do. And I'm sorry but I don't know who you are. And neither does Samantha.'

She'd move on but he has his foot wedged in front of the pushchair wheel.

'Look, can you tell me this. It's terribly important. Do you know her parents? Are you the mother?' He squats at the child's side, examining the features of her face. The familiarity is remarkable. He reaches for her hand, which she pulls away. She buries both her little fists into her stomach, away from his outstretched fingers. She's looking sulky now, pouty, refusing to catch his eye. The young woman glances about, her unease becoming obvious. He stands to confront her. People passing begin to observe them curiously.

'Please,' says Quentin.

'Please what?' She's frowning now. He has a hold on the pushchair handle as she again makes a move to escape.

'Please let me hold her.'

'Will you go away *now*.'

He hates that note of panic that inevitably creeps into their voices, as though he is somebody threatening. Every time it ends up like this, sooner or later.

'Is this man bothering you?'

'Yes,' she says with relief to the man in the suit who has decided to intervene. She looks at Quentin apologetically but defiantly. 'Yes, he is. Can you tell him to go away, please.'

'This is my baby,' says Quentin to the man.

'This is ridiculous. I have never seen him before in my life.'

Another man has stopped now, a younger man Quentin has often seen in a café he regularly goes to. A few paces away a couple has paused diffidently to stare.

The man in the suit takes charge, presses firm fingers at Quentin's elbow.

'Come on,' he says quietly. 'Don't cause trouble. Not on the street. It's embarrassing for you and everybody.'

The woman is pleading. 'Honestly. I've never set eyes on him before in my whole life.'

Quentin stares at the child. Her coppery curls, her pink dress, her tiny white shoes side by side on the bar of the pushchair. She is just a little girl, no different from any other. He's not going to break down but something, some stupid hope within him deflates.

Of course. Of course not. What is he thinking of?

'I'm sorry,' he murmurs. The man in the suit perceives his back down and nods at the woman. She marches away, her skirt billowing around her legs, her shoulders stiff. She doesn't look back.

The man nudges Quentin conspiratorially. 'Someone you met at a party?'

Quentin spins away and hurries to his car, in time to find a meter maid slipping a ticket under his windscreen wiper. He flicks the paper out and tears it into myriad pieces, which flutter to the ground.

In the car, he sits unable to move, trembling, his head slumped against the steering wheel. It has happened again. Just when he thought he was over it, it has happened again. Though this time, this time he was able to walk away without the final scene. Perhaps that is progress.

He sits up and wipes his face, stares at his moist empty palms. Then he looks up to see the meter maid standing poised on the footpath, watching him with concern. He gives her a small wave, starts the car, and pulls out into the street.

CHARLOTTE'S STORY

Looking back now, I can't believe that so many things happened to me, really important things, and all in such a short time. For a while, I didn't know who I was or what to believe. I'd look at people and think of them as actors in a play and wonder what their real life was. As if everyone's life was a pretence, as if they were hiding their real selves from the world. In the salon they'd come to me to get their hair done, and I'd imagine I was dressing them up for the big world drama. Like Shakespeare said. I now know what that means. I knew before, but I didn't understand it like I do now. Some people play the part of chameleons, lying on rocks, trying to fit in with everyone else, so that they're not noticed. And others, well . . . Like, after they wash their faces at night, and lie in their beds, it's the only time they become the real person, thinking about their lines, and how they'll play the next part tomorrow. I suppose I still think that way. I mean, I believe that's how it is, but it doesn't matter any more.

It's not that anything terrible happened, it's just that nothing in my life was what I thought it had been. Nothing or nobody, really.

After the night on the beach I was lying in bed in the flat, just thinking about everything. About the photos and wondering what had happened with Dad, whether he'd slept with the

Swiss girl before he died or whether he'd died first before anything happened, and whether he was unfaithful with lots of women or whether he had suddenly fallen in love. I thought if that had been the case we would have had a different sort of heartbreak, with Dad leaving Mum, like when Brigit's father left her mother for another woman.

Maybe the Swiss girl nursed him, and kissed him on his forehead as he took his last breath.

I reached over and pulled the photographs from my bag on the floor, then I propped myself up on an elbow and looked at them again. Slowly. It was bizarre, it actually hurt; I had this funny pain in my chest that twinged when I looked at Dad. He and the others must have helped the girls fix a puncture on the side of the road or something. I could guess at how it all happened. She was quite beautiful, I had to admit. Lovely eyes and hair. Dad was looking really happy, in one of his teasing moods. He could be so full of fun and teasing. Strangely enough I didn't even feel angry with him. I suppose that was because he'd been punished enough by having a heart attack.

But it did make me realise I didn't know him, and that made me sad because I was thinking that if he had lived longer there would be more to discover about him. But anyway, you can't say *if*. Mum was always saying if only, if only, after he died. I decided then and there that I would never ever tell Mum. About the photos. There wouldn't be any point.

Then I came to the photo of me, then the one of Q. I studied his face so closely, until all the feelings about the beach came flooding back. I stuffed the photos into the packet and thrust them under the bed and rolled over and stared at the ceiling. I felt so humiliated I wanted to die. I thought I would never see him again. In a way I was pleased but in another way I couldn't bear the thought of it.

Then I suddenly heard this little tapping. I took no notice at first, but it became louder and sharper. I looked up and it was Q, outside, tapping on the bay window with a stone. I jumped out of bed, my heart racing, and opened the window. He was standing there in a singlet and running shorts.

'I was just passing,' he said. 'I didn't knock on the door as I didn't want to disturb the whole flat.'

'I'll let you in.'

'No, no. I don't have much time. I'm just out for a quick run. But I . . . I wanted to see if you were all right.'

I sat on the seat and opened the window out wide. He had a chocolaty brown singlet on, and strong tanned shoulders. He wasn't exactly young looking but he wasn't flabby either. He was all warm and glowy from running, and his hair was ruffled. I wanted to reach over and tenderly bounce my palm over the soft dark hairs on his chest. But I didn't.

'I'm fine,' I said. 'Except . . .'

'Except what?'

We were talking really quietly, not quite whispering. A whole lot of sparrows were jumping around on the green mossy lawn behind.

'I feel . . . I feel such a dork.'

'You mustn't,' he said.

'And I'm sorry for being so horrible.'

'No,' he said. 'No, don't say that. You weren't at all. It was a disturbing night. We were both . . . extremely upset.'

'You too?'

'Of course,' he said. He seemed to be looking at me in such a special way. 'I didn't get much sleep.'

'Me neither. Dreams. Weird dreams. But how come you're up so early?'

'I wanted to check that you're okay. Just a quick hello.' He smiled. 'But I have to go now.'

'I'm really glad you came. I was feeling so stupid and depressed but I don't now.'

'That's good. But Charlie, we do have to talk, we have to have a serious talk.'

'Okay,' I said. What about, I didn't ask. I didn't care. Maybe it was to tell me that he was in love with me but was married and was torn in two. Well, if it was okay for my Dad, it was okay for me, just once. I loved him so much then. It was as if I had a premonition that everything was going to change and I had to pluck that moment from the sunny morning, and make the most of it.

'See you then,' he said.

'See ya.' I leaned over and kissed him on the lips. Just lightly. Then he cupped his hand behind my head and he kissed me back, a slightly longer trembly kiss goodbye, but I thought I was going to faint it was so wonderful. It was as if the tremble was the frequency of another magical language, that neither of us could hear. It was obvious to me what it was saying, though.

I felt like Juliet.

After he'd gone I went back to bed.

Quite a bit later one of my flatmates called me to the phone. Said it was Mum.

My mood of bliss dissolved. I thought, oh God, she's just going to spew at me again. I nearly didn't answer. Apparently they'd given her my phone number at the salon. She must have blackmailed them or something. But on the phone she was really nice. I could tell she was tense but she was making the effort to be cool. I started feeling guilty that I hadn't rung her. I hadn't meant it to be like that anyway; it just happened that way. She said that we'd lived together for my whole life and she wanted to be friends with me more than anything in the world, and she found it so hurtful that I could just walk out like that without so much as a howsyourfather. So I asked her around. She said that would be lovely and when could they come. They. I *really* didn't want Steve to come. Something dropped inside me, like one of those balls that bob around on a blast of air until the switch is turned off and flop. Nothing to hold it up. I held the phone tight without answering, not because I didn't want to, but I didn't know what to say. I didn't want to hurt her again. After a bit, she said in a high voice, 'Would you rather I came alone this time?' And I said, 'That would be great.' So she did.

I hung around chatting to Seon and Todd and told them that Mum was coming, then I tidied my room, because I wanted it to look really good for Mum so that she'd be proud of me. I picked some flowers and put them on the desk.

She came early in the afternoon.

She had made an effort to look nice, with makeup on and her hair nicely done and everything. I was stoked, because normally she wouldn't, not for just me. Especially in the weekend. She was dressed for going out. I introduced her to everyone and they said a few chatty things and then disappeared, and so I took her to my room.

Well, right away she said, 'It's lovely, Charlie, but how can you afford it?' She put her shoulder bag on the bed and went over to the window seat, looking out into the garden.

'There're lots of us,' I said. 'It's not too much.'

'On your pitiful wages?'

'It's okay,' I squeaked.

And then she went, 'And what about this boyfriend of yours?' It was as if she thought she'd given me a chance to tell her, right, like thirty seconds, and I hadn't taken it, so she had to tell me she knew.

'What boyfriend?' I asked, which was true because he wasn't my boyfriend. Not yet anyway.

'I was told you were flatting with an old man.'

'Well, I'm not, am I?' I could see it was turning bad. Why couldn't she just be patient, why couldn't she just treat me like an adult? 'Look, Mum,' I said, 'I can't handle this today.'

Of course she got all sniffy. 'Why are you pushing me away? How can we be close if you don't tell me things?'

'You don't tell me things.'

'Don't be insolent, Charlie. Listen, I've been doing a lot of thinking over the week. I can see why you wanted to move out. It disturbs me greatly that you don't get along with Steve. But it's probably better for everyone, as it happens . . .'

'Pig,' I said, and immediately regretted it.

She bit her lip and pulled her cheek. 'But I want to be sure you are doing the right thing and with the right people.'

'I am,' I said.

'Well, what about this man?' She looked pointedly at the double bed.

'What man?'

And then, talk about timing. One of my flatmates, Seon again, knocked on the door and put her head around the corner and said in a hushed voice, 'Um . . . excuse me, Charlotte,' and she looked at Mum. 'Your father's here. Shall I tell him to come in or what?'

I jumped up from the bed and yelped, 'Oh my God.' Seon was standing at the doorway making a funny face, going, 'Uh-oh . . . sorry.'

Needless to say, Mum was looking very perky. 'That's fine, tell him to come in,' she said brightly.

Seon spun away and I said, 'No no,' but I couldn't just leave him there. Mum had decided not to say another thing and had put herself into supercilious observing mode. I rushed off and crashed into Q in the hallway. I put my hands flat on his chest and said, 'Mum's here.' He looked startled and sort of backed off, and then he looked over my shoulder and I knew that Mum was right behind me.

My stomach sank but there was nothing I could do. I hadn't done anything wrong anyway. So what? I could see Seon floating around behind Q, and I decided that before Mum said anything embarrassing in front of my new flatmates I'd better take the two of them back into my own territory. So I said, 'Oh, Q, this is my mother.' She put on her charming voice and said, 'Pleased to meet you, we were just talking about you,' and I said, 'No we weren't.' So we all bumped along in the hallway and I could feel that Mum was triumphant and I just knew that Q was wishing that he wasn't there. And there were a few places I would have rather been in right then as well.

Mum sat on the window seat and then Q sat on the other end, both sort of upright and half leaning against the side walls. I perched on the bed, as if I was going to interview them. Mum glanced at Q, and Q sort of looked at her and they each gave the other a quick forced smile. I suddenly realised that they were about the same age, and that I was the odd one out. I knew Mum would be surprised that he was so good looking and well dressed and all those things she'd expect he wouldn't be. I bet she thought he was going to be a 60-year-old car salesman with dandruff and a diamond in his front tooth or something.

Mum said to him, 'Charlotte was just starting to tell me all about you.' She obviously thought she had the upper hand, she was so superior. And waiting. In. That. Way. Take your time, dears. I have all. The time in the World.

I felt like passing her a nail file. If I'd had one.

Q looked at me questioningly and already I was marsh-mallow inside. 'Oh?' he said, frowning. 'I can't possibly think of what she might have been saying.'

And Mum said, 'I'm sorry, I didn't catch your name.'

And he said, 'Oh, I beg your pardon, I'm Quentin Stanley,' and he reached over and shook her hand in a little tug.

Mum went all red. And then she went white and held her hand over her mouth as if she was going to be sick. She just stared and stared at him. 'Oh no.' And she looked at me and then at him again and said, 'How did you find us? However did you find us? And how did you find out?'

Q looked suitably astonished and I must have too. Mum looked absolutely terrible. Worse than when I told her I was going flatting. Her face went totally blank and staring. Trying to work things out. Then she pulled herself together and said in a choked, haughty sort of way, 'I would have hoped you'd have done the decent thing and contacted me before you contacted Charlotte.'

Q said, 'I'm sorry?'

And Mum said, 'Come on, now. I'm not stupid. I heard Seon or whatever her name is saying that you were Charlotte's father.'

'I didn't know that — I didn't know they were saying that. That has nothing to do with me.'

I said, 'I'm sorry, it was a mistake.'

Mum said, 'Come on you two, there's no point in denying things, it's too late now. I mean . . . why hide it from me of all people, for heaven's sake? I know everything. After all . . .'

What did she know? About the photos or what? About the beach? She was standing up now.

Q was saying, 'I'm sorry, I don't know what you are talking about.'

And Mum said, 'I didn't even realise you knew. Have you or have you not told Charlotte?'

'Told Charlotte *what*?'

Mum shook her head.

'You were, were you not, involved in a truck accident, nineteen years ago?'

Q looked at me quickly and it was his turn to gape.

'Georgia?' he said. 'Is this Georgia?' His eyes were filling with tears. Then he dropped his face into his hands. What was going on? Georgia? What?

Mum jumped across the window seat and was beside him in an instant with her arm around him, staring at me as if she wanted me to leave. Hey come on, I thought, he's supposed to be *my* boyfriend.

'Go and get a drink of water, Charlie,' she whispered. No way. I pulled the flowers out of the glass on the desk and gave her that. She glared and put it behind him.

'What's going on?' I said. 'What's wrong, Q?'

His hands slipped away from his face, his lined, old and ashen face. He stared at me, shaking his head.

'I can't believe it,' he said. 'I've been looking for you for so long but even though I had this fantasy, I didn't *really* think it was you. There have been so many false alarms.'

'No,' said Mum quickly. 'No. This isn't Georgia. Oh dear . . .'

It was about then that Mum realised that neither Q nor I had any idea what she was on about.

'Who is Georgia?'

'Georgia's my daughter. My dear sweet little daughter.'

Mum looked at me and grabbed my hand, so hard, her hand hot and moist.

'This is your daughter.'

Q and I gawked at each other and then at Mum. I suddenly thought that Mum had totally lost it, that she'd gone totally insane and I was somehow responsible.

But it turned out that I am. Q is my father. He and Mum slept together one night when he went to her parents' farm looking for his other daughter, Georgia, who disappeared after a truck accident. But Mum had hardly told anyone, although her mother and father knew and were really pissed off with her. Grandma's dead now but I always had an idea she didn't like me much. So the man I thought was Dad wasn't my father at all, but just about everyone thought he was. I didn't ask Mum whether he was aware I wasn't his child; I don't want to know.

Not yet, anyway. For me, he always will be my dad, even after what he did in the photos.

It ended up being a very emotional afternoon in my flat. Once again.

After that day I didn't hear from Q for two weeks. Nothing. Part of me was relieved because there were lots of things I had to digest as well. I didn't know whether I was angry with the world or what. I was on a real yo-yo of emotion. Brigit came around one night and we drank just about a whole box of chateau cardboard until I was sick. She knew I was freaked about something but I couldn't bring myself to tell her that Dad wasn't my real father, so we left it. She guessed it was something to do with Q but I said it was more to do with Mum and Steve, and that it was their private business. She lost interest then. She knew it couldn't be interesting if it had anything to do with Steve.

Then one night just before I was about to finish, Q came into the salon. He made as if to check his appointment, then asked if I'd like a ride home.

We hardly talked in the car. Q drove to our special restaurant and we sat in the same place where we'd looked at the photos two weeks beforehand.

We selected something from the menu, then Q ordered a bottle of champagne. We weren't exactly sulky with each other; it was just that we didn't know what to say. Neither of us. I could see that he was trying, too. He seemed to be having difficulty swallowing even. We clicked our glasses shyly and said, 'To us.'

I asked him what he really did at work and he told me about that. We were talking politely, as if we were strangers who'd met each other at a bus stop. Funny. When we *were* strangers I couldn't stop talking, but now he was supposed to be my father everything seemed very serious.

He asked me how Steve was, but I hadn't seen him since I'd last seen Q, so I couldn't even start complaining. There was nothing I could think of to say. We drank our champagne quickly, and he poured another. Then that song 'Georgia on my Mind' started playing in the background. He noticed it first, and said sadly, 'Listen to that.' It was as if someone was gently trying to help us along. It's strange how things like that happen. He looked away for a minute, then he said, 'I tried to tell you, Charlie.'

'What?' As if I didn't know.

'I tried to tell you . . . about my life. And everything.'

'When you went out in the boat. Was that after the accident?'

He nodded. He started to tell me all about it then. Things about Georgia, and the accident and how he went mad for a while thinking she was still alive. How he went into a psychiatric hospital, but that mostly he was okay now, but still had this tiny doubt, this little niggle every now and then that she was alive and that he would find her. Every now and then something or someone would trigger a belief that he would find her. Usually something to do with a girl or young woman who would be about the same age as his daughter. And that was why he was supporting me, with the flat and everything, especially when I was so needy. He said he couldn't bury the last seed of hope, just in case. Even when he was being totally rational, there was the smallest pinprick of possibility.

After another glass of bubbly I asked him whether he had loved Mum and what she was like when she was young. And he said that the bizarre thing was that he couldn't recall sleeping with her at all! He said he vaguely remembered her when he went looking for his baby at a river, and gathering mushrooms on her farm, and Mum taking him to meet this wild guy who thought he'd stolen his drugs. He said he remembered that Mum was really understanding but that was

285

all. He wouldn't have even remembered her name if she hadn't turned up like that!

Maybe it was the same with the Swiss girl and my father. Maybe he wasn't feeling well and she was caring for him. Though hardly likely, by the look on his face. Just imagine if she'd ended up pregnant too!

Every now and then I think I should write to that girl in the photos, at that address in Switzerland written on the camera. Sometimes I write letters to her in my head. Sometimes I think I might visit her one day when I go overseas, just turn up on her doorstep and say, 'Oh, I believe you knew my father.' But then I think, well, what if. What if something had happened between me and Q on the beach? What if things had changed at that point? Just suppose. And then eight years later I get this letter from his wife or somebody, saying, hey, what was going on that night? Making it seem like something it wasn't. How would I feel? She might think I'm accusing her or something. So I'll leave it for now. Q agrees with me. He says that some things are better left alone, but that if the time and circumstances are ever right, I'll know.

Q and I still meet for a coffee or a dinner together about once a month or so, after his hair appointment. We met last Friday, just the two of us, and after dinner we went for a walk along the beach. It was a full moon, and warm, and I had my arm in his arm, and we kicked through the sand in a lazy scuffy way, just talking. I thought about that other embarrassing time, and felt as if I'd grown up, as if I was really mature. In comparison. As if I knew so much more about life; as then I was just a kid even though it was only six months or so ago.

I still really love Q, but in a different way, and it's different for him too.

Because I'm still not the daughter he was looking for. But in a certain way we're both pleased to know we belong to each other. No more crying, and moaning about things. He still pays for my flat, and he says that one day he'll introduce me to his wife but, like the other, that the time will have to be right.

Last Friday he was talking about things quite lightly, more freely than usual. Then he said that finding me had helped him a lot.

And I said that finding him had helped me too.

He said, 'No, Charlie, even more than that. You see, you've given me a new kind of trust in life. I never wanted to have another child, because I couldn't bear the thought of losing another one. My wife accepted this, because I was clear about it from the very beginning. But I knew it was a disappointment for her, a regret. She's younger than me, but even so time is getting on. And so . . . well . . . we decided that we would try . . .'

We stopped.

'What?' I said.

'Well,' he said. 'It's a bit frightening but she's pregnant already.'

'Hey, that's really really neat!' I said. And I gave him a big hug, a huge big hug and he held my head in his hand against his chest, stroking my hair, and I looked up and he was gazing out to sea, to the moon's silvery path over the sea. And then we walked on again.

'And that will be a brother or a sister for me,' I said.

'Yes, Charlie,' he said. 'Yes, I guess it will.'

So there you are. I suppose you were thinking that he and Mum would end up getting married and living happily ever after. Now, that would have topped the lot. No — she's still bumbling along with fat Steve, and they seem happy enough. In a funny sort of way I should be grateful to Steve because if he hadn't seduced Mum that night, none of this would have happened. But I'd never admit that to him. And Mum promised that she'd never tell Steve any of this. It's nothing to do with him. It's our secret.

After all this, Mum and I ended up having some huge meaningful discussions. About all sorts of things. I plucked up the courage to ask her whether she loved Q when I was conceived. I really wanted to know that. Or whether I was just a drunken mistake or something. She was a bit embarrassed but she smiled and said that no, it certainly wasn't like that at all. She said that she loved him in a deep and nurturing sort of way, that she wanted to take him in her arms and ease his pain. Oh well! But I still love Dad the best, my real dad — no, my pretend dad — and I know Q will always love Georgia. It's become a habit, you see. To love the other one who is unobtainable. The perfect one, who will always be smiling and innocent and beautiful and floating just out of reach.